SEARCHING

Paperback ISBN: 978-1-7395431-3-6
eBook ISBN: 978-1-7395431-4-3

SEARCHING

a love story

IAN PROUD

INTRODUCTION

I first heard about severe flooding in southern Thailand on Boxing Day 2004 as I drove to a cinema in downtown Bangkok. During the movie, I received a phone call from the British Embassy calling me in for an emergency meeting with the Ambassador, David Fall.

He told the handful of staff still around at Christmas that a tsunami had struck. News was scant, but it was already clear that many had been killed, and the airports were closed to civilian traffic. I suggested we get in a car and travel south immediately. The UK government had been criticised heavily for its slow response to the 2002 Bali bombing and British people would want to know their man in Bangkok was doing something useful. Within two hours, I set off with David, the incredible Khun Amnat from the Embassy's Thai staff, and a driver for the nine-hour journey. Having woken at eight a.m. I would get my first, brief sleep, forty hours later, around midnight on 27th December.

I worked in the disaster zone for thirteen days initially, the first person to go and the last to take a brief break in Bangkok, witnessing things that no one should have to see. The experience had a profound impact on my mental health which I live with still today. But nothing that I have felt since that time can remotely compare to the grief of those who suffered the loss of loved ones, or physical injuries and mental scars that persist.

Searching is a novel that I needed to write for my own healing. Everyone who experienced the tsunami had a life before and after that tragic event. For most, I suspect, life after has been lesser in some way. But I wanted to create an old-fashioned story about two people who loved each other so much that they had the strength to endure the very worst.

Because amidst the grief and suffering, I also witnessed tremendous depths of compassion and human kindness from Thai people and foreigners alike. And love.

The characters in *Searching* are entirely fictional, and I have not drawn on the experience of British or other victims to create them. There is one small exception: the British Embassy official, Nick Evans, who appears occasionally, is a lightly fictionalised rendering of myself.

The 2004 Boxing Day tsunami killed over 225,000 people, including 149 Britons, the majority of them in Thailand. The UK government was roundly criticised for its insufficient response, and for my whole life I will never be able to apologise enough for our failings. Feeling that you've let down your people is and has been a terrible burden to carry. Yet, there were so few of us on the ground and we tried our best, out of service to our country, and because we cared.

ACKNOWLEDGEMENTS

I want to thank my family, including my dad who is still alive, and my late mum, who anxiously picked up my call as I was about to cross the Sarasin Bridge onto Phuket, late on Boxing Day 2004. Through everything, they always supported me, and it was their example which made me want, one day, to have a family and children of my own.

I met my wife Katharine in 2009 shortly after Mum died, and she has been an incredible source of support since that time. Our two wonderful children provide me with endless joy and an escape from thoughts of the past.

As a British diplomat from 1999 to 2023, I worked on many global crises with some of the most dedicated and determined colleagues, to whom I pay tribute. I remain in touch with Britain's former Ambassador to Thailand, David Fall and was fortunate to meet Khun Amnat at the British Embassy back in 2022, as spritely and efficient as he's always been.

Having written endless pithy diplomatic telegrams and policy submissions to British government ministers, I started writing this book with practically no experience of story-telling. I am incredibly grateful to my editors, Emily Ohanjanians, Donna Hillyer and Cassandra Rigg who have patiently and with great insight helped me shape my concept into something remotely readable. Considerable thanks too, to my amazing cover designer, Danna Mathias Steele. I am hugely indebted to my fantastic publicists from FMcM - Emma Mitchell and Kate Bland – who helped me position my beloved book in front of people who might appreciate it.

I wanted to celebrate the wonderful country of Thailand and its incredible people. My best friends today remain Thai people, and I continue to speak fluently in that melodic language. I love them all like family.

Most of all, I wrote *Searching* to commemorate the victims of this terrible tragedy and to pay tribute to all those who did their bit to help in the most harrowing of circumstances.

Glossary of commonly used Thai phrases

Wai	The traditional Thai greeting in which both hands are pressed together under the chin.
Khun	A term of politeness used when addressing people, normally those with whom you don't have a close personal relationship. Always precedes the person's name. Hence *Khun* Monty, *Khun* Hatty. Used on its own, it means 'you' regardless of gender.
Khrap	A polite particle used at the end of sentences spoken by males. Used on its own, it can mean 'yes' or signal affirmation/agreement.
Kha	A polite particle used at the end of sentences spoken by females. Used on its own, it can mean 'yes' or signal affirmation/agreement.
Pe	Used with people that you know who are older than you. Precedes the person's name, Hence *Pe* Alan, *Pe* Aek. Used on its own it is a term of respect for an older person.
Nong	Used with people that you know who are younger than you, hence *Nong* Monty. Used on its own as a term of endearment for a younger person.
Por	Father.
Mae	Mother.
Khob khun khrap/kha	Thank you.
Sawasdee khrap/kha	Hello - pronounced sawat-dee, not sawas-dee.
Yin dee torn rap	Welcome.

PROLOGUE

Boxing Day 2004
Krabi, Thailand

Monty

China cups rattled in saucers, hot liquid sloshing over the sides. Guests voicing alarm raised the noise of the dining room by several decibels.

Monty looked around. Hotel staff bent serenely to their tasks, some cleaning up at tables, while the guests resettled into gay chatter.

'I've never felt earthquakes in Thailand before,' Alan said, concern carved across his face.

'Probably a tremor, not that I really know.' Monty sipped his coffee and, with his free hand, mopped up the spill with a napkin.

'It's a gorgeous sunny morning. Fancy a wander along the beach after, to wake you up?'

He yawned. 'Nah, I'll go back to the bungalow to snooze. I'm still jet-lagged. I want to be awake for our cruise around the bay this afternoon.'

Alan rose to leave. 'I hope you had a nice Christmas with this old fogie.'

'Hey,' Monty said, reaching out to rub his father's arm, 'it's my favourite time of the year.'

'Do you think there'll be another earthquake?'

'Not sure. But it seems to have settled down now.'

'Right, catch you in a bit, then. Love you.'

'I love you too, Dad.'

At the entrance to the ornate Thai dining pavilion, by a crystalline Andaman sea, father and son embraced and bade farewell for the final time.

Back at the bungalow, Monty dozed in the lounge with the TV on. As he lingered in the shallow depths of sleep, he was vaguely aware of a news anchor reporting a major earthquake off the coast of Indonesia.

He sat up with a start, head spinning, and heard loud voices replacing the usual tropical chorus of cicadas. Anxious voices. Voices full of pain and fear. *What's going on?*

From the terrace, he spied guests and staff appearing distracted, staring at the horizon. Some were hurriedly gathering their kids. Someone shouted, panicked, and a stampede started. All running away from the sea. A thunderous noise grew as he stared at the people sprinting in his direction. A gigantic, rolling grey-brown wave rushed in on the beach. Terror gripped him and he screamed at the top of his voice, 'Dad!'

Then Hatty's auburn hair, her emerald-green eyes and fabulous smile flashed into his mind. And a striking fear that he might never see her again. He turned blindly, heart crashing against his ribcage, and ran as fast as his legs would carry him.

Part I

BEFORE

Hatty

CHAPTER 1

Two Years Earlier
August 2002

I'll modernise this one day and add a feminine touch. Hatty strode along the C-Suite corridor, lined with vermillion carpet and buttoned leather chairs. Fusty-framed paintings of tea clippers hung from brass chains. The three-centuries old bank had been started by rich men. Aged twenty-four, she was determined to become the first woman on its board. And a Geordie at that.

As she entered a stylish outer officer, an attractive woman with lustrous shoulder-length silvery-blonde hair smiled from her desk. 'Great to see you again, Hatty, you're looking gorgeous as always.'

'Thanks so much, Deidre.' She pressed down the soft fabric of her knee-length navy dress. As a kid, she'd often worried when her parents' next paycheque was coming, so never splashed out on brands when M&S would do the trick. 'Your new hairstyle looks lovely too.'

A broad grin beamed across her face. 'Thank you. Bob's ready for you if you want to go straight in.'

Robert Thompson, the senior bank vice president, occupied a large corner office. His floor-to-ceiling window offered a commanding view across the tonsil of land at a lazy loop in the Thames.

Bob was trim from regular exercise, his snow-white sideburns and craggy features the only obvious sign of aging. Ushering her to modern armchairs by the window, he said, 'Ah Hatty, thanks for coming up. Do please make yourself comfortable.'

He let her sit before settling himself opposite.

Leaning with elbows on knees, Bob cut to the chase. 'So, there's an opportunity to work out of our New York office for six months next year, and I want you to take it.'

Yes! She mentally punched the air. In her eyes, Bob was one of a rare breed of good guys. No airs and graces. Scrupulously committed to supporting her no less than anyone else.

Calmly, she replied, 'And, of course, I'd love to accept. Are you just sending one person from London? I've heard how highly you rate Montgomery Wiles.'

His inscrutable gaze never left hers. 'The timing doesn't work for Monty right now.'

But it's next year! 'I see.'

'I'm glad I didn't have to choose between you, anyway. It would have been difficult.'

She'd barely spoken to Monty and, having only heard about his apparent brilliance from peers, she was intrigued. 'Why so?'

He pressed his hands together. 'You're like Ice Woman and Maverick in *Top Gun*. Everything about you is cool, calm and collected. When you make a decision, it's normally spot on. Monty does most things from his heart and his instinct, forever cresting the wave but always an inch away from costing us millions.' He chuckled.

Rankling at the faint praise, she asked, 'Doesn't Maverick get all the plaudits in the movie?'

The corners of his mouth tugged into a rare smile. Bob was a wily sod and loved to fan the flames of intra-office rivalry. 'Yes, Hatty. But, you see, Ice finishes top of his class!'

'And Mav is the one everyone likes.' She half-smiled. 'I don't think it's your best analogy, Bob.'

He slapped his knee and roared with laughter before jabbing his finger in her direction. 'And that is why you'll one day be sitting in this office, Harriet Campbell. Because you never settle for second best. Anyway, keep it under your hat for now as there are some issues the people in New York need to square away first.'

By the time Hatty had fired off the news to her parents and sister, she was late for lunch.

Chat and banter filled the bright canteen on the thirtieth floor. Scanning the crowded space for a place to sit, her heart sank. *And there he is!* Montgomery Wiles, the flaming Han Solo of stocks and shares, was sitting alone across from the only vacant seat. *Ugh.*

Despite having joined the bank's prestigious graduate scheme together three years before, they worked on different floors and barely collided, except third hand. Stock traders were anathema to her. Most were men and she hadn't met one who wasn't a chest-beating, cocky cardboard cut-out in chalk stripes and a kipper tie. Calm, caution and a relentless focus on goals had stood her in good stead so far. Together, they created the magic 'p' – predictability.

However, she had to eat.

'Would you mind if I joined you?' she asked primly. 'There's nowhere else to sit.'

He glanced up. 'Err, yes. Please do.'

She placed her salad and smoothie on the table and took a seat. 'Thank you.'

Ignoring her and the plate of fish and chips in front of him, he flicked through a BlackBerry. With sandy, wavy hair and a strong jawline, he looked like a caricature of a *Men's Health* cover model. *Typical southern pretty-boy.*

Broad shoulders filled a tailored striped shirt, adorned with a wide silk tie in bright maroon. She caught the pleasing spicy aroma of his cologne and briefly wondered at the brand. Several women among their colleagues fluttered around Monty like bees on honey, but Hatty steered clear. The type of man who attracted so much female attention was not her idea of a good time. Andrew had enjoyed the attentions of several women behind her back, after all, and when she'd found out, it had near cleaved her heart in two.

Focused on his device, Monty sniffed and flicked a finger across the top of his cheek.

Picking at her salad, she studied him. *Is he crying?*

He glanced at her and sat upright. 'Sorry, where are my manners? It's Harriet, right?'

'You know my name. I'm surprised.'

He looked puzzled. 'Of course I know your name. Everyone knows your name.'

Everyone knows my name? Below the glimmering surface of his blue eyes there was a sensitivity she hadn't expected, so she lowered her guard a touch. 'I'm fairly sure that's not true. And you're Montgomery?'

'Yes. Well, you can call me Monty, now we're having lunch together.' A hint of a smile pulled at the corners of his mouth.

'Well, *I'm* eating lunch. You don't seem to like your fish and chips.'

He looked at the plate and forked a couple of chips half-heartedly before withdrawing into silence.

She sipped her smoothie and thought about the afternoon's plan of work. However, she was distracted by his continued melancholy. *Maybe he's in trouble? Is that what Bob was talking about?* She looked up at the ceiling, trying to focus on something other than him, but her conscience kept poking her. 'Everything okay? You seem a bit down. A problem shared is a problem halved,' she offered.

Pausing, as if considering whether or how to reply, he lay his cutlery down. 'I've just had bad news. About my mum.'

A small corner of her heart thawed. 'Oh, I'm sorry to hear that. What's wrong, if you don't mind me asking?'

Tears gathered in his eyes. 'Cancer.'

Instinctively, Hatty reached out and squeezed his forearm. Her dad's cancer had been found early enough to remove it without further complications. 'Gosh, you must be so worried about her. Where does your mam live? Does she have anyone at home?'

'Just my dad. My parents live in Hampshire.'

And here he was in London. She remembered sitting in her university residence three years ago, feeling helpless, alone and far away from her dad.

Silence fell between them and she returned to her beetroot, walnut and feta salad, which was now less appealing. Sitting back, she considered him again. *Poor guy.* Out of nowhere, she was reminded of her evening plans and her mam's maxim that 'a little bit of kindness goes a long way'. Somewhat against her better judgement, she asked, 'Slightly random question, but do you like ballet?'

He looked up, curiosity in his gaze. 'Men in tights?'

'Or the most beautiful expression of the dancing art form set to classical music.' She arched her eyebrow, determined not to judge him harshly.

'I've taken my mum a couple of times. Why do you ask?'

'Don't take this the wrong way, but I have a spare ticket tonight to see the ballet at the Royal Opera House. My boyfriend was meant to come but can't.' She glossed over the small white lie. While she had originally bought the ticket in the vain hope that Andrew might come, their relationship had collapsed catastrophically the previous month. 'Might be a nice escape for you rather than stewing at home on your own.'

'Aren't you worried about taking a complete stranger to the ballet? What happens if I'm a psychopath?'

'Are you a psychopath?'

For a brief moment, his forehead unwrinkled, and his face brightened into a boyish grin. 'The therapist assigned to me by the police hasn't decided yet.'

She was unable to stop herself from laughing. 'A joker as well, I see.'

He stared off into space, before letting his surprisingly thoughtful blue eyes settle on her. 'You know, the ballet would actually be nice. If you really didn't mind? And if you let me buy the ticket?'

'I really don't need your money. But just promise you won't make any bloke jokes about ballerinas.'

For the first time, *he* laughed, and it was a pleasing, not too boisterous, baritone laugh. 'Okay, I'll try my best. What's the ballet?'

'It's *Giselle*, though I'm sure that means nothing to you.'

'I'm not a complete fool. I do actually know that *Giselle* is about a swan who falls in love with a prince.'

'No dad jokes either, please.' She arched an eyebrow again. His response could have been worse. The evening might not be a total disaster.

CHAPTER 2

August 2002

Hatty glanced to her left. Rapt by the graceful movements of the principal ballerina on stage, Monty's face was in his hands, elbows on knees. It was pleasing, if surprising, to see, and she relaxed enough to refocus on the performance. At least she hadn't given her ticket to someone who would sit there ignoring the dance, trying to find the right moment to touch her knee or put his arm around her neck. She forced the recollection of Andrew's first and only visit to the ballet into a sealed mental dustbin.

After the thunderous applause subsided, and they had filed out of the ornate auditorium, Monty turned to her with a smile. 'Thanks so much for inviting me. It definitely helped take my mind off things.'

'I'm pleased you enjoyed it. It's normally hard to find men who willingly come to the ballet.'

They wandered out onto Bow Street and into the dissipating cloud of smartly dressed theatregoers. Monty was in a clean navy suit and a simple sky-blue shirt without a tie to keep things casual. With her heels, she was just above his shoulder-height, which must have made him six feet one or two.

She walked along the cobbled street, still enthralled by the night's performance.

Monty followed dutifully and asked, 'Fancy a quick drink before we head for our respective carriages?'

He had a quaint southern formality about the way he spoke, and she hadn't decided whether to find it irksome or endearing. Considering him for a moment, she judged the evening had been pleasant, and he showed no signs of trying to hit on her. 'Okay, though just the one. Are you going to take me to a gentlemen's club?'

'Bwahahaha, that's funny. I'll have you know my parents are neither wealthy nor connected enough to get me into a private members' club on Pall Mall.' His smile faded.

She squeezed his shoulder. 'Hey, sorry, was just joking with you.'

He dug his hands into his pockets and pulled out a pack of cigarettes. 'I'm really sorry, would you mind if I smoked?'

'It's a filthy habit, but it's your life.' He hadn't struck her as a smoker, although she figured it might be a response to the stress of his mam's situation.

He lit up and exhaled a large cloud, pausing to stare at the illuminated edifice of the old Covent Garden market. He looked at her, grimaced, stubbed out the cigarette and put it in a bin. 'Sorry, you're right. Can't believe I started up again.'

'Honestly, you don't need to apologise to me. Come on, let's get that drink.'

Monty ushered her into a crowded cocktail bar nearby. She stayed at his shoulder as he edged his way confidently through the bustle.

'What would you like?' he asked, fixing her with those blue eyes again.

He maintained a lot of eye contact, but not in a predatory way. Unlike a lot of men, she noticed a singular chivalry and distance. 'White wine would be fine, thanks.'

'Go on, why don't you have champagne as we've been to the ballet?'

She frowned. 'It's a bit pricey in here, mind.'

'I really don't mind. You got the tickets for tonight. I can buy you a kebab after to level things down a bit.'

You're such an idiot. 'Go on then, Veuve Clicquot, please, with jalapenos and mechanically recovered meat on the side.'

'Veuve Clicquot and a Macallan 18, please,' he said to the barman before turning to her with a sad look. 'I'm sorry, but they only have wasabi-flavoured peas. They do colour match with your lovely green dress, though. And your eyes.'

'Are you saying my eyes look like peas?' she deadpanned.

He coughed. 'No, of course I'm not. It's just the green colour, that's all. Perhaps some might call your eyes emerald.'

Cute. 'Hmm, alright then, I'll let you off.'

With his jacket removed, she noticed again his broad shoulders and a strong chest, which might grace any rugby team or rowing crew. Several women in the bar were checking him out. But he seemed entirely content in her company and paid them no notice. *Interesting.*

He took a sip of his whisky, savoured it, and lost himself in thought.

'Have your parents always lived in Hampshire?' she asked.

He looked at her again. 'Yes, Mum's from Southampton and Dad is from the village near Winchester where they now live. But they actually met in London at university.'

'College sweethearts. That's romantic.' She wondered which of his parents had blessed him with those eyes.

'Strictly speaking, they were best friends for a few years before Dad plucked up the courage. Mum likes to say that she'd almost given up on him.' He chuckled quietly.

'Are you close?' She was incredibly close with her parents and older sister, and somehow presumed he might have a more distant relationship.

'Very. I'm the only child. Apparently, my parents were unable to have another after me.' His smile shrouded a deeper sadness. 'Anyway, tell me about your family?'

'My family's from the north-east, Gateshead area, to be precise. A bit like your parents, really. Not wealthy or connected. Dad was made redundant in the Eighties when all the pits closed and was out of work for a few years before getting a job at Nissan. So it was a bit of a struggle for us, finance wise, but we got through it.' She exhaled heavily and decided not to tell him about her dad's cancer scare, as she didn't want to bring him down.

His forehead wrinkled with concern. 'I'm really sorry to hear about that.'

'Divvin' worry, man. Everything was alreet in the end.' She smiled, replying in the Geordie accent of North East England. 'Anyways, my parents ensured me, and my big sister Martha wanted for nothing, and because I was gifted at school, I got a scholarship to Oxford University. The rest, as they say, is history.'

'Now you're a Geordie lass in a big city bank. You've done really well.'

'Aye, and a ginger Geordie at that,' she shot back, a touch defensively.

He studied her carefully, a grin tugging the corner of his mouth. 'I'd say your hair's a glamorous auburn. Positively Hollywood-esque. Although I'll stop there, for fear of digging a conversational hole for myself to fall into.'

Hatty held his gaze as she sipped her zesty champagne and, in that brief moment, understood that his compliment about her hair had been sincere. Awkward. But probably sincere. She was an auburn, tongues of fire coming out under the summer sun. Though Andrew had teased her about her hair when he was annoyed, usually about something petty.

It was a warm night, and she enjoyed the fresh air and open space as they wandered away from the crowded bar. She'd briefly contemplated staying for another drink, but in the end judged that might have given Monty the wrong impression. And with everything on his plate, she didn't want to lead him on. They soon happened upon Leicester Square, sparkling and chaotic with revellers in the bars and restaurants around central London's party hub.

'Do you have far to travel home?' he asked.

She glanced at her watch. 'I need a train from Charing Cross. No problem if you want to head home, but I might wander for a while as it's such a nice night.'

'Fancy a scenic stroll to Buckingham Palace and back?'

It was a nice idea. He appeared to know his way around a bit better than her, and she was content to follow his lead. The evening had been lacking the awkwardness that she'd feared. He seemed instinctively to understand the boundaries. Outside of the bank, where he was confident and lapped up the attentions of other girls, he seemed thoughtful and modest, with an easy wit. Not entirely as she had expected.

They skirted the National Gallery and crossed Trafalgar Square onto Pall Mall.

'Gosh, London's so lovely, isn't it?' Hatty ventured.

He looked at her and smiled warmly. 'Oh, yes. As cities go, it's pretty hard to beat. And, for me, it's nice that rural Hampshire is only an hour away by train.'

'So do you have a girl in tow, back in Hampshire?' The question spilled out of her mouth before she could stop it, and she mentally kicked herself, knowing Monty would almost certainly ask about Andrew.

'I was dating a girl at uni, but it kind of fizzled out after we graduated. She needed to *find* herself!' He reached into his pocket as if to grab his cigarettes but frowned and withdrew his hand. 'How did you meet your boyfriend?'

A red double-decker bus rumbled by, followed by two rattling black cabs, the noise buying her extra seconds to think. 'We met before I went up to Oxford. He's from the North East, like me. Son of a landowner. It was pretty serious for a while, although we recently broke up.' Continuing to stroll along Pall Mall and keeping her voice calm, she continued, 'I'm sorry. I should probably have told you earlier at the canteen when I offered you his ticket, but I didn't want you to over-think it.'

His brow furrowed and he briefly stared at his shoes as he walked, as if in contemplation, before glancing at her with a considerate smile. 'Well, I'm genuinely sorry to hear that, Harriet. At the very least, I hope this evening has helped take your mind off of things as it has helped me to.'

'Thank you. It has.' She strolled on, lost in thought, then turned to him. Under the street lights, his blue eyes took on a deeper shade, and she saw only kindness and concern. 'I dunno, no offence, but I'm just not sure any man can really live with a woman who's got big ambitions of her own. Anyways, thanks for being so understanding.'

He bowed slightly at the waist. 'I suspect you don't really want to talk about it, especially to a possible psychopath.'

She smiled.

'But I'm a good listener, so if you ever need to vent, or just chat, I'm here for you.'

Gosh, you are going to make some woman happy one day, she thought, a warmth spreading across the shuttered windows to her heart.

They passed St James's Palace and turned onto the broad sweep of the Mall.

'So, changing topic, is it true you played for England in women's hockey?' Monty asked.

She looked at him askance. *How much do you know about me already?* 'At junior level, yes. But after I got into Oxford, I decided to prioritise my studies.' She chose not to elaborate. 'Still play regularly though. And you, any sports?'

'Martial arts, mostly. *Karate* with a bit of *ju jitsu*,' he replied with an even smile, evidently trying not to make a big deal.

She flexed her bicep theatrically. 'Like a good bust up with the lads, then?'

He snorted and cast her a sideways look. 'I was a late developer as a kid and got bullied a bit. Not really the fighting type. I study for self-defence only.'

'Hmph.' She thought back to their lunch, earlier in the day. 'So, can I ask you something?'

'Of course.'

'You said everyone knows my name, and you seem to know all about my sporting life, yet we have barely spoken?'

A wide grin lit his face. 'It just cropped up in conversation. A few of us in the group were talking about who would be the first to reach vice president at the bank and for some reason it boiled down to you and me.'

'So what did you decide?'

'Aha, we held a vote.' He coughed into his fist lightly. 'To cut a long story short, you won.'

Hatty had never been solely driven by career success – a point most men didn't get. She'd just determined never again to set aside her ambitions for a man. 'So, did you vote for me in this . . . ' – she lifted her fingers to make quotation marks – ' . . . "vote?"'

He smirked. 'Now, it would be improper of me to say.'

Her competitive side kicked in, and in a small way she was niggled that he might have voted for someone else. 'Who did you vote for if it wasn't me?' she asked, her tone accusing.

'In case you'd forgotten, Harriet, our British democratic system is built on three things.' He pointed towards Buckingham Palace whose illuminated form dominated the near horizon. 'A constitutional monarch, who lives there.' He turned and pointed vaguely across the darkened expanse of St James's Park. 'A Westminster Parliament, somewhere over there.' Then he met her gaze, his grin growing mischievous. 'And an acceptance among citizens of the outcome of elections, with every vote cast in secret.'

He was being deliberately obtuse which bothered her. But then she remembered her conversation with Bob and her eyes flew open. 'Ha, I got it. You were on the ballot sheet as well and voted for yourself. And I beat you. Admit it!' She did a small dance. 'I beat you!'

His smile enveloped her like the softest robe after a warm scented bath. 'I refer you to my previous remarks, Ms Campbell. I have accepted the unanimous view among colleagues that you will go far at the bank.'

They wandered slowly back along the Mall towards Admiralty Arch, conversation flowing easily. It was only later she reflected that she'd barely thought about Andrew at all. He wouldn't have backed her in a vote. Had they married and had children, he'd have assumed that Hatty should give up her career. And so, cheating on her was probably the final confirmation she needed that he wasn't the life partner she hoped for.

'How will you get home?' Hatty asked as they crossed the cobbled forecourt at Charing Cross train station.

'Ah, I'll just jump on a bus. They're still quite regular at this time of night.' He followed her into the brightly lit concourse.

She didn't need a chaperone to make sure she got on the train, but the truth was she'd enjoyed his company and slightly regretted the evening coming to a close.

Shoulder to shoulder, they stared up at the clattering departures board until it revealed the platform for her train. 'Okay, so that's me then. I'm so glad you came this evening, Monty. I really hope it helped you take your mind off things, however briefly.'

His eyes softened. 'All thanks go to you, Harriet. It was a lovely evening and very kind of you to invite me.'

Without thinking, she stepped up and hugged him, taking in the now-familiar scent of his cologne. 'You are most welcome.' She turned to the ticket gate but then stopped to look back. 'And please, just call me Hatty.'

CHAPTER 3

September 2002

'If you had a guitar and a flat cap for donations, you could put on a performance,' Hatty said, looking down at Monty.

He lounged on the steps of St Paul's Cathedral in faded jeans and a long-sleeved tee, with black sunglasses. So lost in his thoughts that she'd crept up to him. Seven in the evening on a late summer Saturday and the sun hung low in a cornflower sky. While the fabric of his shirt wasn't tight, it clung to his well-defined biceps. Temperature hot.

'I have no musical talent, sadly. Think I'll do better as a banker than a busker,' he smiled out one side of his mouth before jumping up and embracing her lightly.

They'd fallen into the hugging habit after their first night at the ballet. Since then, they'd collided each week, often for lunch or chatting on the phone. It was completely platonic, and he seemed fine with that. Then he'd turned up at her desk to invite her for a Thai meal and she'd agreed without hesitation. Truth was she enjoyed his company and the comfortable, jokey free-flow of their chat, possibly more than she'd prefer.

She nestled her face briefly against the light stubble on his cheek before pulling away to consider him with pursed lips. 'A banker who's over-compensating on the "causal" dress code, I see.'

'These jeans cost a fortune,' he groaned. 'Anyway, you look lovely!' His eyes swept across tanned shoulders that her strappy floral print summer dress showed to good effect. 'I like your hair that way.'

She blushed. Parted down the middle and tied in a ponytail, she'd kept her hair simple as she'd spent the morning on the hockey pitch with her friends. A post-match shower had rendered it frizzy and voluminous. She pushed away an umber strand from her temple, before glancing up at the grand edifice of the cathedral. 'Thank you. This place looks so beautiful on a summer's night, doesn't it? I'd love to have a flat across the river so I could look at it every day.'

'And I believe you will. Hey, stand there on the steps and I'll take your photo.' He whipped a compact digital camera out of his pocket.

'Are you trying to be Lord Lichfield now, or something?'

His eyes hidden by the device, he said, 'No, I just like to capture special moments on film. Sorry, you can blame my parents.'

She was softened by his guileless charm, so struck a pose. 'Come on, I'm hungry.'

They wandered unhurriedly through the historic City of London, past restaurants and vintage pubs with crowds spilling onto the streets.

Soon, the gentle music of a *khim* and an aroma of tamarind and lemongrass enveloped them as they entered the restaurant. Dark wood furniture, gilded figurines and silk tapestries created the feel of ancient Siam. A Thai lady in ankle-length silk sarong and fitted gold tunic pressed her hands together in a *wai*, which Monty returned in an easy movement. They were seated in a secluded, intimate booth.

'You know, I've always wanted to go to Thailand,' Hatty said. 'I have a great uncle who is buried in a Commonwealth War Grave.'

'You should, it's incredible. My parents' best friends from university are Thai and we've visited them every year since I was a toddler. Strange though it sounds, it's a peaceful, idyllic spot out where the Japanese built the death railway, and the cemeteries are beautifully tended.'

Like soft catkins, Monty's brows, crept towards each other over his nicely proportioned nose.

'Gosh, I may need you as a tour guide.' In that moment, Hatty felt an irrational urge to reach across and kiss him on the lips. Then she remembered New York, how romance was definitely not in her plan and how she must tell him before things went too far.

He chuckled. 'With pleasure. Did you want champagne with your dinner, or . . . ?'

'A beer will do just fine, thank you very much,' she replied, pertly.

A waiter appeared, and Monty ordered, speaking in the lilting Thai language.

'Are you trying to impress me by talking the lingo?'

'Heaven forbid, no. Was just trying to impress the waiter. We were gossiping about you, and in the fun of it I forgot to order any food.'

'You didn't, Montgomery Wiles!' She slapped his forearm.

The waiter reappeared, placing two glasses of Singha beer and a bowl of prawn crackers before them. 'Your food will be here soon.' He smiled.

'Anyway, what are you reading?' Monty pointed at the paperback sticking out of her handbag.

'*A Town Like Alice*. It's my favourite.'

'Suppose that makes sense with your great uncle having been a prisoner of war.'

She raised her eyebrows sceptically. 'You've read *A Town Like Alice*?'

'Too right.' He struck a dodgy Australian accent.

'You sound like Crocodile Dundee.'

There was a pause. 'Don't knock it. Could be an allegory for us. Sophisticated, flame-haired high-flier meets rugged rough-around-the-edges yet handsome man from the backwoods.'

'You must be confused. Suits don't exactly scream "rugged" in my books. Mind you, maybe in Hampshire that counts as rugged.'

He laughed his rich baritone, comforting like hot chocolate after a cold walk.

After a sumptuous Thai meal, as they wandered past Spitalfields Market, Hatty instinctively hooked her arm through the crook of Monty's elbow. 'Thanks for tonight, I had a really lovely evening. You've really inspired me to go to Thailand now.'

He glanced sideways at her, 'You should. I think you'd love it there and Thai people would love you.'

'Are you always this sweet, Montgomery Wiles?'

He squeezed her arm gently in his, before stopping to stare at an illuminated billboard. 'Hey, look! The Bolshoi Ballet is performing *Swan Lake* in London!'

'Have I turned you into a ballet nut all of a sudden?'

'Think of it as a *very* belated birthday gift. Treat's on me this time.'

What? 'Hold on, how do you know my birthday?'

'I've got my sources.' Grinning from ear to ear, he whipped his mobile phone from his pocket and punched in the booking number.

She stared at him incredulously. 'What are you doing? It's past ten at night!'

Phone pressed to his ear he nodded towards the billboard. 'Twenty-four hour booking line. Oh hello, yes, I wanted to ask if you have any tickets left for *Swan Lake* . . . Oh you do . . . ? Only in the stalls . . . How much for two . . . ?' Leaning to his right, he ruffled around in his pocket, withdrew his wallet and awkwardly prised a credit card out of its slot.

So is this what he's like at work? Has an idea, goes for it? Everything in her life was planned down to the last detail and he was now loosening the straps of her self-control. *But* Swan Lake *with the Bolshoi Theatre. And with kind, funny . . . fabulous Monty?* Swept along in a whirlwind of his spontaneous energy, Hatty was petrified lest her feelings run too far yet unwilling to stop them. She needed to stick to the plan.

CHAPTER 4

14 December 2002

The train zipped through Surrey and then Hampshire. Hatty sighed and stared out at the slate grey sky above the glaucous blur of woodland. She *must* rip off the 'New York' plaster before the day was done. At the very least it would fix permanently in her mind the idea that they were, and would only ever be, just friends.

Yet here they were, on a pre-Christmas excursion that Monty had planned. They'd spent so much time together since that magical night at *Swan Lake* that they might as well have been dating. Except they weren't. And Hatty struggled each day to convince herself that she should stick to 'the plan'.

In Winchester, she admired the old-fashioned English station with its dagger-board fascias, a brief wave of sadness washing over her. 'We could have dropped in on your parents, you know?'

Monty's shoulder pressed into hers and he smelled so nice as he leant across to look out the window. 'That's alright. I'll be back tomorrow. Actually, I've decided to move back home for a while, as I think they need me around.'

'Your mam will appreciate that. How's she doing?'

He shook his head, the corners of his eyes reddening. 'Months, not years, apparently.'

She looped her hand through his arm. 'Oh, Monty, why didn't you tell me?'

His forehead uncreased, red blotches on his cheeks fading to nought, and he gazed at her, pupils like planets, stroking her cheek affectionately with his thumb. 'Mum wanted us to have a nice day together.'

She frowned. 'You've told her you're swanning off to a football match with me?'

'Yeah.' His smile lit up her world, making her want to cry.

Saint Mary's football stadium in Southampton was packed. Holding cold lager in plastic cups, they settled into cramped seats, legs pressed together. In an ocean of people she thrilled at occupying her own private island with Monty. Whenever he turned to her, their faces were so close, his warm breath caressed her cheeks.

'Smile!' He held his camera out at arm's length and she nestled into him, a boundless smile on her face.

As she'd never followed football, and with an in-built tendency to self-preservation, she remained fixed in her seat when Newcastle scored just after half time. Monty cursed, and she poked him in the ribs, which forced a grunt and reluctant half-smile.

Then he erupted out of his seat with the crowd, as Southampton equalised. She leapt up and down like a lunatic with him, hugging him and yelling at the top of her voice. He held her shoulders, his joy overflowing, pulled her in and kissed her lips.

It happened so quickly that she didn't have time to react to the delicious sensation of his warm mouth before they continued leaping up and down. It was just Monty being typically in the moment and catching her off-guard. *He doesn't really like me that way. Does he?*

It was dark when they joined the slow-moving exodus from the floodlit stadium.

'Fancy pizza?' he asked, as they walked back into the city centre, his voice hoarse from shouting during the match. 'I know a really nice place.'

She glanced at her watch before squeezing his arm. 'Sure, why not. What time train do we need to get back?'

'We've got loads of time,' he replied, with a Delphic smile. 'Did you bring something fancy to wear?'

'Oh, yes!' She'd almost forgotten. 'Is Southampton known for posh pizza then?'

He bumped into her shoulder on purpose. 'Not especially.'

She narrowed her eyes. *What are you up to, Montgomery Wiles?*

Before long, he ushered her through the glass door of a tiny Italian restaurant across the street from the civic centre. It was almost full, though there was a spare table for two, and he politely checked with the waiter that it was free.

As she pulled off her coat, she was struck by the simple décor and the unctuous aroma. The waiter placed two inviting pizzas on the adjacent table making her mouth water. 'Well, this all looks lovely.'

'I've lost count of the number of times I've been in here. It's a real family favourite and I'm nothing if not a creature of habit.'

She glanced at the menu briefly before looking up at him. 'Hm, I never pegged you as someone who likes routine.'

'I've been going to the same holiday destination in Thailand with my parents since I was in nappies and I can barely get by a week without seeing you, so . . .'

She leant forwards and touched his nose. 'That is because I'm the best friend you ever had, Montgomery Wiles.'

He traced the shape of a heart on his chest. 'Harriet Campbell, you complete me.'

She fell back in her chair, peals of laughter bursting from her as the waiter appeared to take their order. 'You've been to one sporting event and now you're rocking Jerry Maguire quotes?'

Within minutes, the waiter set their pizzas on the table, thick golden crusts, lightly charred from the wood-fired oven. Hers was fabulous chunks of spicy Italian sausage in a rich tomato sauce with lots of gooey mozzarella.

Once they had eaten, Monty headed to the restaurant's bathroom to change into smarter clothes, leaving Hatty sipping her mineral water and wondering about the next intriguing part of their excursion.

After she'd changed into a simple, purple dress, it didn't escape her notice how much he'd stared when she returned to the table.

'You look beautiful.'

She glowed inside yet grew sombre as her eyes settled on his. She'd been putting off and putting off the New York conversation. He needed to know. And she needed to tell him, for her sake as much as for his.

'Look, there's something I wanted to ask you about.'

He smiled eagerly. 'Sure, what's up?'

A bell tinkled as the restaurant door opened and a couple walked past in search of a table.

'Hey, Monty?' the man asked.

Monty jumped up and pumped the man's hand. 'Josh, you old scumbag, how are you?'

Josh was a tad shorter even in a winter coat, appeared in similarly good shape. 'I'm good, it's been ages, matey, how've you been keeping? Look, this is Tilly, my fiancée.'

'Fiancée? You kept that quiet.' Monty smiled expansively at the petite woman, her curly brunette hair cut into a stylish bob.

'He just proposed last month,' Tilly said, holding up a delicate hand with a sparkling diamond on a gold band.

Exaggerating his movements, Monty bent at the waist to study it close up. 'Well, I never. Really happy for you. Look, this is my best friend Hatty from work. Hats, this is Josh, my old schoolmate. He must be a much nicer person than when we were kids to have convinced such a wonderful young lady to marry him.'

Josh play-punched him on the arm.

'Congratulations. It's lovely to meet you both.' Hatty smiled and extended a hand. 'You'll have to tell me what a scoundrel Monty was at school.'

Monty put a hand to the side of his mouth and called to the waiter, 'Can I get the bill please? Need to leave in a hurry,' whereupon they all fell into laughter.

'What brings you back down to Southampton?' Josh asked. 'I heard your mum was sick. Mate, I'm really sorry.'

Monty clapped him lightly on the shoulder. 'Cheers, I appreciate that. No, we just went to see the Saints draw against crappy Newcastle.'

Hatty poked him.

'You don't exactly look dressed for football. Or maybe you do, as you're a City boy now.'

'Ah, well, we're off to the ballet next.'

'The ballet?' Hatty squeaked, near dumbstruck.

Tilly's grey eyes studied Monty and then moved to Hatty, her pretty face upturned into a knowing smile. 'You should take me to the ballet sometime, Josh.'

Parrying the suggestion, Josh asked, 'So do you get down this way often, Monts? We should meet up for dinner next time you are down.'

'Not as often as I'd like, to be fair. But yeah, maybe we can organise an evening sometime in the New Year?' He turned to smile at Hatty.

Hatty blinked. *I won't be here.* 'Excuse me,' she said in a bid to change the subject, 'would you mind taking a photo of us together please?'

She cuddled into Monty again for the shot and smiled, her emotions in a spin.

Having bade farewell, they walked down the hill to the Mayflower Theatre.

'What was that thing you wanted to ask me about?' he asked, as they joined the madding crowd of ballet enthusiasts.

She sighed. *Now's really not the ideal time.* 'Oh, nothing urgent.'

On the late train to London, she dozed with her head on Monty's shoulder, vaguely aware of the rocking of the train and his arm around her.

'Wakey, wakey,' he whispered at Waterloo Station.

Opening her eyes, she blinked against the light. 'Gosh, have we been here long?'

He grinned. 'No longer than an hour.'

She sat up suddenly. 'We haven't?'

'Just got here. Come on, still time to get the last tube train.'

As the escalator plunged them deep under the streets of London, Hatty became melancholy and stroked his shoulder. 'Monty, why are you always so lovely to me? Today was simply magical, and I really don't deserve it.'

He turned to her from the step below, took her hands in his and smiled. 'Ssshh, you make *my* miserable world magical, Harriet Campbell.'

For the second time that day, Hatty wanted to burst into tears. Grabbing the lapels of his jacket she shook him gently, 'But, I'm a truly terrible person who cares about my career more than people.'

He put a warm finger softly to her lips, and whispered, 'Hey, hey. You're not. You're the start and end of every day for me, and you don't realise how much that helps.'

A cloud of drunken noisy revellers surrounded them as they exited the escalator, shuttering their conversation. The final train of the night clattered out of the tunnel and drew to a halt, everyone piling aboard when its doors swished open. They found seats in the packed carriage and Hatty sat pressed up against his shoulder for the short journey, wanting desperately to talk more but embarrassed to do so in such a public place.

When the train arrived at her stop, she kissed his cheek and stared into his eyes. 'This has been such a wonderful day, Monty, I can't even begin to tell you how much.'

'Thank you for travelling south.' He grinned. 'Have an amazing holiday with your family. I'll call you on Christmas Day.'

Of course he'll call me on Christmas Day, she thought miserably as she stepped off the train, and watched it disappear into the black tunnel, taking with it a man she was struggling in vain not to fall desperately in love with.

CHAPTER 5

Christmas Day 2002

'Wilma Flintstone?' Martha exclaimed in a high-pitch, putting the vegetable peeler down on the worktop.

'That's right,' Hatty replied, leaning against the fridge in her big sister's kitchen.

'Doesn't she have bright orange hair?'

'Yes, why?' She fiddled distractedly with a net of Brussels sprouts.

A touch shorter, after their dad, her older sister had a Hollywood smile and feminine curves accentuated by the birth of two children. Her look now was incredulous. 'You used to hate it when Andrew called you Ging Girl when he was in a huff about something. But now you love it, do you?'

'Monty's always complimentary about my hair.' She stared at her fingernails. 'Everyone has been asked to wear costumes to the bank's New Year's party. He says all our computers at work are Stone Age, so the Flintstones seemed a good call.'

'Oh, it was *Monty's* idea, was it? Harriet Campbell, I don't think I've ever seen you dress up in costume in all your twenty-four years.'

The siblings were personality polar opposites, though they couldn't be closer.

'Always nice to try something new.' She smiled elliptically.

'Hold on a minute. Is this the fella you went to the football with?'

'Uh huh.'

'And the one who is forever organising nice trips to the ballet for you, according to Mam?'

Hatty didn't look up, continuing to unpick the vegetable net with her fingernails. 'Mmm hmmm.'

'Would you pass me those bloomin' sprouts, please?'

She handed across the Brussels, then picked up the bag of carrots and returned to fiddling.

Martha pushed the thick brunette curls from her forehead with her wrist and fixed her brown eyes on her kid sister. 'You're in love!'

'I've only known him a few months,' she protested. She was going to New York *precisely* so she didn't have to confront the increasingly troublesome *L* word with Monty.

'Is he a great kisser?'

'Martha!' Hatty protested, trying to force the thought of her lips against Monty's magazine-cover mouth from her mind.

'Who is Monty, Mam?' Martha's five-year-old son Jimmy wandered into the kitchen in pyjamas, clutching a cuddly wombat.

Hatty ruffled Jimmy's thick mop of blond hair and, glaring at her sister, replied, 'Oh, he's just my friend at work, darling.'

The boy looked up at his beloved aunt, hugging her leg. 'Is Monty your special friend now you don't like Andrew anymore?'

Martha strangled a laugh. 'No, sweetheart, auntie Hatty says he's just a *friend*.' On the final word, she surreptitiously fluttered her eyelashes and puckered her lips.

Hatty knelt to look into her nephew's aquamarine eyes. 'Do you want some Cheerios, pet?'

He nodded solemnly.

'Okay then, I'll get that sorted for you. Can you go and ask Maisie if she wants some too? Nana and Grandad will be round soon to open Christmas presents.'

'Okay,' the little boy said as he ran happily out of the room.

She gathered the cereal box and a couple of plastic bowls from the cupboard and glanced sideways at her sister. 'I can't believe you told Jimmy about me and Andrew.'

'I didn't tell him anything. I think he must have eavesdropped me and Steve the other night. You know how he sometimes sneaks down the stairs after bedtime.' Martha dried her hands and smiled coquettishly at her sister. 'Anyways, tell me more about Monty.'

'Sounds to me that you've got all the information you need from Mam already.'

'The way Mam talks about fancy hats, I keep thinking you're about to get married?'

She fetched up a potato and scraped it distractedly, wrestling with the urge to visualise Monty in a tail coat at church. 'He's just a lovely, lovely guy. A real friend.'

'So, as he's such a good "friend"—' she threw her fingers in the air in exaggerated air quotes '—he probably doesn't mind you going away to New York then?'

'Ugh.' Hatty peeled with increased vigour.

'You've not told him, have you?' For a change, her big sister's gaze was serious and searching.

Tipping her head back to stare at the ceiling, the confusing pattern of decorative Artex swirls symbolised the emotional maze she'd found herself in. 'I've kept putting it off until it feels like this huge obstacle, and I now feel terrible.'

Martha's voice softened. 'His mam's dying of cancer and he's clearly crazy about you. You need to be straight with him, Hatty, love.'

She wiped a tear from the corner of her eye. 'That doesn't make me sound like a selfish cow now, does it?'

Laying down her utensils, Martha threw her arms around Hatty, kissing her forehead. 'You're the best lass in the whole wide world, Harriet Campbell. Straight-A student, kind, successful at work, love your family, utterly gorgeous. You've got the lot. It just seems you really like this canny lad and are pushing him away because of what happened with Andrew.'

'I do like him. More than I am probably even ready to admit. But I don't want to make sacrifices again for a bloke, *any bloke*, who might let me down again.'

'He doesn't sound even remotely like that pratty bloke Andrew.'

'Monty's lovely. But I've concluded that men are scared of women who want a successful career and a happy family. I'm searching for a perfect that doesn't exist.'

Martha sighed. 'Well, that's depressing. Anyways, you'll have to let me sort you out with a costume for the party.' In a flash, her smile shone like a glitter ball over a ballroom packed with couples in finery. She knew when not to push too hard.

'Just a simple white dress should be fine. I mean, just like Wilma, nothing else.' Fancy dress was way out of her comfort zone, but slap bang in the middle of Martha's.

'Oh no! I'm going to *zhoozh* you up, darlin'.' She stood back and admired Hatty. 'Something to show off that gorgeous figure of yours. Although,' she said, glancing down, 'I'm not sure it needs any help.' Eating healthily, plenty of sleep and time on the hockey pitch had blessed her little sister.

Hatty's phone buzzed. Perfect timing. 'Sorry, need to take this call.'

'Monty, I assume?'

She flashed a dazzling smile.

CHAPTER 6

New Year's Eve, 2002

'You look ridiculous,' Hatty giggled when she laid eyes on Monty in the bustling hotel lobby.

'That's no way to talk to your husband,' he huffed. His calf-length orange smock with black spots was complemented by a shaggy black wig. Padding bulked out his torso, a portly look betrayed by muscular arms.

She flung her arms around his neck and pulled him into a hug. Nestling her head into his chest, she breathed in his wonderful smell. 'You know I'm just teasing, Fred.'

'And my life would be the lesser without it, sweetheart.' He kissed her nose sending tingles down her back, before helping her out of her coat.

'How do I look?' She spun around to face him. Martha had worked wonders. She adjusted an old white dress to give it a single strap and a jagged hem, tailoring it snug around Hatty's narrow waist. A charity shop necklace of big white beads and flat leather sandals, completed the look. But her hairdo was the pièce de resistance, a pompadour and bun combo, with a temporary dye that elevated her natural auburn to a fiery ginger.

'Honestly, you look swell, Wilma.'

Colleagues from the bank milled around in all manner of costumes.

'Hey, you two look groovy together,' said a colleague in a dusty pink velvet jacket *à la* Austin Powers.

'Would you take our photo together please, mate?' Monty said, whipping his camera from goodness-knows-where under his smock.

Hatty sidled up and Monty wrapped his arm around her shoulder while they posed. She was acutely aware that the thinnest layer of fabric separated her hip from his warm powerful thigh. While they hugged often, this was something new and thrilling.

The ballroom had been transformed with tables set for a banquet, with the finest crockery and champagne on ice. At one end, a dance floor with glitter balls and an enormous net of balloons suspended from the ceiling.

The DJ intoned over the microphone. 'Right, for all you fans of Eighties power pop out there, here's "Leave a Light On" from Belinda Carlisle.'

'Oh my goodness, Belinda Carlisle's my favourite. Time to see you boogie, Fred.' Hatty grabbed his hands and drew him towards the crush of people dancing under a kaleidoscope of light.

'But I can't dance,' he spluttered.

'Don't be a southern wuss.' She steered him into a small pocket of space on the dancefloor and let her body move fluidly to the rhythm of the music.

Shaking his head, Monty started to dance in stiff movements.

'Is that how you danced at Eton?' she shouted in his ear.

'You know I went to a state school,' he growled, his sparkling blue eyes raking down the front of her dress, before holding her gaze.

Raising both hands over her head, she rolled her hips in figures of eight, before pouting and turning away from him, heat coursing through her thighs.

The next few hours fizzed by in a whirl of dancing. He seemed content to let her set the pace, and she was freer and happier than she could recall ever having been.

After jumping up and down like crazy to Van Halen, the DJ's voice came in again. 'Okay, it's getting close to midnight, folks, so we are going to slow things down a bit.'

The lights dimmed and the gentle intro to Savage Garden's 'I Knew I Loved You' becalmed the dancing masses. Couples fells into each other's embrace, leaving the two of them separated by an emotional canyon.

Suddenly unsure of herself, Hatty stared at Monty.

'Did you want to dance?' he mouthed.

Without replying, she took his left hand in hers. He placed his free hand in the middle of her back gently, as she placed hers on the powerful curve of his shoulder. She looked up into his shimmering eyes, her heart racing.

Moving slowly with him as one, his even breaths caressed her cheek, his heart thumping rhythmically against her. Everything was so unforced and natural in the intimate world she'd created for them.

Briefly, she rested her face on his chest. Feelings erupted in her heart, leaving her dizzy and confused. Just like that, she'd stepped beyond friendship, without thinking, into a world of emotions that she'd tried to keep on a distant horizon. *You've got to tell him about New York*, her conscience screamed! But, here and now, immersed in the touching lyrics and cocooned in his arms, she silenced the rational voice inside.

Looking up into his eyes again, she discerned gentle flames of attraction with a warmth much richer than base desire. *Gosh, I'm falling for you, but am too scared to admit it.* Having held his gaze for what felt like an eternity, she lay her head on his chest, pulling him closer still. Then in an instant, the song ended when she wished it had lasted all night.

Prince boomed over the dancefloor with '1999'. Reluctantly, she let go and smoothed the skirt of her dress.

Monty stood close, staring at her, breathing hard like he'd sprinted for a bus.

'We should probably get a drink as it'll be midnight in a few minutes.' She squeezed his hand, before walking off the dancefloor with him at her shoulder. She needed to sit down briefly and compose her thoughts. *Please, please just tell him and end this torture.*

'Yeah, definitely, I'll go and grab us some bubbles.' He stroked her shoulder lightly, tingling her arm.

As he wandered to the bar, her gaze lingered on his back. At a different time, she might have slipped the tightly fastened tethers of her desire and released every tempestuous impulse he incited in her.

But she wasn't ready. Not even close to ready for a relationship.

Then he was walking back, in each hand a crystal flute brimming with champagne. His face, a picture of . . . *nerves*? Whatever he was nervous about, she was every bit as nervous. *Time to rip off the plaster.*

'Your drink, honey,' he said, tightly, smiling down as she took the stem of the glass between her fingertips.

Glancing up to look at him once more, his eyes melted another ice block in her defences. Remembering herself, she asked, 'Hey, what time is your taxi collecting you?'

'Oh—' he checked his watch '—in around fifteen minutes.' Sadness crept across his face.

She wondered whether it was the thought of going home to his sick mam, or the impending end to their fabulous evening that pressed more heavily on his heart. Another block melted. She took his warm hand. 'Glad we are getting to see in a New Year together. It's going to be "dino"-mite!'

The familiar boyish grin and baritone laugh erupted from him, abruptly deafened by an acoustic screech from a microphone.

Vice President Bob tottered onto the stage, whisky tumbler in one hand, dressed as Captain Hook, clearly the worse for wear.

'Good evening all you dashing rapscallions,' he opened to a chorus of cheers from the crowd. 'It's been bloody brilliant year and I just wanted to thank each and every one of you, and wish you good luck for 2003.'

His glassy-eyed gaze fell on Hatty, sending dread down her spine.

No no no!

'Ah Hatty, there you are. Hatty is going to be fantastic in New York, isn't she? Let's give a round of applause to Hatty here. Happy New Year everyone!'

Monty's body stiffened and when she glanced at him, his eyes were focused on the stage, eyebrows furrowed. 'New York?'

Hatty swallowed hard, anguish on her face. 'I . . I wanted to tell you but—'

'Ladies and gents, it's almost time to welcome in the new year. Ten, nine,' the DJ led the countdown.

Hatty wrapped an arm around Monty's waist, his arms slack at his side.

'. . . two, one.' Big Ben chimed midnight as a blizzard of balloons and sparkly chaff rained down from the ceiling. Other couples hugged and kissed. 'Happy New Year!'

Hatty turned to kiss his cheek at the precise moment he did the same. Their noses collided, and she pulled back, giggling, before aiming for his other cheek and brushing his nose again.

'Sorry,' he said, nervously, his eyes a mess of confusion, his face millimetres from hers, his breath scented with champagne.

Hatty's eyes narrowed, her lips pursed between flushed cheeks, mind scrambling to regain control. 'No, I'm sorry. I'm so sorry.' Placing a hand on his collar bone lightly, she leant in, brushing her nose against the edge of his, deliberately this time.

As he repeated the movement, she blinked slowly, a shudder rippling through her. She touched his nose with a fingertip and ran it over his lips, watching its path with studied concentration.

He pulled her closer still. 'You're the most beautiful person I've ever known, Harriet,' he murmured. His fingertips explored every shallow hillock up the valley along the centre of her back, and she shivered as he reached her neck.

No, don't say that, please don't. She met his gaze. 'Happy New Year anyway.' Her voice was quiet, yearning, and she kissed the point below his mouth where her finger had been.

Lowering his face, his lips met hers, softly at first, him sighing deeply as if she'd breathed life into him.

Opening her mouth, her tongue danced slowly around his, warm, electrifying. Reaching across, she placed her champagne flute on a table, before cupping his face with both hands, and pulling him with more urgency and hunger into the kiss.

His hands charted every inch of her back, fingertips pressing into her flesh like explorers of old searching for the most prized treasure.

Locked in a kiss, her fears were cast in a messy heap on the dance floor. They had become a two-part jigsaw made perfect, her breasts pressed against his abs, her thighs against his legs. The friction of each small movement fanned a fire in her softest places.

Then, someone bumped her shoulder, throwing a bucket of iced water over her trance. Pulling away, she closed her eyes and pressed her forehead against his chest, hugging him tighter. 'Sorry,' she whispered.

'Don't be.' His voice was tight. Again.

When she looked up, anxiety was etched over his face. She smiled, half-heartedly. 'I just . . . I wasn't expecting this to happen.'

'Me neither.' His mouth was smiling, but his sorrowful eyes were not. 'Although I'm not sad that it did.'

She took his hand. 'Come on, let's go talk. Your taxi will be here in a minute.'

They walked hand in hand out of the ballroom and into the hotel reception area, which was largely empty. Her head was screaming at her to let go of his hand, but her heart was uncommonly stubborn.

She turned to face him. 'I'm sorry, Monty. I'm sorry I didn't tell you about New York, I told you I was a terrible person.'

'You're really not.' He rubbed her shoulders, his eyes suddenly flat. 'I'm sure you had your reasons.'

They took a seat on a sofa in reception, their bare legs pressed together. 'Monty, you have been the most amazing surprise. Every moment we've shared has been magical, beyond words.' She swallowed, her mouth drier than cotton. 'I'm just not ready for anything more than friendship.'

'We don't need to rush anything. You give me a reason to smile when I wake up each day and before I go to bed and that won't change while you're away, you know?'

She closed her eyes. Her heart was screaming at her. But she just couldn't take the risk on a relationship, and it wasn't fair on him to wait for her to change her mind.

'You're just the most amazing guy, Montgomery Wiles. So many girls at the office think the world of you. You should . . . ' she whispered. 'With me going off to New York, I think it would best if you started dating someone who's better for you.'

His eyes hardened, yet his voice remained soft. 'You don't mean that.'

Out the corner of her eye, she spotted a black taxi pull up outside. Sitting up straight she stared into his eyes. 'Your taxi is here, I know you need to rush home.'

'It can wait a few minutes.'

Desperate to cry, she continued, 'Honestly, Monty, you're better off. You'll have a free run to reach vice president with me off the scene.'

He stared her impassively. 'How much do you think I give a monkey's about that right now? I've moved in with my parents and I'm commuting to London every day to make rich people richer.'

She was panicky and unsure of what to say. 'But we're big rivals remember? There was that big vote. You told me about it. You voted for yourself.'

He chuckled grimly. 'I voted for you, Hats.'

'Did you?'

'You're the superstar.'

'I don't deserve you being so nice.'

'Well, let's not disagree.' He flopped his hands heavily to his sides. 'Look, I've got to go. I've, you know . . . '

A cold knot of tension twisted her diaphragm tightening her voice. Yes, she knew. He needed to get home quickly. He'd put so much care into making her feel incredible at New Year, with his mam declining and his dad needing his help. 'I know . . . '

His voice hushed. 'I'm in love with you, Harriet Campbell. Completely in love with you.'

Without another word, he kissed her on the cheek, stood and strode out of the hotel.

She watched him go, adrift in an ocean of tears held back by her reserve. 'I love you too, Monty,' she whispered, as he waved before stepping heavily into the cab. 'More than you'll ever know.'

CHAPTER 7

April 2003

A robin fluttered onto the weathered lych-gate and considered the scene before flying across the grey slate roof of the Norman church. There was but the gentlest spring breeze. The hearse pulled up slowly and Hatty stood to one side, among the other mourners. Pallbearers lifted the ornate casket onto their shoulders. A magnificent sea of white and yellow flowers adorned the coffin, their perfect blossoms radiant in the sun and defiant in the face of their impermanence.

Hatty hadn't thought twice about booking a flight home after Monty's heartbreaking call last week with the news that Daisy had lost her final battle. Suddenly, her high-life in New York was cast into irrelevance by his pain.

The funeral party processed slowly towards the sturdy oak door of the church, Monty following behind in a dark suit, gripping his dad's arm. Her face flushed and she dabbed her eyes with a handkerchief.

Something poked her and she turned to Penny, a junior colleague from the bank. Petite, pretty, fresh out of Oxford and overflowing with ambition.

'Hi, Hatty, it's really good to see you here. So nice you flew back from New York.' Her tone suggested a question.

'Hello, Penny. Yes, lovely to see you too. I'm just here to pay my respects as Monty and I are friends.'

'Oh, I didn't know you were friends. He hasn't mentioned it, and we are, well, pretty inseparable.'

Monty and Penny? He hadn't mentioned it – hadn't even mentioned her. Why wouldn't he have told me? We chat on the phone every week. 'So, you and Monty are . . . ' Before she'd finished talking, Penny cut her off abruptly.

'Yes, we're an item. He is such a great guy. People say we make a real power couple.'

Penny's words thudded into her like punches to the stomach. 'I'm sure you do,' Hatty replied with a smile, her heart shattering. She took a seat towards the back of the ancient nave, while Penny sat at the front, immediately behind Monty and Alan.

'Let me introduce you to Dad.' Monty gently took Hatty's arm and steered her to a different corner of the lounge, in his family home. 'Dad, I wanted you to meet Harriet, my best friend.'

Alan was a touch shorter than his son, with salt and pepper grey hair, but with a similar athletic build of someone who kept an eye on his weight and exercised often. Facially, softer and more rounded, his thoughtful blue eyes were nonetheless striking like Monty's. 'Hello, Harriet. Thank you for coming today. Monty has told me so much about you.'

Told him so much about me? She kept a tight lid on her tears. 'Thank you, Mr Wiles. I was heartbroken to hear about Daisy's passing. Today's service was beautiful. I could really feel your love and how special your marriage was.'

'That is such a nice thing to say, Harriet. Thank you.' He reached out and took her hand in his. 'And please, just call me Alan.'

'I'll try my best, but do call me Hatty.' She hugged him, and noticed he wore a similar cologne to his son.

Hatty hadn't wanted to get in the way during the wake, so floated around the room, talking to other guests. Browsing family photos, it was clear that Monty was the likeness of his mam. A smile spread across her face at a photo of him as a boy, still the same height as Daisy, his arm around her on a tropical beach.

'Finally, I get a little time to talk.' Monty appeared beside her, glass of sherry in hand.

She stroked his arm lightly. 'I love this photo of you and your mam.'

'Yeah, I love that one too. It was taken in Thailand.'

'Do you think you'll get back there with your dad?'

'Yes, of course. Mum would want us to. It's our family ritual and, as much as anything, we have close friends there. They're here somewhere.' His eyes swept the room.

She glanced towards Alan, deep in conversation with the vicar. 'I think your dad must be so proud of you for the way you've helped.'

'Ah, well—' he shrugged '—any child would do the same.'

I'm not entirely sure about that. 'So then—' she poked his arm playfully '—tell me about Miss Moneypenny.'

He scratched his hair. 'Hmm, yes. We're just kind of, you know. Nothing serious.'

'She seems pretty keen on you, mind. I could almost picture her measuring up the church pew ends for wedding flowers.' Immediately, she kicked herself for letting jealousy turn her mean.

He grimaced. 'Hope not. Got too many other things on my plate.'

She was doubly annoyed with herself for making Monty awkward when he was struggling to hold it together. Looking around she asked, 'Where has she gone by the way?'

'Oh, she went home about ten minutes ago. Has some engagement with her friends in London later this afternoon.'

He drifted off to talk to other guests, and Hatty continued to float, chatting with people who were lost for company.

An Asian couple stood to one side, the man in a dark suit and the woman in an elegant dress, and pearls, her eyes rimmed red.

'I hope you don't mind me saying hello, but I think you must be Alan and Daisy's friends from Thailand?' she asked, politely.

The man smiled at her broadly, his eyes crinkling at the edges. 'Why thank you. You are quite right. My name is Aek and this is my wife, Mai.'

She remembered Monty telling her about Thai culture and pressed her hands together beneath her chin in a *wai*. 'It is really nice to meet you *Khun* Aek and *Khun* Mai.'

'Oh hoo, you know Thai culture? I'm impressed,' Aek returned the wai, his smile like tropical sunlight. 'Have you been to Thailand?'

'No, not yet, but I'd love to visit one day. I have family reasons and Monty has said so many wonderful things.'

Mai considered Hatty inscrutably before asking in perfectly accented English. 'May I ask, are you *Khun* Harriet?'

She took a half step back. 'Gosh, yes, I'm Harriet, but please call me Hatty.'

Khun Mai smiled serenely. 'My dear friend Daisy told me a lot about your friendship with Monty. It made her so happy.'

'I'm really sad that I never met Daisy.'

'Ah, you've met Hatty I see,' Alan said, appearing at her side and briefly wrapping his arm around her shoulder. 'Isn't she lovely?'

Aek grinned, less formal than his wife, his eyes twinkling. 'She is beautiful, and it is our honour. I can see why *Nong* Monty likes her so much.'

Mai cast her husband a stern look and spoke *sotto voce* in Thai. Silence fell, the three old friends turning their eyes warmly towards Hatty as if she were a member of their extended family.

Alan reached into the drawer of a nearby cupboard, pulling out a camera. 'While I've got you all here, why don't I capture a picture?'

'Oh, let me take a photo of you and your friends, Alan,' Hatty offered.

'That's okay, dear. It'll give me a lift to keep a photo of you with our dearest friends.'

Aek and Mai dutifully flanked Hatty and faced Alan who clicked a couple of times.

Suddenly awkward, she asked, 'Do you know where Monty is? I should see if he needs help.'

'I think he's in the kitchen, dear,' Alan replied.

Head spinning, she bade farewell to the group, *waiing* to Aek, Mai and Alan, who returned her respect.

Empty sherry glasses and plates were scattered around the room on side tables and sills, so she gathered them on her way to the kitchen.

Monty hunched over a sink overflowing with suds, sleeves rolled up, furiously washing glasses.

'Oh, hello, I was wondering where you'd got to,' she said softly.

Without looking up, he replied, 'Just so many glasses to clean.'

She stroked his arm. 'You okay?'

He turned, his face flushed. 'Mum used to hate it when the kitchen was in a mess.'

'Oh, Monty.' She wrapped him in a hug and rubbed his back as he sobbed into her shoulder. 'I'll help you get through this, I promise. Come on, if you wash, I'll dry. Get it all tidy, just as your mam would want it.'

He smiled through his tears.

There were fewer guests when she returned to the lounge a while later.

A slight, elderly lady with a mop of white hair and a black home-knitted cardigan caught her eye.

'It was very nice of you to collect up the glasses, deary,' she said, a lily of the valley scent emitting from her, the deep creases of her face softening with her smile.

'Oh, thank you, that's kind. I thought I should do something to help.'

'That's exactly the sort of thing Alan likes to say, you know? Always the calm and helpful one.'

'Ah, that's nice to hear. I've only just met him today, but he is a lovely man.'

'Has Monty not brought you down before? Oh, tut tut, that really won't do. Nice girl like you.'

Hatty blushed. 'Ah, well, you see, me and Monty are just friends, that's all – and I live in New York now.'

The lady leant in and fixed Hatty with her watery eyes, touching her arm with a pale, bony finger. 'You know, I remember Alan saying Daisy was just a friend when I first met her, too.'

'I see you've met Mrs Wyeth.' Monty kissed the old lady on the cheek, looking at Hatty with a warmth that expressed gratitude beyond words.

The old lady crooked her arm through Monty's and smiled sweetly. 'I've known this handsome young man since he was a baby, crawling around naked on the floor in here. He's really quite the catch.'

Hatty drove out of the picturesque English village on the outskirts of Winchester, the narrow road hemmed with thick rivers of white and yellow daffodils. Flicking on the radio, she listened to the soulful voice of Lee Ann Womack and cried for the first time since she met Monty. He'd found another woman. Super-intelligent, pretty, perky Penny. And the worst part was, she'd encouraged this and was denied the catharsis of being cross at him. She'd pushed the man she loved into the arms of another, creating the most dreadful Gordian love knot that she couldn't now untangle. Because she was never going to fight another woman for his favour. Not after what happened with Andrew. Not ever.

She pulled into a layby and sat staring out at the clover green slope of St Catherine's hill, the trees blurred by her tears.

CHAPTER 8

July 2003

Hatty stood in the mirror, sorting her make-up. Her hair was frizzy and curled at the temples after the hockey match she'd helped her team win with a late goal. But she rather liked the Austen-esque look it created. Except that Lizzie Bennett would not sport sparkling eye shadow, nor have her lips coloured to a high gloss. Or wear a figure-hugging Chinese cheongsam, in gold with jade flecks, and a long slit up one thigh.

Connie sidled up to her, in a short and glittery purple dress, which showcased her lissom legs. 'Mm hmm, the men of New York are gonna be in trouble *tonight* when they see us!'

'Talk for yourself, you look like Naomi Campbell, but somehow even more amazing.'

The African-American had become an instant friend when she moved to New York. Super smart, kind and funny. One of those people who, when they put their minds to something new, can master it quickly, as she had with what she insisted on calling 'field' hockey.

A touch taller, with high cheekbones and the most gorgeous burnt caramel eyes, she draped an arm over Hatty's shoulder. 'You just keep talking like that, sister, and I ain't gonna let you go home tomorrow.'

They shared a cab across Brooklyn Bridge, the midsummer sun a molten orb above the skyscrapers of Lower Manhattan. Friends from the bank had gathered to bid farewell at the end of Hatty's six-month stay.

It was jam-packed at the cocktail lounge in Exchange Place when they arrived, but Connie bustled through and found their normal crowd, on sofas in the far corner. Helium balloons tethered to champagne bottles floated above low tables.

A cheer rang out and someone handed Hatty a glass of champagne.

Connie bossed two of the guys off of a sofa, so she and guest-of-honour Hatty could sit in the prime spot.

Another cheer went up when a tall, *extremely* well-built man, with blond hair in a crew cut appeared, a champagne flute in one hand. Still in workwear, his shirtsleeves were rolled halfway up thickly muscled forearms. Having ditched the tie, his top two buttons were undone, showing a tanned valley between his pecs. Monty was in great shape, but this guy looked like a body builder in business attire. Hatty couldn't help but stare at his square, lean features, before his predatory grey eyes scorched into hers and she dropped her gaze.

'Who the heck is that?' she whispered.

'Who that?' Connie glanced across. 'All you need to know is that—' she paused for emphasis and sass '—*that,* sister, is trouble. His name's Trent. Just joined us from Goldman Sachs or, according to the rumours, Goldman Sex.'

'I can well imagine,' she said, returning her gaze to him and getting a flirty wink.

'Now, don't you be fooled by his homesy charm, sugar. Trent is old money New York. This boy right here,' she twirled her finger in his direction, 'he'll probably marry some southern heiress called Willow who gives him six kids and ignores him screwing around.'

After a while Connie left to chat with others, and Hatty fell into conversation with the people around her.

And then, inevitably, Trent flopped into the sofa beside Hatty, his weight causing her to tumble into him.

'So you're the lady of the moment, right?' he said, wrapping an arm around and pulling her closer. He didn't care about her personal space and his hot breath seared her cheek.

'That would be me.' He didn't wear cologne like Monty, and his smell was dangerous.

'So what's a beautiful, single girl like you doing in a bar like this?' His grin revealed perfect white teeth.

She shoved him away and sat upright. 'What makes you assume that I'm single?'

'I see no other guys here. So, you got a boyfriend back in London town?'

'No. Well, just a good friend, Monty at the London office. Kind of close. It's complicated.'

'Monty Wiles? Hey, you know Monty?' a female colleague asked.

'Yeah, that's him.'

'He's dating a friend of mine. She says he's dreamy.'

Irritated, Hatty looked up into Trent's eyes, which didn't waver. 'That would be Penny, pretty, perky Penny.' *More money, more honey, Penny.*

'Not Penny, Miranda,' the lady clarified.

'Miranda?' Hatty exclaimed. *Who on earth is Miranda?*

'Hey, don't you worry about no Penny or Miranda.' He pulled her close and ran his fingers in figures of eight up her arm, making her shiver. 'Let's get some shots going over here.'

'Oh, I don't normally drink hard liquor,' she said, anxiously.

'Come on, it's a celebration, right?' Dimples like canyons appeared on his cheeks.

Trays of tequila appeared. The first shot burned the back of her throat, making her cough, but her inhibitions dropped a touch.

Not having eaten after hockey, she was light-headed, but tossed down another fiery shot. Between cracking loud jokes, Trent had nothing interesting to say as the evening rolled by. But Hatty's mind was elsewhere and she sunk deeper into gloom.

Why didn't Monty tell me he'd moved on to another woman? They still spoke every week. Why the secrecy? She was furious about Miranda, drunk, and resentful that he should move on so quickly. And that she hadn't.

'You look dynamite in that dress.' He stroked his fingers gently through her hairline.

She pushed his hand away.

'Boy, am I sorry you're going home tomorrow.' He downed another shot and grabbed two more for them both, pushing his hand high up her bare thigh as he leant forward.

Fury bubbled within her and she slapped his face. 'Don't touch me!'

Trent's eyes flew open as she stood, staggering slightly, steadying herself on the edge of a sofa.

Every eye in the room focused on her.

Then Connie was at her side, shooting the others a warning look. 'Let me get you out of here, missy, I'm struggling to breathe with them male egos fillin' the room.'

Hooking a hand under her arm, Hatty followed her friend out of the bar.

It was still warm outside, though she trembled as a yellow cab approached.

Connie slid into the rear seat beside Hatty. 'You're not much of a drinker, huh?'

Hatty sat forward, head in her hands, spinning.

'I think you better get back to London for your own safety, girl. Things that boy Trent wants to do with you is damn naughty.'

'Ugh, don't.'

'He's got you really riled up, hasn't he?'

'Thinks he's got a licence to feel me up because he's got lots of money,' she slurred.

'I didn't mean Trent, but that guy in London you speak to every week. Monty, right?'

'He's dating *Miranda* now, apparently.'

Connie chuckled. 'But wait now. Didn't you tell him on New Years that you weren't interested?'

'Can we stop the cab please?' She suddenly needed to vomit.

Walking through duty free, Hatty pulled her sunglasses over her eyes to shield them from the fluorescent lights. To catch the early flight, she'd slept just three hours and still had a dull headache, despite drinking water and orange juice non-stop on the plane. *Ugh.*

Then, backlit by a shaft of evening sunlight, appearing through the crowd, like a handsome jeans- and polo-clad knight, was Monty. She'd not seen him since the funeral, but it could have been yesterday. His familiar, cheeky, boyish grin erupted. He spread his arms wide as he approached, and she nestled into his embrace, releasing her suitcase and dropping the carrier bag to run her hands up his back.

Gosh, how I've missed your smell. Her grumpiness dissolved and her brain fog dissipated, just a touch.

He kissed the top of her head as she clung to him, before grabbing the handle of her case. 'Can't tell you how nice it is to have you home again, Hats.'

CHAPTER 9

September 2003

Hatty effervesced with excitement as Monty looked up from across the trading floor and spotted her, his eyes not leaving hers as she approached nonchalantly. He'd had his thick hair cut recently, which looked glossy and perfectly shaped with whatever product he'd added. She wondered if *Gaynor* had got him to use that, then shoved the thought aside.

'You're up to something, Campbell,' he accused, with narrowed eyes.

'What, *moi*?' She pressed her fingertips to her collar in mock surprise.

'*Mais tu ne parles pas français* – but you don't speak French.'

'Oh, now you are being clever.' She stamped her foot.

'There's a decent language laboratory in Greenwich if you fancy doing French lessons after work sometime?' His usual smile returned, the one that seemed reserved just for her.

She gazed into his deep-blue eyes. 'Only if I can show you how to play hockey in Battersea with my club.'

'Hockey skirts must look good on you, but they wouldn't flatter *my* hips.'

Looking him up and down slowly, her eyes finally fixing on his, she whispered, 'Oh, I dunno. Maybe let me be the judge?'

Tipping his head back he laughed out loud. 'Alright, you got me. Did you come down here for anything in particular, or . . . ?'

Since they'd kissed nine months ago, he backed off whenever she flirted and it bothered her, given the seemingly carefree nature of his recent dating life. 'Well, sorry to disturb your ever so busy schedule, but I organised a treat for your birthday.'

He stared at the buff envelope in her hand. 'Oh, you really didn't have to. What is it?'

She proffered the envelope and he prised it open, revealing two tickets for the Sadler's Wells Theatre.

'It's *Swan Lake*,' she explained.

'I can see.' He flicked his forefinger alternately between himself and her. 'Is this some "I take you to ballet for your birthday and you take me to ballet for mine" thing?'

Her spirits lifted at the reminder of *her* birthday treat; box seats for *Sleeping Beauty* after champagne tea at Claridge's Hotel. It had been a perfect, well, almost perfect, evening with Monty. 'Unkind! I just know how much you love the ballet now.'

His eyebrows crept up his forehand as he studied the tickets again. 'Harriet Campbell, I think there has been some sort of dreadful mistake. You've got me tickets to *Swan Lake* performed entirely by men.'

Grabbing the tickets with a theatrical flourish, she stared at them. 'Oh, really? Gosh, they must have run out of tickets for the show with women swans.'

He stared at her and for a brief moment she wrung her hands, worried that she'd gone too far. Everyone was raving about Matthew Bourne's all-male take on Tchaikovsky's classic, and she'd wanted to go for ages.

His forehead un-creased, unadulterated warmth returning. '*Man Lake*, eh? Alright, good one. I'll get my legs waxed.'

Excited chatter blended with the rumble and rattle of red buses and black cabs on the road outside.

Hatty buttoned her overcoat against the autumn chill and glanced up at Monty, hoping he'd loved the performance as much as she had. 'Fancy a wander before we head home?'

'Feels a bit early to call it a night.' He smiled easily as their post-show routine followed its accepted path.

They crossed into Spa Green gardens, its trees up-lit a luminescent green, and turned south, towards the Thames.

'So—' she nudged his arm '—what did you think?'

'I was wondering whether those feathered pantaloons might suit me at the office fancy dress.'

A molten glow erupted in the base of her tummy at the thought of him, torso bared, dressed as a swan. 'Can't imagine the eye make-up on you, though, if I'm being honest.'

He paused to look at her, his eyes burning through her outer defences. 'Perhaps you might dress as the swan princess. All tutu and legs that never stop . . .' He paused, before whispering, 'dancing.'

The warmth crept up her neck and she blushed, hoping he wouldn't notice. 'Now that's something you'll never see me do at a work party.'

'Pity.' He strolled on. 'I just think you'd look great. Convincing eyes, persuasive lips.'

'Wait.' She laughed, turning to shake the lapels of his jacket. 'Are you hitting me with Belinda Carlisle lyrics now?'

'Sorry, I can't speak when I look in your eyes.'

'Oh my God. What are you like?' Crooking an arm through his, they continued out of the gardens and onto the busy road once more.

Up ahead, two men in hoodies approached, their voices laced with sarcasm and lager. The taller called out, 'Look at these posh love birds in their fancy clothes then? Wa-hay.'

Alarm bells jangled loudly in Hatty's head, her shoulder muscles tightening like springs.

'Not going to give us a smile, love? Beneath you, are we?' he leered.

Monty strolled on regardless. She glanced up to see a big grin light his face.

'Alright lads. You having a nice evening then?' he asked, with no hint of anxiety.

The taller shrugged his shoulders, disarmed by *bonhomie,* and stared back with bloodshot eyes. 'Yeah mate, just having a few beers and a laugh that's all.'

'Top job, glad you're having a great night, buddy.' Monty stretched his arm out with a clenched fist inviting the man to bump him, which he did.

'Where you two off to then?'

'Just going to get a drink. Recommend any place decent?'

The second, slightly shorter, man jabbed his thumb behind him. 'Yeah. There's some decent bars just down the street, fella.'

'Cheers, man.' Monty fist bumped him too.

'That your girlfriend then?' the taller man asked, less aggressively.

Monty wrapped his arm round Hatty's shoulder and kissed the top of her head. 'Yeah. Isn't she gorgeous?'

They laughed, fist-bumped him again and continued noisily up the street.

A few hundred yards further on, chatter spilled out of a softly lit cocktail bar with stylish décor.

'Come on, let's get one for the road,' Monty said.

Exhaling sharply, she replied, 'I think I need one.'

In his usual way, he navigated through the well-dressed throng with ease. 'A glass of Veuve Clicquot and a Macallan 18, please,' he asked the bar-lady politely.

For a man who in most things was spontaneous and spur of the moment, he clung to their routines and rituals, as if they were a sacred part of his canon.

With all the tables occupied, they found a pillar with a shelf to rest their drinks on.

'That was pretty scary,' Hatty said after a sip of champagne.

'I'm a big scary animal.'

'Who you trying to kid?' She parried, the stress tumbling off her shoulders.

'Ha!' His grin lit up her world. 'Anyway, those two lads were harmless enough. Just having a bit of fun.'

'Why did you tell them I was your girlfriend?' His words had felt uncomfortably nice.

He smiled evenly. 'It worked, didn't it?'

'What do you mean?'

'If I'd got all defensive it would have just got their backs up and raised the temperature. A friendly, happy couple is non-threatening.' His eyes lightened like sharpened steel. 'And a subtle reminder not to try anything silly.'

'Oh, okay.' She stared into her glass. That's all it was; a ruse to shake them off. Reality crashed home that they were lodged forever in the friend zone. Maybe, that was just their destiny. Monty loved her – indeed he'd told her so at New Years – and would fight for her if needed. But he'd put himself into a box that she'd closed, too upright to press her on whether the lid might be ajar. 'Just seemed a bit over the top,' she said, more petulant than she would have liked.

'Anywayyy,' he ran his hand down her arm, breaking her heart with his smile. 'Loved *Man Lake*, thank you so much.'

'Me too. Might be the last we get to see each other for a while.' She inhaled hard. 'Monty, I've been offered a promotion back in New York. It's what I've been working hard for.'

He stared into his whisky tumbler, his broad chest expanding with each breath, before meeting her gaze. 'You've done so brilliantly and deserve this chance. I think it's genuinely a fantastic opportunity.'

She wrinkled her brow. 'I sense there's a "but".'

'No buts. You are totally amazing, Hatty. I'm not going to lie, I missed you before and I was rather getting used to you being around again. So I'll miss you. Not a lot.' His face softened. 'Just a bit.'

Whenever she felt so moved that she wanted to lean in and kiss Monty, she could never break through the thick protective glass around her heart. 'I'll miss you too,' she whispered.

'It's only New York. We can still talk on the phone. And I'm sure you'll be back sometimes to see your family. Hope you'll find a smidge of time to see me too.'

'Of course I will, you know that,' she stared into his eyes and knew he'd always be available for her, wherever she was.

'It's a pity, in a way, because someone mentioned a new ballet production next year; *The Nutcracker* performed by drag queens. *The Dance of the Sugared Plums Fairy* sounds especially notable.'

Laughing so hard, tears came to her eyes, not all of them joyous. She flung her arms around his neck, uplifted by his warm reassuring cheek against hers. 'I'm sure they'll make heaven a place on earth.'

'That was dreadful.' Monty groaned, whipping out his camera. 'Time for a quick photo?'

'Go on then,' she replied, nestling into him.

Since she broke up with Andrew over a year ago, her career had blossomed and that had felt enough at first. But at the end of her life, she probably wouldn't weigh success solely on her career, but what she had done with her life. And, one day, hopefully, with her family.

Everything Monty did seemed to be driven from his heart, more than his head. She loved the unconditionality of his affection for her but was too scared to trust in it. The painful truth was that having pushed him way, she loved him too much to remain close and watch him marry someone else. Maybe her fate really did lie in New York.

CHAPTER 10

25 December 2003

Caught up in Twister, Hatty was tangled among the skinny limbs of her nephew and niece.

'Your phone's buzzing,' her mam Evie said, from the armchair.

Threading her leg free from Maisie's arched body, she got up and stretched cramping toes. Grabbing her phone, she sat on the sofa beside the family's border collie Billie, who thumped his tail lightly and rested his white muzzle in her lap.

No number was displayed, but it didn't matter, as it was Christmas Day, after all. In her thickest Geordie accent, she answered, 'Stargate chippie, what would you like to order?'

'Are you taking orders on Christmas Day then?' Monty asked from Thailand, his voice tinny.

She pictured his puzzled face and smiled. 'Wey aye, kidder, of course we are. Just letting you know we have mince pies on special.'

'What's in them, then?'

'*Mince.* Are you trying to be funny with us?'

'Oh.' There was a pause. 'Do you have mushy peas? Only, when I get lonely, I like to spread them over my naked body and let a dog lick 'em off.'

'Montgomery Wiles, that's disgusting!' she squealed, somewhere between indignant and intrigued.

She wandered out the lounge and upstairs to her childhood room. Kicking off her slippers, she settled into the familiar comfort of the bed and brushed stray strands behind her ear. 'I'll never eat mushy peas again after you said that.'

'Which makes me incredibly sad. Anyway, happy Christmas, Hatty.'

'Merry Christmas, Monty.' She touched the rare autographed first edition of *A Town Like Alice* on her bedside table. 'And thank you for the gift. It's incredible.'

'Ah, you know, what says friendship more than buying someone a second-hand version of what they already purchased brand new.'

'Stop it,' she laughed. 'It must have cost a fortune.'

'Anyway, thanks for the digital photo frame. Every time I look at it, your image torments me in a different way, which is priceless.'

She giggled. The choice had been easy – he loved taking snaps of them together and she couldn't wait until the next one.

'Finally dragging you out of the Stone Age, Fred Flintstone.' The words spilled out before she could stop herself, and her spirits sunk at the reminder of their *almost-could-be*.

'Why, thank you, Wilma,' he replied, without missing a beat. 'How's your day in Bedrock?'

'Ate too much turkey, Dad fell asleep, farting on the armchair where I normally read, we watched the Queen, then played twister with hyperactive children on a full stomach, which has made me queasy.'

'Can I come to yours next year?'

'Sure. Though I don't think Billie likes mushy peas, mind.'

His laughter echoed from five thousand miles away.

'Have a really lovely Christmas won't you, hinny,' Hatty said to the unkempt man as he took his dessert. The queue of people patiently waiting for their Christmas pudding snaked around one side of a Tudor hall in Newcastle.

'You're an absolute angel.' He offered a toothless smile before moving on.

'Give us a bit more custard, darling,' another diner said.

'Go on then, there you go.' She obliged with a smile. Talking to Monty had offered a poignant reminder of how close they were, yet also how far apart. Helping Dad with Christmas dinner service at the local community kitchen had felt like a nice way to recharge emotional batteries ahead of her return to New York.

With the crowd dispersing, she scoured one end of the hall, filling a binbag with used napkins, plastic cutlery and other sundries. 'Do you want me to help sweep up when I'm done, Dad?' she called to John, folding away chairs.

'Aye, can do.'

It was almost eleven by the time she sank into the passenger seat of John's van.

'Life's a bit simpler and less complicated up here compared to London and New York, eh?' he said, as he pushed the gear stick into first and drove into the remnants of Christmas night.

'Wey aye,' she replied quietly.

'I hope you know how proud of you we all are, Hatty. Not just me and Mam, but Martha, Steve and the bairns.'

'No pressure, then.'

'Hey, there's never pressure from us. You've always worked hard at everything, and you don't need to prove anything by flying to the States.'

'The main reason I work so hard is to ensure that, maybe one day, my family doesn't need to worry about money like you and Mam did.'

'We did okay in the end, didn't we?'

'Aye, we did. We had an amazing childhood.' She stared out the window across to the south bank of the Tyne River as John drove along the Scotswood Road towards home.

'Just don't forget to live your life, kidder, that's all.'

She sighed. Andrew had grown up with no financial worries and no great care for people less fortunate. Cheating on her hurt most because, in accepting him, she'd made a bad decision. Monty had always met a need in her heart that Andrew *never* could fulfil. 'It's hard for me to trust another man after Andrew, you know?'

John glanced at her from the driver's seat. 'Well, Andrew let you down, there's no doubt about that. It's just that I never once saw you as happy *with* him as I've seen you on the phone to this Monty fella. What do you think he'd say about you volunteering at a community kitchen anyways?'

A grin warmed her face. 'I'm not a betting girl, but I'd put money on Monty jumping straight in. He has a good word for everyone at work, from the cleaners to the receptionists. He's the most naturally kind man I know.'

'After me, you mean?'

She giggled. 'Wey aye.'

'Well, you being in New York might finally prove if he's as nice as all that. Absence makes the heart grow fonder, and all.'

'We'll see.' It weighed heavily that she wouldn't see Monty before she flew to the States, and tears rolled down her face.

John flicked on the hazard lights and pulled over. 'Come here and give us a hug.'

She sniffled miserably into his shoulder for a few seconds.

He patted her back softly. 'Do you think he really knows how you feel about him?'

It was a rhetorical question. For all the fabulous moments, Hatty had never been brave enough to trust Monty enough with the knowledge of how dearly she loved him. And, if she could never do that, then her rational mind told her that, perhaps, she should move on.

CHAPTER 11

April 2004

Hatty forked at the avocado salad distractedly as she read the next message on her BlackBerry. Lunchtime differed from desk time only in the provision of food. Although this message was from her New York partner in crime, Connie, currently in China researching companies.

'You working and eating at the same time?' Trent plonked himself uninvited into the chair opposite.

She peered above the parapet of her device and noticed again the chatter of the bank's canteen, high above the bustle of Wall Street. And Trent, slouched back, top button of his expensive shirt undone, an over-confident smile on his chiselled face.

'Some of us have a lot of work to do, you know?'

'Hey, I'm busy.' He held his hands up in that characteristic, *I'm so innocent and harmless fashion* before glancing left at an attractive female colleague who walked by.

Already growing bored, she asked, 'Did you want anything in particular?'

'Someone said you like Broadway. Was going to ask if you wanted to catch a show sometime?'

She studied him. 'I didn't see you as a culture vulture?'

He pushed his chair back onto its rear legs and laughed, brushing his fingers down his powerful chest as he did so. 'I'm not saying I am. Just thought it would be nice to extend a hand of friendship to an English woman in New York.'

'Hmm, I'm not short of friends. Just saying.' She returned her attention to the BlackBerry. After their first, difficult encounter last year, Hatty had kept the cocksure American at arm's length though had sat at the same table over lunch a few times, with others. He'd seemed genuinely embarrassed and had apologised for getting her drunk and acting inappropriately on their first meeting. That was a slip up she'd determined never to repeat.

'Give a guy a chance, will you? Someone told me that *Mamma Mia* show is great, and I thought you'd like to go, that's all.' His dimples assumed their full craggy canyon effect bracketing his tanned face as he smiled.

Mamma Mia was a show she hadn't seen yet, so despite her reticence, she was tempted. Monty was dating yet another woman, goodness knows *her* name, and why shouldn't she dip her toe in the chilly, frog-infested waters?

Hatty was enthralled by the dazzling, colourful tapestry of Abba songs woven into a chaotic but no less joyous storyline. At certain points she sang along quietly, although 'My Last Summer' sent her thoughts flying to Monty on the steps of St Paul's Cathedral.

'Can you believe that guy?' Trent whispered loudly, his lips almost touching her ear, his knee bumping her leg lightly. He kept his arm draped over the back of her chair, so he could stroke her shoulder with his fingers whenever he made comment on the show.

She re-focused, not allowing herself to mind too much about his repeated invasions of her personal space. It had now been almost two years since her break up with Andrew and she was trying to loosen up a bit. Trent was not someone she could see a future with, but why not enjoy the company of an interested, good-looking man for a change?

'Thank you so much for organising tickets for tonight,' Hatty said, as they shuffled out of the Adamesque auditorium of the Winter Garden Theatre following the show.

He briefly clamped an arm around her shoulder before hurriedly releasing it. 'Sure, no problem. Hey, have you been to the top of the Rock? There's some great views up there.'

She turned her mind to the Rockefeller Centre and its supposedly fabulous views of the New York skyline. 'Actually, no I haven't visited yet, so I don't mind if you're offering to be tour guide?'

'No problem. It's just a five-minute walk.'

Midtown Manhattan was vastly different from Central London at night-time. Like a gaudy *son et lumière* of billboards, yellow cabs and bustling sidewalks. It did brash by the bucketload, a bit like her companion.

'So, what did you think of the show, Trent?'

'It was okay though a bit kooky.'

She glanced at him, his eyes fixed ahead at the crowded pedestrian crossing. 'Bit too European for your liking?'

Turning, his eyes bore into hers, hotter than the Mojave in summer. 'Ha, maybe. Just didn't get the whole thing with her mom having slept with three guys and she doesn't know who the father is, thing.'

'That's such a bloke thing to say,' she harumphed.

'What's that supposed to mean?'

'Aside from the "that not being the point of the show" thing, I don't think you'd take the same view if it was about a guy who slept with three women.'

'Suppose you've got a point.'

She poked his side playfully with her elbow and jested. 'It's about powerful, independent women, a concept that I'm sure must terrify you, Trent Morgan!'

'My mom's the most powerful woman I know, so I'm not all that hung up,' he grumbled.

'"Wisdom and Knowledge shall be the stability of thy times,"' she said brightly, admiring the Art Deco sculpture above the main entrance to 30 Rockefeller Plaza. It seemed fitting to a woman like her who valued understanding and careful study.

'Yeah, it's a nice one.' Trent admired the ornate entrance. 'It's a biblical quote from the Book of Isaiah. Actually, Lee Lawrie, the guy who made this, also has a similar sculpture in the United States' Senate.'

She raised her eyebrows. 'That's actually very interesting. And to think I had you down as a one-dimensional caveman.'

His chest heaved up and down as he laughed. 'Hey, I'm a New Yorker, what do you want from me? So I joke around a bit, but it doesn't mean there's nothing going on in my head.'

'Come on, let's go up and see the view from the top.'

They stepped out the lift at the sixty-fifth floor, into a glamorous, Thirties-style cocktail lounge, hemmed on all side by ceiling height windows with skyline views. A tuxedo-clad *maître de* stood attentively, his eyes lighting upon Trent. 'Good evening, Mr Morgan, how ya doin' today, sir?'

'Hey Davey, I'm good, thanks. Great to see you again, how's the family?'

He broke into a wide grin. 'They're doin' great thanks. You joinin' us for cocktails?'

'Yes please, if you got space, I know you must be busy. Just bringing my friend all the way from London, England to see this amazing place.'

Trent was slick with the charm, she had to give him that.

Davey ushered them into the beautifully appointed space, skirting a circular dancefloor on which the well-heeled turned and wheeled to Thirties music. Chatter and laughter popped like champagne corks, high above the liquor drinkers on the sidewalks outside.

They were seated at a table by the window with a view across the Empire State Building, whose lights twinkled in the night sky. Without asking, Trent ordered cocktails. 'Can't come to New York and not have a Manhattan.'

Sitting back, Hatty studied him, white candles casting shadows across his face, the glint in his steely eyes creating an inextinguishable light. 'Now you are a man who is used to getting what he wants.'

He raised his hands again. 'Who doesn't want to get what they want?'

A waiter placed Martini glasses before them and an assortment of delicate canapés.

Savouring her cocktail, she peered at him over the rim. 'My friend told me that you are trouble.'

'What's the trouble with dating a beautiful lady like you?'

'Who says this is a date?' she countered.

'Okay, so it's maybe not a date. But maybe you'll still agree to a dance?' His strong mouth flipped into a smile.

Gazing at the crowded dancefloor, the first lick of alcohol warming her tummy. 'Go on then, why not?'

He took her hand and led her to the dancefloor whereupon the band struck up a waltz.

'I haven't danced ballroom since I was at university,' she squeaked, her voice an octave higher.

Smiling into her eyes, he explained, 'It'll come back easy. Just put your right hand on my arm here and take my hand with your left. We'll take it nice and slow.' His left hand pressed gently against her lower back, fixing her pelvis against his upper leg. And then they were off.

Expertly, he led her around the polished floor.

The moves came instinctively, following dance lessons when she was a teen, and she moved effortlessly with the rise and fall of his steps. Andrew used to get cross at her waltzing with other men at a ball when he refused. Now, stress swept from her shoulders as she circled with longer strides, arching her back and turning her head at every spin.

Her flowing red dress swirling around her legs, she felt more beautiful than she had in a long time. Then he stopped, suddenly, tilting her body back, allowing her to lengthen her neck and flash a brilliant smile towards the guests sat at their tables.

There was polite applause when the tune ended there and she clapped her hands, skipping slightly. 'That was amazing, Trent. The caveman can dance!'

Lifting her fingertips, he deftly twirled her around before pulling her close again. 'Now the caveman will show you foxtrot.'

In the taxi, Hatty flopped her head back on the seat, dizzy from two hours of non-stop-dance. 'You are quite the surprise, Trent Morgan.'

'Good surprise or bad surprise?'

Narrowing her eyes, she replied, 'Still figuring that out.'

'Have you figured out enough to agree a second date?'

'Hmm. I didn't think this was a date. But anyway, possibly. We'll see.'

CHAPTER 12

July 2004

'I'm sure Monty can't possibly be as nice as you've said, so I'm prepared for disappointment.' Martha grinned.

'Good,' Hatty replied. 'That way you won't go over the top.'

'I'm choosing not to be offended by that. Anyways, do you want something to eat before your fun day out?'

'Go on then.' Hatty reached into her sister's cool bag and fished out a large Tupperware box, laying it on the picnic blanket.

'So, how are things between you and this fella you've got in New York?'

'I wouldn't describe him as my fella. I've been on a couple of dates, and he gave me a lift to the airport, but I'm choosing to go slowly.'

'So you've not . . .' her sister flapped her fingers in the air lasciviously.

She pushed her sister's hand away indignantly. 'Martha, no we haven't. He's nice enough, in some ways. But third date?'

'Did he know you were coming back for your birthday?'

'He didn't seem to,' Hatty turned and scanned St James's park.

'Oh.' Martha rolled her eyes. 'It's nice to have you home anyways.'

'Do you two want one of Grandad's sausage rolls?' Hatty called to Jimmy and Maisie who were kicking around a football on the grass nearby.

They ran over excitedly and sat next to their aunt, who put a selection of food on cardboard plates for them. She checked her watch again, wondering if Monty would be on time, how he'd look, how he'd smell. And how she'd feel.

'Looks like we might have company,' Martha said.

Through the treeline Monty approached from the direction of Buckingham Palace. In one hand, a bulging carrier bag, a rucksack slung over his shoulder. He looked great in knee-length denim shorts and polo shirt, with Aviator sunglasses against the hot summer sun. *Lovely as he ever was.* She waved, and he responded with his free hand.

'Mind if I join your party?' he asked politely.

Hatty stood and hugged him briefly before kissing one cheek, anxious not to show her sister and the kids the emotions fizzing inside.

Martha jumped to her feet. 'I'm Martha, and it's so nice to meet you Monty, after everything my sister has said. Come on, let me give you a hug.' Without awaiting a response, she wrapped her arms around Monty's neck and squeezed him until his face turned red.

'It's so nice to meet you too. Hatty talks about you all the time.'

'Nothing bad, I hope?' she gushed.

'Only good things,' Hatty intoned evenly. 'Although that could change.'

Monty grinned, mischief dancing in his eyes.

'Come on and sit down, we're just enjoying a birthday picnic for our Hatty,' Martha replied, fussing around him. 'I bet you must have missed her.'

He turned his azure eyes to Hatty's. 'Ah, you know, I can't imagine a World Without You.'

She burst out laughing, slapping his shoulder.

'What you laughing at?' Martha quizzed.

'I'm not even going to try to explain.'

Monty sat cross-legged by the kids who remained seated and wide-eyed. 'I reckon you must be Jimmy and you must be Maisie? I've got something you might like.' He reached into his bag and withdrew two packages.

Hatty helped the kids pull off the gift-wrap to reveal a box of Alien Eggs for Jimmy and a Luv Cub teddy for Maisie.

He'd also brought a large box of Krispy Kreme donuts for everyone to share.

'Are you trying to make us fat?' Martha gushed.

'No donut could spoil either of your fabulous looks.'

She melted into a fit of giggles, like an eleven-year-old being asked to slow dance for the first time at a school disco.

A few minutes later, Martha gazed dreamily at Monty playing football with the kids. 'Is he always like this, or is this just for show?'

Hatty took in the spectacle. 'You know what, I've never seen him with kids before but yes, this looks pretty much the full Monty.'

'Well, I'm ovulating just looking at him, so I can't imagine how you must feel.'

'That's outrageous!' She picked a fingernail. 'Anyway, he's too busy on the hamster wheel of dating.'

Scratching her manicured nails on Hatty's knee, she pouted. 'Maybe you just need to root around in the hamster cage with him.'

'Martha!' Hatty's face flushed crimson, and her voice dropped to a whisper. 'You know my views.'

'Wey aye. And I'm only saying. But maybe one reason he's scurrying around other lady hamsters is that you disappeared to New York and have refused to admit that you love him.'

'Thanks for the reminder,' she groaned.

Her big sister shuffled up and wrapped an arm around her shoulder. 'So, tell me what has he planned for your big birthday surprise?'

'I have absolutely no idea. But knowing him, it will be unexpected in the most amazing way.' She smiled, continuing to watch her best friend lark around with the kids. *Best friend?* Her smile faded.

'Hey kids, come over and have some cake,' Martha called. 'I think your aunty has to go soon.'

'Would you mind if I took a photo of you all together?' Monty asked. 'To remember this lovely day.'

Martha raised an eyebrow at Hatty, before gathering her kids around her. 'That would be absolutely lovely.'

Hatty jabbed her in the ribs.

The train sped through the glaucous coppice and heathland of the New Forest. They stopped in leafy Brockenhurst and historic Christchurch before eventually drawing to a halt in the seaside town of Bournemouth.

As they wandered down the hill towards the centre of town, seagulls floated in the cornflour sky, and the smell of saltwater grew.

'Do you mind if I have a quick look in here for some things?' Hatty asked, at a department store.

'Sure, we've got plenty of time.'

She mooched unhurriedly around the women's fashion section with Monty trailing behind. He waited patiently outside the fitting rooms, offering supportive comments about this or that jacket or dress she tried on. It occurred to her that this was the first time she'd been shopping with a man for several years. In the lingerie section, she held up a pretty set of green lace knickers and matching bra.

The pattern is so nice though I wonder if it's a bit see through for my liking? She tended to the practical when it came to smalls, but she suddenly wanted something that made her feel attractive and confident. Sexy. Holding the set up in the mirror, she noticed Monty a few yards behind. 'Oh,' she turned, blushing, 'I'd almost forgotten you were there. Do you think these ones look nice, though?'

He glanced down at the delicate underwear, his eyes returning to hers, mouth ajar, nodding imperceptibly. 'Err, yep. Yes. Definitely look nice.'

She held his gaze, the heat rising within. 'I might get these then as they're pretty.' Raising an eyebrow, she continued, 'Actually, now you've brought me to the beach, I might as well get a cozzie.'

He checked his watch. 'We've got plenty of time for a swim so, yeah, sounds nice.'

She led him through to the swimwear section.

'How do I look?' Hatty stepped out of the public changing rooms on the promenade a while later. She'd chosen a simple bikini in summery lemon and aqua-marine colours, that tied at her neck and hips with soft laces. It wasn't excessively skimpy and covered her modesty, but she liked the way it emphasised her slender waist and feminine curves.

Monty's eyes were sapphire as he took in her appearance. 'You look like the weather,' he said huskily.

'What does that mean?' She knew he thought she was hot but wanted him to admit it.

Standing close, his pupils bigger than comets, he took her hand in his fingertips, sending bolts of energy through her secret recesses. 'Harriet Campbell,' he said, leaning so close his nose brushed hers, 'I think you know the answer to that.'

She didn't let go of his hand as they walked onto the beach, their rucksacks and towels slung over their shoulders.

'Shall we go in then?' Monty peeled his t-shirt over his head, to reveal the muscular figure of a middle-weight boxer.

'Last one in is a sissy.' Hatty raced across the sand at full pelt, as keen to cool the fire raging inside as to beat Monty in a sprint. She reached the shallows first.

However, he sprinted past and dived headlong into the onrushing surf, a cloud of water spraying over her and puckering her skin.

'I'll get you for that.' She dashed after him, splashing water with her hands.

He stepped to one side catching her off-guard and lifting her high above his chest, before dropping her into the deeper water.

Gasping from the cold water, she charged at him, fuelled by a potent mix of vengefulness and arousal.

He turned in mock horror to run away, but she leapt onto his back, wrapping her legs around his torso. With all her strength, she twisted to one side, spinning him back under the water with her.

Tumbling over in the surf, air bubbles exploding all around, she pressed her feet into the sand and propelled herself up, breaching the surface, elated and bursting with laughter.

Erupting out of the sea, water cascading down his chest and abs, Monty wrapped his arms around her and kissed the top of her head.

Clasping his broad back, their hips pressed together, she knew how he longed for her.

Walking out of the sea hand in hand, they let their bodies dry in the warm sun for an hour and chatted lazily about nothing in particular.

Hatty couldn't recall a time when she'd felt so at peace with life, and so happy in the company of a man. *My man.* She'd finally sprung the soda can on suppressed feelings of love and attraction for Monty. Deep down, she wondered how it might feel to mess around on the beach with him in twenty years with their kids.

'Hey, they've got a Harry Ramsden's on the front. Fancy some fish and chips before our big adventure?' he asked after a while.

Having dozed, she opened her eyes to the sun's glare, a throbbing in her temple. 'Ooh, actually, I'd love that.'

They showered and changed, before strolling along the sea front past Bournemouth pier, the beach still crowded with bathers.

At the restaurant, they found a table by the window looking across the crystalline sea.

Hatty studied the menu. 'So, were you going for mushy peas with your fish, or . . . ?'

He looked around the dining room. 'Nah, I don't think they allow dogs in here, so . . . '

She sniggered.

The food came quickly. It was delicious although she couldn't finish it with the beginnings of a headache. The day had been perfect in every detail, and she didn't want to make a fuss, given the trouble Monty had gone to.

Brow furrowing, he studied her carefully. 'Are you okay, Hats?'

'Yes, I'm fine, thank you. I maybe didn't drink enough water today.' She rubbed her temple and downed a full glass of water, whereupon he topped it up.

'I hope you'll be okay this evening.'

She reached across and took his hand. 'Don't be silly, I'll be just fine. This has been the best birthday treat already, so thank you.'

Looking deep into her eyes, he said, 'I've got to make the most of this time with you, as you'll be off to New York again soon. Will miss you more than I can say.'

Right now, she wished he knew how much she'd missed him this past six months. She rubbed her neck and a short burst of pain made her squint. 'Why don't you try to say, then, Monty, just this once?'

'I miss you all the time, Hatty, you must know that?'

'Is that what you say to the girls you date? Like, who is it now? Beatrice?'

He shifted in his seat. 'I haven't seen Beatrice for ages.'

He always threw the shutters up to any conversation about his dating, which was fine most of the time. They were, after all, *just friends*. But now she chafed at the conversational tramlines he'd set for their friendship. Especially after the time they'd spent messing around like lovers on the beach.

'Anyway, sorry. I wanted to ask if you knew Trent, in the New York office?'

'Err, yes, I know about Trent. Seen him in the London office a few times.'

'We've been on a couple of dates and he keeps pestering me to, you know, get into a relationship. Just wanted to ask what you thought?'

He whistled as he exhaled. 'You know he has a terrible reputation?'

'And you think you've got a great reputation with the ladies, do you?'

'I mean, I think you could do better. You deserve better.'

'Sayeth the expert in human relationships.' The headache had grown in intensity, making her uncharacteristically mean.

'Ouch.' Forking at his remaining chips, he fell into silence and glanced out of the window.

She remembered the New Year's party, their slow dance and that identical look of deflation after she scotched his hopes.

Reaching forwards, she squeezed his hand. 'Hey, I'm sorry for killing the mood. I've just had the most amazing day with you. Sorry, jet lag must be giving me a headache.'

'That's okay.' His face creased with concern, and he rubbed her forearm, her goosebumps now sore.

'Shall we get out of here? It's a bit stuffy and I could use the fresh air.' She fished into her bag and pulled out some paracetamol, which she took with water.

'Are you sure you're okay? We could just head home now if you like?'

'No, I don't like.'

They were soon in a taxi.

'So, I hope you like Eighties music.' Monty bumped into her shoulder.

'Course I do,' she replied sleepily.

'Got six acts performing tonight including Kim Wilde, Paul Young and, drum roll, Belinda Carlisle.'

'No way?' Excitement rose in her chest.

'Wey aye, man!'

'Oh, shut up! That's crazy.' She slumped into him and kissed his shoulder, leaving pink lipstick on his sleeve. 'Thank you so much.'

The approach to Dean Court stadium bustled with fans heading for the *Here and Now Tour*.

They found a place on the pitch area of the stadium, close to the stage. When The Human League opened to flashing lights, she jumped up and down and screamed in unison with Monty. As they closed their set with 'Don't You Want Me', she provocatively sang the female lyric, before turning her back to him and swaying her hips.

He'd packed a large bottle of water, and she kept taking big gulps as it was as hot as Hades in the crowd.

By the time Belinda Carlisle was announced, she felt her head might explode with painful elation. With 'Circle in the Sand' echoing into the cerulean sky, she rested both hands on his shoulders, as he held her waist, and they circled as one, their hips pressed together.

Hatty stared deep into his eyes, high on a cocktail of adrenalin and painkillers, desperate to leap the emotional canyon and kiss him with no plan for what next. Blinded by the stage lights, the headache pounding in her temples, she drank the last of the water.

Paul Young slowed the tempo with a selection of his biggest hits. Her neck was stiff and painful, so she leant back and rested her head on his shoulder. Moving in time with the music, she mouthed the lyrics to 'Everytime You Go Away', tears scalding her face, her fingers entwined in his.

Why don't you see how I am so utterly in love with you, Montgomery Wiles? Why can't you just see it without me telling you? You must surely know.

Her vision blurred, her migraine unbearable, his soft stubble tearing her skin. She turned and wrapped her arms around him, burying her face in his chest and slurring. 'Monty, sorry, but I'm really unwell.' Only later would she recall collapsing into his arms before blacking out.

CHAPTER 13

August 2004

Hatty clamped her eyes shut against the light.

'It's Mam, can you hear me?'

Something squeezed her hand. She opened her eyes, slowly, and focused on Evie, perched on a plastic chair next to the unfamiliar bed. *That's strange*. 'Mam, what are you doing here?'

She leant across and kissed her forehead. 'We've been here with you the past two days, darling. You've been really sick.'

John appeared behind his wife, rubbing his reddened eyes with the sleeve of his fleece. 'Am I happy to see your beautiful eyes open again, pet.'

'Where am I?' She studied the drip canula strapped to the back of her hand.

'You're in the Royal Bournemouth Hospital. You collapsed at the concert with a nasty virus,' he said.

An ice-cold fear gripped her heart. 'Where's Monty? Is he okay?'

'You can ask him in a minute. He's gone to fetch me and your mam a cup of tea.'

She sunk her head on the soft pillow and closed her eyes, exhaling heavily. Colourful fragments of recollection connected in her mind. She smiled and closed her fingers around an imaginary hand. 'Monty's okay.'

Voices percolated through her senses, and she opened her eyes again. The room was so white and sterile. Footsteps echoed along the corridor and grew close.

'Thank you, son, that's very kind of you,' her dad said. 'Hatty just woke up.'

'That's fabulous news, Mr Campbell. God, I can't imagine how relieved you must feel.'

It's Monty. Her spirits soared.

'Are you talking about me?' she croaked.

He stepped around to the side of the bed and knelt beside her, his smile like shattered glass. 'Hello, you. I can't tell you how relieved I am to see you awake. I knew my dancing was bad, but I hadn't expected it to put you in hospital.'

'I reckon I'd look good in Michael Jackson's *Thriller* video at the moment.'

'Don't say that.' He laughed, stroking a loose hair from her forehead. 'Your face isn't *that* green. You're ghoulish chic; it's the new thing in London right now.'

'Always the charmer, Montgomery Wiles.' She gripped his hand and her eyelids grew heavy.

'I should probably leave you alone now with your mum and dad. You're only meant to have two visitors at one time and I've already had to snog the nurse just to stay this long.'

'You didn't?'

'He insisted.'

She chuckled and her head hurt. 'Don't make me laugh, I'm sick.'

He bent over and kissed her forehead. 'Can't tell you how relieved I am to see you.'

His soft lips and the smell of his cologne were more healing than antibiotics and she yearned desperately for him to stay. 'You'll come back and see me, won't you?'

'Course I will, beautiful. I've rented a house nearby with Belinda Carlisle, to remain close.'

'I hope she's a decent cook.'

He rubbed his eye with his fist. 'She just sits around singing all the time. No bloody use.'

'Stop it.'

'You get well soon, you hear? I'm Mad About You.'

'Oh my God, Monty,' she laughed, painfully. 'Did she teach you that one as well?'

'No, that's all me.' He stood to leave and was intercepted at the door by Evie getting on tiptoes to give him a massive hug.

John then pumped his hand, until she worried it might snap off. 'Monty, you've done us a really big turn by looking after our daughter.'

'Honestly, no need to thank me. Like you, seeing Hatty on the mend is all I want.'

Immediately he'd gone, she missed him grievously.

Her mam sat beside her. 'I tell you what, I know I wanted to meet Monty, but I wasn't expecting him to be such a lovely lad, mind. Martha said he was in tears, when he phoned her to say you were in hospital, and he's been here every day since.'

'Martha always exaggerates,' she countered.

'Ee, well, your sister does exaggerate. But she doesn't usually make things up.'

Bitter tears came to her eyes.

Three weeks later

'Are you absolutely sure you are well enough to travel to New York?' Monty asked, loading her suitcase in the boot of his Mercedes. He'd parked outside an attractively gentrified building near Tower Bridge, where Hatty had invested in a new flat, with a view across the Thames to St Paul's cathedral.

'The doctors say I'll be fine.' A warm breeze ruffled her hair and she popped on her sunglasses to protect her eyes, still sensitive to the light.

She'd settled on a sporty look, with leggings, and a stylish loose-fitting top, which was perfect for a long flight. 'How do I look?'

'Like a cover model for *Women's Health*, as always.' He opened the passenger door.

'Charmer.' She cast him a dazzling smile before easing into the passenger seat.

Monty drove along the cobbled lane, before turning onto the busy highway for the drive south.

He'd visited her in hospital every day until her discharge. But, of course, with her family members there, they'd had little chance to talk alone.

And as soon as she got home, she'd booked a flight to New York. Four more months to decide whether she should make a move to the States permanently. Maybe cut her losses with Monty. She stared out the window.

The Thames sparkled in late summer sunshine as they passed the Archbishop of Canterbury's Residence at Lambeth Palace. They tracked the north bank of the river past the Royal Chelsea Hospital before crossing into Richmond and on past the towering Rugby stadium at Twickenham.

'Are you sure you don't mind lunch with dad before I take you to Heathrow?' Monty glanced at her before refocusing on the road.

'Of course, I don't mind. It will be lovely to see your dad again in happier circumstances.' She offered a Delphic smile before returning her gaze to leafy countryside as the miles zipped by.

Monty had clicked awkwardly back into the friend zone with her. And now she was counting down the minutes to board her flight, which may represent the final point of embarkation from her hopes and dreams with him.

The car slowed and she looked up to see they had left the motorway.

'Almost home.' Monty drove along a narrow country lane in the lea of green and pleasant hills on the outskirts of Winchester.

'It's so beautiful here. Almost as nice as where I come from.'

He grinned briefly. 'You never invited me up to yours, so I wouldn't know.'

His handsome face was captured in a verdant frame and her heart became heavy. 'Well, maybe I'll take you, one day.'

'Wey aye,' he replied, under his breath.

He drew to a stop with a gentle crunch of gravel outside the white thatched family home, set back from the road.

Alan stood on the front step, in a blue button-down shirt, corduroy trousers and suede slippers, his grey hair neatly combed in place.

Monty hugged him and turned towards her. 'Dad, may I introduce you to Hatty? Actually, you've met before.'

'Yes, of course I remember Hatty. I'm so glad you're feeling better. Do come in, won't you?' He smiled warmly.

Instinctively, she leant in and embraced him. 'It's lovely to see you again.'

'Well, I am definitely happy to see you, as Monty talks about you all the time.'

'I literally never talk about you at all,' Monty yelled from inside the house.

Alan reduced his voice to a whisper. 'Don't believe a word he says. Now can I get you a drink, Hatty? Cup of tea or a cold drink? As it's past twelve, I have some Veuve Clicquot in the fridge, which Monty says is your favourite.'

'Oh, I couldn't take your expensive champagne, Mr Wiles. A cuppa would be lovely, thank you.'

'Very well. Come on through and do please call me Alan. I'd much prefer that.'

Passing through the lounge, they walked onto a patio overlooking terraced gardens leading down to a river lined with trees, their branches looping above a gently flowing river.

'Oh my goodness, it's so beautiful here, Alan,' Hatty exclaimed.

'Let me show you around,' he gestured towards a set of steps down to a lower level filled with rose bushes of every colour, still in bloom.

'Your roses are stunning.'

'Daisy really loved gardening.' He sat on a bench beneath a wooden arbour covered in fragrant pink flowers and patted it for her to join.

She let her eyes explore this garden of Eden. 'That's lovely. Monty often talks about what a wonderful woman Daisy was.'

His eyes never left hers. 'She really was. This pink rose is the first we bought after our marriage when this was all just lawn. We'd often sit out here on the bench in the summer, thinking about new plants to buy and deciding which ones to prune.'

Her face crumpled and tears rolled down her cheeks. Alan's mourning love seemed so pure and alive in the beautiful garden he tended as a living memorial to his wife. 'You must miss her terribly.'

'Oh, now, don't cry, Hatty. We enjoyed thirty years of blissful happiness.' He glanced towards the river. 'Everyone is parted by death, but I believe when my time comes, I'll be reunited with my Daisy in heaven.'

Monty wandered down the garden, a champagne flute in each hand.

'Fire's on. Blimey, Dad, Hatty's just got here, and you've reduced her to tears.' He extended a bubbling glass to her. 'Here, drink this, to relieve the pain.'

She laughed, before wiping her nose with a hanky. 'Joyful tears, Monty. You wouldn't understand.'

'We were just having a lovely chat about your mum.'

Monty frowned before heading back up the garden. 'I'll sort out the barbecue then. But no need to help! I can do it all on my own.'

The sarcasm was betrayed by his relaxed, playful tone.

'I normally cook Sunday roast, but he insisted we do a barbecue. It used to be a family ritual, and we've fallen out of the habit since we lost Daisy.'

'Your son never ceases to surprise me.' She sighed.

'He's got a soft heart, has Monty, which he masks with his joking around.'

'Some people tease that we're like a married couple with our habits and in jokes.'

'You are uncommonly at ease with each other, so I can see that.' He chuckled. 'Daisy and I were also friends for a long time too, you know? I loved her from the start. But in our first year at college she said we should just be friends. Turns out, she wanted something deeper with me from early on. But I was too anxious to spot the signs.'

'I can see so much likeness between you and Monty when you say that.'

'Well, one thing I'm certain of —' Alan pressed his fingers to his chest '—is that my son loves you.'

'Sausages are on the grill,' Monty's distant voice called.

'I'm just scared about breaking the impasse and getting hurt again one day.'

'When you spend a lifetime with someone there will be moments of pain and difficulty. Daisy and I had ours.' He sighed deeply. 'But, you know, getting through those made us a stronger team.'

'Amen to that.' Hatty smiled.

After a sumptuous barbecue, enriched by joyful conversation, she insisted on taking photos of Monty and Alan in the family garden. She enjoyed a second glass of champagne and thought how nice it might be to visit Alan at weekends, with Monty. Briefly, she imagined him one day playing with grandchildren, her kids, but quickly pushed it aside.

'So, here we are again,' Hatty said, clipping open her bag to retrieve her passport and boarding pass. They stood to one side of the security gates, to avoid blocking other passengers. She'd lost count of the number of times she and Monty had dropped off or met each other at Heathrow airport. Now she wondered whether the joy of it might fade in future. Or whether this may be the last time.

'You've definitely got everything you need?' Monty asked.

'Yep, I'm ready to fly!' she replied, not wanting to go, yet desperate to say farewell.

Hands thrust in his pockets, he stared at his feet. His wavy hair flopped over his forehead, and when he looked up, his deep-blue eyes burrowed into hers. 'I'll miss you.' He ran his hand down the light stubble that dusted his jaw. 'I always do.'

'You always miss me?' she teased, lightly tugging his shirt, above the button at his collar, her fingertip brushing the soft, fair strands of his chest hair.

'Yes.'

She glanced at the queue waiting to go through security, before smiling up at him. '*Okay*, Montgomery Wiles, I'll miss you too. You've finally made me admit it! Happy now?'

Eyes narrowing, he asked. 'Have things changed for you, since *that* New Year's eve?'

She froze, her mind scrambling. 'You mean, the fancy dress ball?'

'When we kissed. When I told you I loved you.' His eyes were like the afterburn from a fighter jet, 'It's just that on your birthday—' he paused to gulp '—before you collapsed. Something was different with us, closer, more intimate. At least for me.'

Fireworks exploded in her mind, and she was unable to order her thoughts. 'I'm just about to get on a flight to New York, Monty, and I might not be coming back any time soon. You do pick your timing, don't you?'

'You'll come back at Christmas. Or if you decide to stay, I could come to New York.'

'What would you do in New York?'

'I dunno. Don't see myself in banking forever. Maybe I'll sell bagels.'

'I didn't know you liked bagels.' She didn't know what was happening. The door to his heart had reopened and now she was trembling, wondering whether to step through.

'You know, lightly toasted, cream cheese, smoked salmon, bit of dill, pepper.'

'That's a lot of detail.'

'Squeeze of lemon juice.'

Pursing her lips, she glared at him. 'Monty, you're dating other women!'

'I *was* dating other women, but not now.' His unrelenting eyes remained locked on hers.

She was confused and frustrated. 'So I'm next in line, am I?'

His voice remained even. 'I've wanted to be with you, and only you, since we met, but you said you didn't want a relationship.'

'Okay, but I didn't think you would go through most of the women at work!'

'That's not exactly fair or accurate.'

'Perhaps. Though I hope you'll forgive me for not wanting to spend my life looking over one shoulder at the competition.' Her cheeks flushed with anger, pent up anxiety boiling out of her.

He closed his eyes for moments that felt like forever. 'They didn't mean anything to me.'

'*She didn't mean anything to me.*' Andrew's words flooded back and her temples throbbed. 'Do you even know how unkind it is when men say that about women they've slept with?'

'I'm sorry, I didn't phrase that very well.' His eyelids drooped.

She braced herself emotionally against a dump of unsavoury facts about him she'd spent so long insulating herself from or plain denying.

He snorted like a caged bull, wrestling with how to reveal the ugly truth. Then he met her gaze, his eyes becalmed, the doors to his soul open to her as never before. 'I didn't sleep with any of them.'

'You've been *celibate* all this time?' Like a volcano's cap had cracked, her words burst out like emotional magma.

A family of four walked by, the dad gripping his young daughter's hand protectively.

Monty grimaced. 'You might want a microphone, Hats, as there's a slightly deaf person in Terminal 5 who didn't hear you.'

'I'm sorry, it's just—' She raised both eyebrows, her eyes wide. 'What were you thinking?'

'About you, pretty much,' he deadpanned.

'Wow.' She shook her head, trying to grapple with a revelation that had flipped her assumptions about Monty on their head.

'Okay, so have a good flight then.' He theatrically turned to leave.

'No, don't.' She tugged the sleeve of his shirt and pulled him back to her insistently, before wrapping her arms around his neck and holding him close. Nestling her head against his chest, breathing in his familiar, comforting scent, she continued. 'I can't believe you did that.'

'They weren't you.'

'It's just, I never believed you'd put me first.' She paused. 'Andrew made me give up my dreams, like playing hockey for England.' She balled her fist and tapped it lightly against his firm chest.

'I'm not A—'

She pressed a finger to his lips. 'Sssh. We don't need to mention his name ever again. I just wanted you to know. Maybe to help you understand me a bit better.'

He kissed the tip of her nose. 'I want to spend a lifetime getting to know you, Harriet Campbell. You've been the Circle in my Sand since we met.'

She laughed. 'And I suppose Belinda Carlisle taught you that one while you were house sharing, did she?'

'Nah, she'd moved out already. Got fed up with me talking about you all the time.'

Glancing at the security queue, she groaned heavily. 'Ugh, I really have to go now, you silly man.'

He smiled boyishly, his handsome face more affectionate than she'd ever seen. 'It's okay. I'm sure we'll figure things out, when you get back from New York or if you decide to stay. We're a great team, you and I.'

'We really are. In fact we're the best team.' She straightened his shirt collar, before looking anxiously at her watch. 'Let's do this properly at Christmas. We can have a nice dinner when I get back and put everything on the table. Spend all night catching up.'

He raised an eyebrow, pushing a strand of hair behind her ear and sending shivers rippling down her spine. 'Do you think all night will be enough time?'

'I worry it might not be.'

'How worried?'

Hatty pulled Monty into a lingering kiss before staring deep into his eyes. 'Really not worried at all.'

His eyes glittered under the fluorescent lights. 'You go and be brilliant over there, as always. I'm so proud of you.'

CHAPTER 14

22 December 2004

Hatty was stressed because yesterday's flight from New York had been cancelled last minute. Mercifully, she'd got a standby, waiting six hours at a packed-out JFK to luck-in on the 'next available' seat. The western masses were migrating in the annual whirligig of winter travel and she, too, had waited months to reunite with the person she most loved at Christmas.

The delay had destroyed their romantic dinner plan, and he was flying to Thailand in the morning with his dad. But she was here now, and joy swept her anxieties aside.

Monty leant against a table, a bow tie hung loose against his dress shirt, whisky tumbler in hand and chatting with a work mate. She could almost smell his cologne.

The colleague wandered off and he turned his wrist to check the time.

Light as a feather, she arced away from his field of vision, in the hopes of surprising him. It worked. 'Of all the gin joints in all the towns in all the world, you walk into this one, Montgomery Wiles?'

He spun around with a smile that sparkled like an ocean under an azure sky. 'You've been in the States for a year and now you're Humphrey Bogart?'

She batted her eyelids. 'Do I look like a Humphrey?'

'No.' His eyes scorched hers and, considering her with a sly smile, he continued, 'Anyway, I remember *this* dress.'

'Really? I was running late so threw on the first thing I could find in the wardrobe.' She knew full well it was the green dress she'd worn on their first night at the ballet and wasn't worried a jot about wearing a two-year-old dress to the Christmas party.

'Is that so?' He rubbed her shoulder affectionately with his thumb before drawing her into his arms.

Running her hands up the firm contours of his back, she breathed in his spicy citrus aroma and set her soul on recharge. 'I'm so sorry I'm late. Had a nightmare with flights back.'

'Don't be. I wasn't going anywhere until I saw you.'

'Come on, let's get a drink.'

In a rush, she'd put her hair up into a flurry of Jane Austen-esque curls. Stray wisps clung to her damp temples, but she couldn't care, conscious of his admiring glance at every step. Finding a space at the bar, she ordered. 'A Macallan 18, straight, and a glass of Veuve Clicquot, please.' *Their unique combo.*

When the drinks arrived, she passed the heavy tumbler to Monty, took his free hand, and steered him towards an empty table.

Wonder filled his gaze. 'I missed you. Not a lot, just a bit.'

She arched an eyebrow. 'Only a bit?'

'A big bit.' He reached across and drew her hand to his lips, kissing it lightly.

Warmth pulsed through her at his touch. ''S'pose I did too, then.'

A pretty woman with raven hair appeared in a figure-hugging black number, her eyelids heavy with mascara. 'Hey, Monty,' she said, ignoring Hatty completely. 'A group of us are going to that cocktail bar I told you about, in Shoreditch. Fancy coming along?'

'I'm sorry, Lucy, but I'll pass. I haven't seen my girlfriend since the summer, and we've got a lot to catch up on.' He squeezed Hatty's hand, his skin warm and dry.

The woman turned on her stilettoes and stomped off.

Before Monty had opened up at Heathrow, Hatty might have been bothered about a pretty woman hitting on him. But not now. No other woman stood a chance against her. 'So, I'm your girlfriend now, am I?'

A smile played across his lips. 'I've never wanted anything more.'

'Well, if you say that, I might just have to keep you forever.'

He laughed, took both her hands and kissed them. 'It's nice to know that We Dream the Same Dream.'

She pulled him into a lingering kiss, goosebumps tingling down her neck. 'And there'll be no more house sharing with Belinda, mind. I'm as possessive as I am passionate.'

'There'll never be anyone else, howsoever long I may live.'

And she knew it with no greater certainty. She sighed. 'What time do you need to go, darling?'

The bar was still crowded with party-goers and right now she just wanted to be alone with Monty. With her *boyfriend*.

Monty frowned at his watch. 'Fairly soon. Haven't packed yet and I want to get down to Dad's by seven in the morning.'

'Shall we get some fresh air before summoning carriages?'

'Absolutely!'

At the cloakroom Monty grabbed his briefcase before helping her into her coat, tenderly kissing her neck before smoothing the cashmere over her shoulders.

Considering his leather attaché, she asked, 'Did you bring your work to the Christmas party?'

He grinned and shook his head.

Outside, the wind was sharp from the frost that set in the day before.

Hatty looked down the street towards a line of black cabs waiting for customers at closing time. 'Do you have time for a stroll by the river?'

'I'm not in *that* much of a rush. I'll have twelve hours to sleep on the plane.'

She put her arm through his crooked elbow, and they strolled unhurriedly along the cobbled lane, towards the river.

Tower Bridge glowed against the midnight sky and spotlights illuminated the triple turrets of the museum ship, *HMS Belfast.* Couples promenaded by the Thames, and Monty politely asked a man to take their photograph.

'You must be looking forward to Thailand with your dad?' Hatty said.

He leaned against the chrome railings to gaze across the river briefly in silence, before facing her with a smile. 'I am. This may be the last time we holiday like this for a while.'

'I don't expect you to stop doing things with your dad just because of me, you know?'

White vapour burst from his mouth into the chill winter air. 'I know. I'm not about to abandon him and he knows that. It's just—' he squeezed her hand '—I want to prioritise us.'

She rested her hands against the cashmere lapels of his overcoat. 'You're a great son, Monty, do you know that?'

He shrugged. 'I lucked in on the parent front. They gave me an example to strive for if I have kids one day.'

A big unanswered question about Monty was checked off. They'd never spoken about children, and she'd only briefly seen him play happily with her nephew and niece. But she knew he'd make an amazing dad. Peering into the indulgent depths of his gaze she feigned doe-eyed innocence. 'Can celibate men have children then?'

His chest shook with his deep baritone laugh as he hugged her closer. 'Very funny.' Bending his head to her upturned face, he kissed her lightly on the lips.

She entwined her fingers through his hair to pull him closer, her lips parting, their tongues dancing gently together.

Wrapped in each other's arms, they danced slowly across the path to a bench illuminated by the tender glow from a Victorian lamppost.

Monty pulled her gently onto his lap and she lost herself in his electrifying embrace for many minutes more.

After a while, she snuggled into him, starting to believe in a future with the man she loved as no other. 'Would you really come to New York and sell bagels just to be with me?'

Running his fingertip down her nose and pressing it lightly against her lips, he said, 'Of course I would. I love you, Harriet Campbell. I've loved you since the day you reached out and touched my heart.'

'I love you too, Montgomery Wiles, so very much.' She hadn't had the faith to believe in it for so long. Those three sacred words were more precious than any gift, and she prayed they'd never tire of uttering them over the years. 'I just don't want you to feel you have to lose out on anything for us.'

'I feel like the winningest man alive right now. Talking of which, I got you a Christmas present.' He pulled a rectangular parcel from his case.

'Ooh, what is it?' Hatty peeled away the wrapping to reveal a leather-bound album. Leafing through its pages, she gasped. He'd curated all the photos from their times together into a beautiful collection. 'Oh my goodness, Monty, I love it. Gosh, the Flintstone photo is my favourite. Look at my hair. Look at your hair!'

'I hoped you might like it.'

'I've got your Christmas gift at home, but in the rush didn't bring it. I wondered whether we could do a mini-belated Christmas lunch and gift giving when you get back?'

'I'd love that. We could make it our first new tradition as a couple.'

'We have a lifetime to create our own memories and traditions.'

'We do.' He pulled her into another, unhurried kiss. 'Can I ask you something?'

Alarm rose in her chest. She knew beyond all certainty that she would marry Monty in the not too distant, but a rushed proposal before his holiday didn't feel the right time. 'Yes, sure.'

'How would you feel about me re-training as a teacher?'

She sat up in his lap and considered him. 'Less batty than selling bagels, but also a big change in your life. Are you sure it's what you want?'

'I've done well out of banking. But it's not my passion. I think my parents' zeal for helping kids rubbed off on me.'

She'd never seen him so relaxed and at ease. 'Then it's a lovely idea.'

He kissed each of her fingers one by one. 'My mortgage is paid off and I have plenty of money in the bank. So I can afford to study and keep house for you in New York, while selling bagels on the side.'

She grinned from ear to ear. 'Then you might be better off studying in London.'

His eyebrows climbed up his forehead. 'Why so?'

'I got offered the dream promotion in the London office.'

His laugh echoed among the trees lining the boardwalk. 'You leave it until now to tell me? That's brilliant.'

She stroked his cheek. 'After we spoke in Heathrow, I thought it would be easier to visit your dad and my family in Newcastle if we are London-based.'

'You've got this all planned out, haven't you?'

'That's why you love me.'

'One of so very many reasons.'

She kissed him once more. 'Then come back to me safe and sound from Thailand, you hear? I can't do without you now.'

Part II

AFTER

Monty

CHAPTER 15

Boxing Day 2004

'I can't do without you now.'

'Hatty!' Monty screamed before spewing fetid salt water. Wiping his lips with the back of his hand he lay still, listless, before his world again faded to black.

But she was still there. Her auburn hair bathed in light, her emerald eyes beacons. A smile impossibly beautiful and kind.

His eyes popped open, and he squinted against a blinding sun. He shoved at a rough concrete beam that pinned him down, but the effort caused a searing pain. Blood carved a muddy crimson stream along his right arm.

'Hatty!' Every painful word rattled in his throat. With all his strength, he pushed the beam again, grinding his teeth against the agony, until it fell away with a crash.

A scream startled him. 'Help me, please help! Somebody.' A man's voice. Desperate.

Monty sat up. His shirt and shorts torn, exposed skin raw as if scrubbed with wire wool. All around, biblical carnage. *No, Hatty isn't here. She's safe.*

Rolling to one side, he vomited again.

Debris tore at the soles of his feet as dizzily he stood and looked around. *I'm on a roof.* He gripped a twisted handrail and hobbled down steps, pain shooting through his ankle.

A wrecked car was lodged in the entrance to the building. Mud, tree branches, books, clothing, garbage everywhere. And bodies. A woman in a fitted green tunic, her head at an impossible angle, her lifeless eyes staring. '*Sawat-dee kha, Khun Alan.' I'm in Thailand.*

Terror gripped him. 'Daaaaaaaaaaad!'

Heart racing, he shuffled through the lobby, passing a man and a young boy by the stairs, clinging to each other in death.

Outside, the tear-shaped pool, a septic pit of mud, sun loungers, corrugated sheets, and more bodies. In the distance, sirens and the thwack-thwack of a helicopter sounded.

'Daaaaaad!' He coughed, bringing up muddy phlegm. 'Alan!' he tried instead.

He tried to stagger past a man in swim shorts, his torso criss-crossed with blood, but the man, wild-eyed, grabbed his arm.

'I'm looking for a boy,' said the man, his gaze frantic. 'A small blond-haired boy aged eleven, called Hendrick. Silver trunks. If you see him, come find me, okay?'

'I will. I'm looking for my dad, around five-foot-ten with short grey hair. Alan Wiles.' Monty remembered paddling in the sea as a child while his parents read books on their sun-loungers. He liked to be able to see them to know that everything was fine. *Poor Hendrick.*

He stood on shaky legs and struggled on until the ground span and he sat heavily on an upended tree trunk, a dull ache creeping down his right arm. *Must find Dad.*

Everywhere, brightly coloured boats were upturned, bodies scattered amongst them. Some people knelt to inspect the dead. Others tended those with injuries or in great torment.

A member of hotel staff ran towards him, tunic ripped and torn. 'Are you okay, sir?' Her muddied cheeks were crazed with tears.

Monty *wai*'d weakly. 'I'm okay, are you alright?'

But she hurried off and he laboured on. 'Alan, Alan Wiles! Daaad!'

Fifty yards ahead, Monty saw grey hair. Terror stopped him in his tracks but he had to know and soon stood above the corpse. The man's eyebrows were raised above closed lids as if in surprise. A tattoo decorated his right shoulder. *Not Dad.*

Then something else. A child's body, covered in sand and scratches. Monty knelt and studied the silver swimming trunks and the blond hair matted with blood. *Just eleven years old.* He wept, his lower jaw shaking as he thought of his dad, Alan Wiles, the kindest headteacher, talking to all the anxious, wide-eyed students at the start of each school year. '*A verbal hug to make them feel safe and welcome,*' he liked to say.

'I'm so sorry, Hendrick,' Monty sobbed.

Hyperventilating, he put his head in his hands. 'Where the heck are you, Dad?' His energy faded and he slipped into a fraught, unconscious world illuminated only by Hatty's anxious smile, and words he could not discern.

CHAPTER 16

27 December 2004

'Hatty?' Monty's eyes popped open. Something warm dabbed his arm, which throbbed in pulses.

He stared at a young woman in a white uniform and old-fashioned nurse's cap cleaning his wound.

All around was a hubbub of people, Thai and foreign, staff and tourists. Many wore fresh bandages while others bore open wounds. Some wept, and a man with a scarred face and bloodied t-shirt shuffled along the beds, scrutinising other patients.

'Where am I?*' he asked.*

She lifted her head, revealing a delicate face and almond eyes. 'You are in Krabi. At hospital.' She took his wrist and glanced at her watch. 'How do you feel?'

'Not great.' He coughed, his breath short. 'I've lost contact with my dad. Do you know where I can get some information?'

'I'm sorry, but I do not have information now. There was a giant wave. Thousands of people injured, missing and. . .' She glanced away. 'You almost drowned. Lucky to be alive. We treat your wounds and rehydrate you first, okay?'

Sweat broke out across his brow and his heart thumped against his rib cage. *I can't afford to hang around here while Dad's missing.* 'Okay. Thank you.'

'Just relax. I need to make stitches. You want a drink?' Her accented English was good.

'Yes, please,' he croaked.

She called out, and an orderly appeared with a bottle of water. 'Just sip. Do not drink fast.' She lifted a straw to his mouth.

The water was cold. Monty took another sip and laid his head down on the soft pillow.

The nurse prepared a tray of instruments, disinfectant and gauze. 'I give little injection now, for pain.'

He winced briefly, then watched as she threaded black stitches into his arm before applying a bandage and inserting a cannula. 'What's your name?'

The nurse looked up at him. 'I am Fah. And you?'

'Thank you, *Khun* Fah. I am Monty.'

'You know the word *khun* already? *Phut phasaa Thai dai lor kha, khun Monty*?' Can you speak Thai, Monty?

'*Dai nit noi khrap.*' A little bit. His racing heart slowed as he recalled eating Thai food in London with Hatty. 'Do you know where I can use a telephone please? *Thorasap?*'

'I try to find information, when I can, including about telephone, *kha.*'

'Okay. Thank you.'

She moved to the next gurney to attend to a young woman with a large, violet scar on her torso, as if something had slewed a large chunk of her flesh.

Monty lay back and drifted in and out of consciousness. When he woke, it was dark outside. He blinked in the light from fluorescent strips. A constant noise of vehicles coming and going rattled in his head. Urgent Thai voices accompanied each new arrival. Despite the air conditioning he sweated heavily. *I wonder if Dad has come in on one of those trucks? Maybe he's unscathed and looking for me. He could've been taken to a different hospital. There must be injured people all over the place right now.*

A lady in a beige uniform arrived to take down the details of his travel insurance. 'Hospital very busy. Need insurance to get more equipment and medicine.'

Thankfully, he knew the details of his travel insurance company, though not his specific policy number. But it was enough to satisfy the official, for now.

Two Styrofoam cartons and a bottle of water had appeared on the mattress beside him while he slept. The first carton contained fried rice with an egg and a segment of lime, while the other, chicken and oily rice with a dark sauce.

After the lady had gone, he took a sip of water and gingerly ate a spoonful of rice. It tasted good, and he realised he hadn't eaten since the previous night, devouring both cartons of food. With a sigh, he lay back and drifted into a fitful sleep.

'It's just a light swell,' Alan called from the waterline as the wave roared in. Monty tried to run to him, but his legs were stuck in the mud. Suddenly, he was lying in the blazing sun, hotter than the fire of Hades. Hatty's face appeared bathed in sunlight and spoke in a strange voice.

'Monty. Monty. Wake up.'

He opened his eyes, unable to comprehend the brown eyes looking at him. 'Hatty?'

'No, my name is Air. You have fever now. I come to take you to different ward, *kha*.'

Two orderlies wheeled him from under the patch of ceiling he'd come to know.

He looked down the corridor and saw hospital beds lined up three-deep. 'But I need to get out and find my dad.' His voice cracked, tears rolling down his cheeks.

'*Khun* Monty, we make you better, then you go look for your dad, okay?'

Wiping his face he stared up as the strip-lighting and air-conditioned chill changed to darkness and tropical heat.

The orderlies led him under covered walkways to a different annex where light and chill washed over him once more. Eight spaces occupied the ward, one of them empty. Each bed occupied by a soul with a scratched-up face and bandaged limbs.

Air thanked the orderlies, put a thermometer in Monty's mouth, and wrapped a blood pressure cuff around his left arm. 'Your fever get worse. Doctor already said you need an antibiotic injection. Do you have an allergy to antibiotic?'

He shook his head. She administered the dose by injection and made him take two painkillers with water. She provided a plastic urinal in case he needed to pee and hooked up another bag of saline.

'*Khun* Monty, I check on you later, okay?' She looked at him with a kindly smile and a furrowed brow.

He hurt all over, was burning up and bone dry with a raging headache. But his mind couldn't settle. He turned to look at the man in the neighbouring bed, head bandaged and face covered in thin crimson cuts.

The man stared back. 'Where are you from?'

'I'm British. You?'

'Australian.'

'This is bloody terrible. I can't find my dad.'

Tears ran down the man's face. 'I lost my wife and kids.'

Alan's coffin was carried along the beach by pallbearers in tattered swimwear. At a gravesite next to piles of rotting bodies, Daisy cried with other mourners. He tossed and turned, pain hammering the inside of his skull. He was hot and sweating yet cold to his bones. Still in her green party dress, Hatty called out to him from a lectern.

'*Khun* Monty.'

He opened his eyes, blinking in the light.

Nurse Fah sat beside his bed. 'I promised to come back to check on you.'

'That's kind, thanks.' He forced a weak smile. Breathing was still hard, but the drugs were starting to work.

'I'm sorry, I could not find much information. Many people are missing.' She looked down at her hands, folded in her lap.

'It's okay.' His spirits slumped.

'I got you a telephone, so you can call people.' She placed a mobile phone and charging cable on the bedside table. 'Maybe people here can use it too.' She gestured to the other patients.

'Thank you very much. How much did it cost?'

'A company came to hospital and gave telephones to people for free. You can make international telephone calls. I borrowed this for you.'

When she'd gone, he grabbed the phone and punched numbers into it. It took several attempts to get a connection, but finally, he heard a faint ringing.

'Hello?' Hatty answered, a delay in her tinny voice.

'Hatty, is that you?'

She crumpled briefly before composing herself. 'Oh my God, Monty?'

'Yes, it's me.'

'Thank goodness it's you. I tried and tried to phone the Foreign Office, non-stop since yesterday, and I couldn't get through. Are you okay? Where are you?'

'I'm in a hospital. In Krabi. I'm a bit busted up but it could be worse, all things considering.' He squeezed his eyes tight at the reminder of Alan.

'Oh, darling. I'm coming out to get you. I'm going to Heathrow right now and getting on the first plane.'

'You shouldn't. It's bedlam here.'

'But I'm worried sick,' her voice broke again.

He rubbed his temple. 'Could you go to my place and get my travel insurance policy? It's in my study. I've got a spare house key in my desk at work. Oh, and I need to find a helpline number for my bank so I can get some money sent out.'

'Okay, I'll go into the office as soon as we finish talking.' Her voice was now calm and collected, his gorgeous, super-competent girlfriend. 'I'll just send you some money via Western Union then you can get everything else sorted when you are back, okay?'

He imagined her at home with her work face on, a study of concentration, ready to solve any challenge. His amazing Hatty. 'I'll pay you back.'

'Don't be silly. It's enough to know you are safe. Is your dad there?'

'No. He's not. I haven't seen him since yesterday. I'm hoping I can find him so we can fly home together in a few days.'

'God, I'm so sorry, darling. I'm praying you find him.'

Tears welled in his eyes, and he coughed. 'Yeah, me too. Look, I'd better go, so others can use this phone. I love you, Hats.'

She sobbed. 'I love you too, Monty.'

Monty sat up and offered the phone to the Australian in the next bed.

His head throbbed non-stop as he listened to the man crying uncontrollably about losing his wife and kids, before the phone worked its way around the ward.

Throughout the day, visitors appeared; mostly young tourists who came by to chat. A buddy system had been established with the uninjured helping the injured. Mostly it was keeping people company during their time of need. Some offered practical help. Others prayed while a few tried to counsel those who were bereaved.

Monty chatted with every visitor, but none could answer his fundamental question: Was there any information about how he might locate Alan? At six in the morning, exhaustion overcome him, and he slept.

Monty woke to find a youngish man in an Adidas t-shirt and khaki jeans sat by the bed, writing in a notebook.

He looked up, dark rings around his eyes. 'Hello, are you Montgomery Wiles?'

'Yes. Who are you?'

'My name is Nick. I'm from the British embassy in Bangkok.'

'Oh. Hello. What date is it?'

'It's the twenty-eighth of December.' He glanced at his watch. 'Just past four o'clock in the afternoon.'

I've been here two days? 'Have you only just arrived?'

'I'm really sorry it has taken so long. Got here this morning and have been rushed off my feet. As of now we have fourteen staff covering a coastline of several hundred miles.'

'Wow.'

'Would you mind if I asked a few questions? I've been told your dad is missing.' He collected detailed information about Alan, including when and where he'd last been seen.

'What can be done to find him?'

'The whole area's a disaster zone. We've got thousands of casualties that we already know about and a much larger number of people who are currently unaccounted for. Right now we're gathering as much information as we can about missing persons.'

He slumped into his pillow and clamped his eyes shut, to hold back tears. 'I just can't get my head around what's happened.'

'I'm really sorry. We're trying our best and more people are on the way.' Nick didn't appear hugely confident in the latter assertion. 'Right now I can help get you evacuated back to Bangkok. The Thai authorities are running planes and buses out of here pretty much 24-7.'

'Not being funny, but with my dad missing, I'd sooner stay here and keep searching. Can you help me find more information about casualties?'

'There's a temporary mortuary at a Chinese temple in the centre of Krabi. The Thai authorities have posted photos of deceased people collected there on the internet. Be warned, you'll need a strong stomach.'

Monty shuddered. 'Thanks.'

'Look, I'll check in with you again tomorrow. See how you're getting on. Here's my card. Call me anytime, okay?'

'Okay.' Chest tightening, he reached out and shook Nick's hand. *No further forward.*

That evening, Monty waited patiently to use a computer in the hospital lobby. He found the body identification website. Over three hundred images had been posted for Krabi alone, and he clicked through them one by one, eyes on stalks, head thumping.

Some of the deceased were untouched by injury, others ravaged with wounds, some serene, others stared out in terror, faces frozen in time. Every time he clicked on a file, his neck muscles tightened like metal coils, then he'd whistle out softly when the body wasn't Alan. *It's easier to look at when their eyes are closed* – a mixture of bare-shouldered or swimwear-clad tourists and fully-clothed Thais. With only a handful of files left to view in the ghastly gallery, his hopes lifted and he thought about getting a solid night's sleep, before resuming the search in the morning.

Then the gunmetal grey hair and eyebrows flashed on the screen, and he doubled over as if he'd been thumped in the stomach with a sledgehammer. *No, please no.* He ran his fingers over the screen, incredulous, tracing the shape of the nose and the teeth, as the mouth was wide open. 'No, Dad.' His voice rose and tears streaked down his face. He leant closer to study the jawline, occluded by jagged black scars like a demon's teeth. A recollection of Dad with a scratched up jaw after a fall crashed into his mind. Heavy sobs burst from deep within his inflamed lungs and he cried uncontrollably. 'I'm sorry, Dad. I'm so sorry.'

An arm wrapped around him and he was aware of an American accent. 'Hey, man, you okay?'

'Sorry.' Pain ripped through his chest like his heart had been torn asunder. He stood and staggered out of the reception area towards his ward, people milling around him in an amorphous blur. Barely conscious of his movements, a whispered litany of grief spilled quietly from his mouth. 'It's all my fault.'

CHAPTER 17

29 December 2004

Monty had barely slept when the doctor discharged him.

Dressed in baggy donated clothes, he hobbled out of the air-conditioned ward, the heat hitting him like a furnace. The sun was blinding and the grass outside was pale and parched.

Fah approached from another building and bowed her face to her fingertips.

'*Khun* Monty, are you leaving hospital?'

'Yes, Nurse Fah.'

'You will go home now?'

'No, I'll stay in Krabi to search for my dad.' He fiddled with the bag in his hands.

'Ah, I see. Did you find any information about him yet?' Her brow wrinkled with evident concern.

'I found a photo online.' He ground his teeth, thinking about the grim task ahead.

Sadness swept across her face like a cloud blocking the sun. 'Oh. I am sorry, *kha*.'

'You've been so kind, Nurse Fah.'

'Thank you, *kha*. I was doing my duty.'

'I left the phone you gave me in the ward with the nurse. I hope someone else can make good use of it.'

She considered him. 'I'm sorry that bad things happened to you in Thailand, but I hope you may come back one day.'

After a polite exchange of *wais*, Monty continued into the reception building which remained a hubbub of activity. Beds still lined the corridors, though many were now empty. Photographs of the missing covered makeshift noticeboards.

Pausing, Monty stared at a photo of a woman with long ginger hair and a beaming smile, a crystalline sea in the background. *Trisha Davis. Please contact Graham on this number if you have any information on her whereabouts.*

He was transported to the beach in Bournemouth with Hatty, her spectacular smile and how he'd never felt so happy. He shivered. *The hope of seeing her is the only thing keeping me sane right now.*

People, mostly western tourists, huddled around talking about flights to Bangkok. But he wandered out of the hospital and into the scorching sun. A military truck pulled up, nurses in blue uniforms dismounting and filing into the hospital.

A 7-Eleven stood across the road where he bought a pack of cigarettes, a lighter, and two cans of beer. Sitting on a low wall, he lit his first smoke since that first night at the ballet with Hatty two and a half years ago. *Feels like a lifetime. Ugh, she won't like me smoking.* He cracked open a beer and took three gulps. *God, that tastes good.* He took another drag, finished the beer, and opened the second can. Staring across the road at the hospital, his mind numb, he downed the rest.

A Thai family – husband, wife, and young daughter – approached. With some encouragement, the girl stepped up to Monty and held out a food carton and bottle of water.

'*Khob khun khrap* – thank you.' He pressed his fingertips together beneath his chin, tears gathering in his eyes. *How are Thai people able to be so kind when they must be suffering terribly from what has happened?*

A white Land Rover parked up at the hospital entrance and he limped towards it, wiping his face with his wrist.

Nick Evans stepped out of the car, speaking into a mobile phone. He waved, finished the call, and stared at Monty intently. 'Hello. How're you feeling today?'

'I've been better. I guess you're still busy?' He lit a cigarette and took a drag, blowing smoke through his nose.

Nick glanced back into the bustling hospital entrance. 'Yep. Still busy.'

A woman approached with a bundle of documents and a clear plastic bag with wallets and tattered passports.

'Monty, this is *Khun* Aew, who works with me at the embassy. She'll accompany you and help with translation if needed. There's another Brit – the girl I told you about – who should be here in a minute, okay?'

Soon a young woman in a shapeless donated dress appeared and introduced herself as Serwah. Her ebony legs bore angry pink welts and her thick black hair was tied in a bunch at the back.

They drove into the centre of Krabi. Aew sat up front and either chatted with the driver, spoke into her phone, or made small talk. Pick-up trucks and mopeds filled the streets. Shops were open, and food carts lined crowded sidewalks, steam billowing from woks. Everything seemed eerily normal.

Monty was dizzy from the beer and dozed but then sat up with a start when his head lolled forwards. *God, I wish Hatty could help me through this.* Then he balked. Did he *really* want her to see him in this broken diminished state, sobbing his heart out every five minutes? Inconsolable. Not the confident, everything-going-well man who had persuaded her to love him in return. He rubbed his knuckles hard against his forehead. He'd come so close to the ideal of happiness. So close. *What use am I now in this state?* He tapped his head repeatedly against the window.

'You okay?' Serwah asked.

He looked at her, balling and un-balling his fists. 'Ugh, sorry, just really not looking forward to this.'

'Me neither. I'm glad we don't have to do it completely alone.' She smiled thinly.

Eventually, the Land Rover came to a stop by a low white building with red roof tiles and Chinese sculptures. He *stepped out and immediately gagged, pulling his t-shirt over his nose. It stinks a hundred times worse that rotten meat in the fridge.*

Aew handed him and Serwah surgical masks and a small tub of ointment before disappearing into the complex.

Serwah's rich brown eyes were wide with fear as she snapped on her mask.

Hand shaking uncontrollably, Monty rubbed a messy smear of the ointment on his upper lip before putting on his mask. *Now death smelled of Tiger Balm.*

People milled about, tourists, locals, and others in a variegated array of uniforms.

Aew returned with an official. 'This man help you to find the people you are looking for, okay?'

The man shuffled along a narrow corridor to a cramped, stuffy room with trestle tables inside. Body bags lay on four of the tables, one of them child-sized.

Monty's every step was leaden. Sweating profusely and struggling for breath, he handed the man a piece of paper with a reference number on it. Serwah did the same.

After what felt like forever, the man returned, followed by workmen carrying two thick plastic bags, that sagged in the middle.

Monty wheezed raggedly, unable to take his eyes off the bags.

Serwah stared at him, her eyes wet. 'Shall we do this together?'

'Please.' He put an arm around her, and they stepped up to the first table.

She flinched when the man nodded at her.

The workman unzipped the bag and pulled back the upper cover.

All the vitality driven out of his soul, Monty looked at the body of the young South Asian woman in a purple bikini. Her dull raven hair was tangled with sand. Despite terrible wounds, her greying face was untouched. He retched but put a lid on the contents of his stomach that threatened to spill out of his mouth.

Serwah slumped in his arms and sobbed.

He squeezed her close, 'I'm sorry.'

'No,' she replied in a whisper. 'It's not her.'

The man unzipped the second bag, and Monty shivered as if racked with fever.

'Be strong,' she said quietly.

Reluctantly, he cast his eyes upon the body of a man with grey hair. The torso was naked, though Monty figured any clothing may have been removed. Chunks of flesh had been sheared away, and the face, already darkened by decomposition, was crisscrossed with black wounds. His head spun so he gripped Serwah's shoulder.

She wrapped an arm around his waist and squeezed him. 'It's okay, I'll support you.'

It was dreadful to look at the cadaver, the shape of the nose, the eyebrows, the dull, lifeless hair, but he couldn't take his eyes away. He shook his head, struggling to grasp mentally and emotionally what he was seeing and unfolded again the piece of paper with the reference number on it, reading it over and over. He never made mistakes with numbers and was sure he'd written it down properly. 'It's not the same person I saw,' he croaked, angry that he'd endured the unquantifiable anxiety of preparing for this heartbreaking scene yet perversely relieved that the dead person was not his dad.

'Come on, let's get out of here.' She led him through the quickest exit, away from the fetid room.

They passed into the central courtyard of the temple. Refrigerated containers sat at the far end. The doors were open to one, and men carried body bags and handed them to people inside. In front of the containers, more than a hundred body bags, and bodies wrapped in random plastic sheeting, were laid in neat rows. Closer to Monty, corpses lay on the scorching concrete, brown like dried figs, waiting to be packed.

The combination of heat and stink was overwhelming. Finding a patch of shade to one side, he sat on the rough concrete floor, put his head in his hands and cried. He was at his wits' end and desperate to talk to Hatty.

'Can I drop you somewhere?' *Khun* Aew asked as the embassy Land Rover pulled away from the kerb.

'I need to pick up money and buy things, a telephone and stuff like that,' Monty replied.

Within minutes, they pulled up outside a modern-looking shopping centre which, like the rest of the town, was operating as normal.

As soon as he stepped onto the pavement, he lit a cigarette. 'Do you want one?' He gestured to Serwah with the open packet.

'No, thanks.'

They sat on a low wall in silence for a few minutes while he smoked.

'I need to withdraw money at the Western Union too. My parents sent it out,' Serwah said after a while.

The prompt jolted him back to the real world. 'Yeah, me too. I could also use something to eat.'

An hour later, carrying plastic bags with various necessities, they found a busy food court. Brightly coloured stalls framed the space with tables in the middle. The air was rich with the aroma of tamarind, chilli and grilled meat and noisy with hawkers and customers.

They bought two cartons of pad Thai noodles, with a papaya salad to share and a large bottle of water, before finding a vacant table.

Monty fired off a text message to Hatty so she knew his new number. *Thanks for the money. Got a new phone as have been discharged from hospital. Will call later. I love you. M xx*

'So, how did you get caught up in this?' he asked, mixing various condiments into the noodles before spooning some onto her plate, in the Thai custom.

'Thanks. Ugh. I was on Phi Phi with a girlfriend. The wave hit the narrow strip of land where we were, from both directions. Just awful. Lakshmi, my gorgeous friend from Chennai . . . That's who I was looking for today.' Serwah took a forkful of noodles and a gulp of water, before wiping her eyes with the back of her hand.

He squeezed her forearm gently. 'I'm sorry. I really hope you find her.'

She forced a weak smile. 'Thanks.'

'Did you meet Lakshmi on holiday?'

'No. We're dental students and met through a university exchange.' She sniffed.

'Sounds like a great programme.'

'It is. And you? How did you end up here?'

'On holiday with my dad, who I was looking for today.' He munched on noodles, not conscious of their flavour.

'I'm sorry. What are you going to do now?'

'Right now, I'm so confused. I thought the photo I saw was Dad, then this today.' He pressed his fingertips into his temples. 'I don't know what's real.'

They finished their food and walked back outside.

Having exchanged numbers, he hugged Serwah awkwardly before summoning a motorbike taxi.

CHAPTER 18

29 December 2005

Smartly dressed, Alan called insistently from the pile of bodies. Whenever Monty approached and however hard he tried, Dad always moved beyond reach until, eventually, he disappeared.

A shrill ring brought Monty to life in the darkened room. Confused and disoriented, he saw the illumination of his phone.

'Hello.'

'Monty. Are you okay, darling?' Hatty asked.

'Not great.' He rubbed his eyes. 'Sorry, I must have nodded off.'

'That's okay. What's happened?'

'Just had a dreadful day, love.' He didn't want to go through all the details again.

Silence at the end of the line, then sniffing. 'I'm so, so sorry. Where are you now?'

'I checked into a hotel. Pretty empty now as lots of tourists have left.'

'Won't you please let me fly out to help you.'

His shoulders slumped. He didn't want Hatty to endure this. To see these terrible scenes with the odour of death on every street corner. 'The picture's so confused right now.'

'Then come home, at least for a little while. We're a great team remember? I can look after you and we'll figure out a plan.'

He scratched his head. 'There are still things I need to get organised, like a temporary passport and to visit other hospitals, in case Dad's there.'

'Then how about I book a ticket for you in a couple of days?'

What about Dad? What if I need a bit more time than that? He didn't have the energy to argue it out with her, but if he didn't want her to fly out, what else could he do? He flopped back onto the bed. 'Alright then, but maybe get a flexible ticket in case I need to stay longer?'

'Perfect! I'll do that.' Her voice brightened.

'Thank you.'

'You never need to thank me. I thought I'd lost you and right now just want you home. I really love you.'

'I know.' He pressed his fingers into his temples. 'I love you too.'

After the call, he hobbled to the bathroom. A haggard man with a scratched-up face and wild hair stared back from the mirror. *Jeez what would Hatty think now? Not exactly the man she fell for.* After his first shave since Christmas Day, he took a long hot shower.

The bedside clock said 9 p.m. so he made a strong coffee, gulping it down and scalding his throat.

In the empty garden restaurant, his newly purchased shirt was soon soaked and stuck to his back in the oppressive humidity. Lacking enthusiasm, he ate a bowl of curry with rice, while nursing a beer and chain-smoking.

His phone rang again. 'Hello?'

'Is that you, Monty?' Serwah's voice was quavering and slurred. Loud music and the sound of chatter filled the background.

'Yes, it's me, Serwah. Are you alright?'

'Can you come help me? I'm a bit drunk.'

His pulse throbbed in his temples, and he scrunched his eyes. 'Do you know where you are? I'll come and get you.'

'At the Dolphin hotel.'

He soon clung to the pillion of the motorbike taxi, hot air streaming through his hair on the short ride to town. Walking into the ground-floor club at the hotel he spotted Serwah, half-slumped at the bar. Towering over her, a tall older man in a German police polo shirt was speaking to her, focused and predatory.

'Really glad I found you, darling,' Monty said with a broad smile, easing past the other man to join her.

She stared at him with glazed eyes and flung her arms around his neck. 'My hero, come to save me.'

'That's me, sweetheart. I think you need to get to bed.' He turned his head and winked at the man, who bristled, thought about arguing the toss, then lost interest and left.

She got down from the stool and slumped against him.

'Are you staying in this hotel?' he asked once they were in the reception.

'I dunno.'

'Blimey, alright.' He rubbed the side of his face. 'You can stay at mine, then.'

Several taxis were parked outside so he gently bundled her into the back seat, his leg aching from the effort of supporting her.

Back at his hotel, Monty flicked on the lights and was followed into his room by Serwah. Warm tropical air washed over him as he opened French doors to moderate the arctic air conditioning. He stepped onto the balcony and looked across illuminated gardens, shuddering at the distant sound of the waves.

'Wow, this is awesome.' Serwah appeared at his side, suddenly rejuvenated, and wrapped her arms around his waist.

He turned and hugged her briefly. Her getting drunk prompted him to consider whether the stock of booze in the minibar would be enough to get him through this night. 'I don't suggest you sleep out here as you'll get eaten by mozzies.'

'Thank you for saving me from the pervy man,' she mumbled, her head buried in his chest.

'That's alright. I was glad to help.'

'Today was really awful and you were just amazing.' She leant in, drawing closer, her lips parting, the smell of alcohol strong on her hot breath.

He cupped her face in his hands, pulled away a little and smiled gently. 'You are very drunk, Serwah, and I have a girlfriend.'

'A girlfriend.' She lifted a finger and considered him with glassy, bloodshot eyes. 'Can I use your toilet?'

'Sure. Go right ahead.'

She zig-zagged away and disappeared into the bathroom. He grabbed a bottle from the minibar and took it onto the balcony.

Loud retching jolted his senses as he was sloshing vodka into his glass. Stubbing his cigarette, he rose from the balcony chair and stepped back into the room. Seeing the bathroom door still open, he rapped the frame. There was a stifled groan then more retching.

He peered in and Serwah was collapsed on the floor, hugging the toilet basin, her head half inside. Her body convulsed and she vomited again.

Grabbing a bottle of water and tissues from the wash basin, he knelt beside her and rubbed her back. 'Better out than in,' he said softly, remembering what Alan would say whenever he was sick as a child.

The following morning, he woke on the sofa bed to the sensation of workmen hammering the inside of his skull. The sound of running water stopped, and Serwah appeared wrapped in a towel.

'Oh, good morning,' she said, timidly.

He sat up in his makeshift bed and pulled on a t-shirt, squinting. 'Morning. How are you feeling?'

'Better than last night.' Her brow wrinkled, and she pointed at the bed. 'Did we?'

'We didn't.' He smiled.

'Whew.' She gathered up her handbag from the bedside and retreated to the bathroom.

He pressed paracetamol tablets out of a blister pack and took them with water. After slipping on shorts, he grabbed his mobile phone. A goodnight message from Hatty brought a half smile to his face.

Serwah reappeared, freshened up.

'How's your head?'

'Ugh, rubbish. I never drink that much.' She smiled, half-embarrassed. 'Sorry.'

'Don't be.' He tossed her the paracetamol. 'Take a couple of those with a big drink of water. Do you fancy breakfast? It's meant to be good here.'

She looked unsure.

'It's already paid for with the room, so don't worry,'

'If you really don't mind, that would be sweet, thank you.'

The blinding sun outside made his dull headache worse, so they sat in the shaded part of the breakfast area. A long food service table lined one wall of the outdoor area, weighed down with hot and cold breakfast dishes to suit western and Asian tastes. Except that the number of hotel staff vastly outnumbered the handful of remaining guests. He piled his plate with sausages, bacon, and hash browns, while Serwah returned with fresh fruits, yogurt, and a large glass of orange juice. A waitress poured them coffee.

'Thanks for taking care of me last night,' she said, before taking a long draft of juice.

'That's alright. Figured we should look out for each other after the crap day we had.'

'Aww, it's like you're a big brother, rescuing me when I get into scrapes.'

His mind drifted to Daisy and her inability to conceive after him. 'You know, as a kid, I often imagined what it would be like to have a sister.'

With a huge smile, Serwah stood, reached across the table and gently squeezed his shoulders. 'Well then, welcome to the Osei family! I've only got sisters, so you make a welcome addition.'

He grinned. 'Have you phoned *our* family yet?'

'Oh, my word, yes, spoke to them yesterday. My mum cried so much. Most of my relatives were at home and they all wanted to talk to me, so it turned out to be really emotional, not to mention expensive. How about you? Have you been able to speak to anyone back in the UK yet?'

'Yes, I'm in touch with my girlfriend, which has helped.' It would be the middle of the night in London and he calculated that he'd need to wait six hours or so before calling again. A vast emotional vacuum was opening up in his chest caused by their separation.

She smiled sheepishly. 'Ah, yes, I vaguely recall you saying something about a girlfriend. She didn't come on this holiday, then?'

'It's a long story. Well, not that long actually. We clicked romantically just before I flew out here, though we've been best friends for over two years.'

'Besties,' Serwah cooed, her face melting into a wide smile. 'That's so sweet. Lucky, in a way, she wasn't here, given everything that happened.'

Monty lit a cigarette and blew a cloud of smoke away from Serwah. 'Yep, lucky her.'

'I reckon the only thing she's thinking right now is about you being okay.'

'Maybe.' He scrunched his eyes to blank out images from the day before.

'Do you love her?'

He stubbed out his cigarette and replied cagily. 'Direct question.'

Her laugh was deep and hearty. 'Well?'

'Well . . .' He paused. 'Yes, I do.'

'You're overwhelming me with your enthusiasm, Monty.' She smiled, displaying perfect pearly teeth.

'Sorry. Felt a bit weird admitting it to you. Don't know why, to be honest.'

Her eyes sparkled. 'I thought we just agreed that I'm your sister now?'

'Hmph.' He fiddled with the edge of the cigarette pack but decided against smoking another, so sat up straight. 'Truth be told she's the love of my life. I loved her from practically the first moment we spoke properly.'

'She must be super special.'

'She is. Beautiful, smart, amazing at everything she does, but more than that, she's just such a deeply wonderful soul. You know? She found me at a low point in my life and just wrapped me up in warmth and kindness. And she's funny. Oh, my Lord, she's a wonderfully dry wit. Even if we lived to a hundred, I reckon we'd still be cracking jokes in the old people's home when our grandkids visit.' His voice trailed off.

Serwah dabbed at her eyes with a napkin. 'Never let go of that image.'

He exhaled sharply through his nose. His mind flashed back to waking up on the shattered roof of the hotel and he shook his head vigorously, before taking a sip of the strong coffee. 'I just can't believe all this has happened.'

'You'll be home with her again soon.'

'Well, I'm not completely sure when I should go home. After yesterday, I want to find out what happened with my dad.' His body shook involuntarily. 'What about you? What will you do next?'

'I still need to find Lakshmi. I spoke to some people yesterday who said volunteers are helping at the big body collection site up the coast in Khao Lak. As I've got dental training, I might put my skills to good use and continue the search.'

'Sounds horrendous. Will you be okay doing that?'

'I hope so. At least I will be doing something productive. I've seen dead bodies during my medical training. Yesterday was just a bit weird as I was looking for my friend.'

Weird is certainly one way to put it.

After breakfast, the hotel concierge summoned a taxi to take Serwah back into Krabi. Monty wrote his email and UK phone number on a piece of paper and handed it to her. 'Get in touch with me at any time, okay, kiddo? We're kind of stuck with each other now.'

She stepped forwards and hugged him. 'You too, brother Monty. Thanks for looking after me yesterday and last night. Go back to Hatty soon, okay? That reunion kiss will be the best medicine.'

CHAPTER 19

30 December 2004

The whitewashed walls radiated heat from a relentless sun and Monty's shirt was soaked in the moments it took to walk from the taxi to the hospital entrance. The hustle had subsided, and he paused at the lonely noticeboard, zeroing in on another photo of a missing redhead. She had a dazzling smile frozen in a fleeting moment of joy that might never be repeated . . . *I'm looking for my wife, Jenny. Please contact Trevor on the following number if you have any information.*

He shook his head and pulled a sheet of A4 paper from a buff folder. Picking an empty spot, he pinned the notice among the others.

A photo of Alan, rendered black and white by the photocopier and the words.

Desperate to find Alan Wiles. If you have any information, please contact his son, Monty Wiles on . . .

He stepped back to check the image and writing were clearly visible.

'Monty?' a voice called.

He turned to see a Thai man in light chinos and a cream button-down shirt.

'Uncle Aek?' Monty's knees buckled against the emotional force of seeing the family friend he'd known since birth.

'Oh, my God, Monty, you're okay. We've been worried about you.' A touch shorter than his best friend Alan, Aek's hair was a smartly combed bonnet of salt and pepper grey.

Monty wrapped his arms around him and sobbed. 'It's so good to see you.'

'Sorry it took me so long to come. The airports were closed for a while.'

'It's okay, I understand. Is Aunty Mai with you?'

'No, she is in Bangkok, phoning hospitals there to see if they have any patients who match your and *Pe* Alan's description.' He used the affectionate Thai '*pe*' prefix to denote Alan's seniority in age.

'I haven't seen Dad since it happened.' Tears streamed down his cheeks. 'I saw a photo, then when I went to see the body, it wasn't him. I, I don't know what to do.'

Frown lines formed deep furrows across his Aek's forehead. 'I can help you now. We'll keep searching, okay?'

'I need to figure out what I can do next, to search for Dad, though Hatty's is booking me a flight for New Year's eve.'

'*Nong* Harriet, your friend? Oh, she's so kind. Come back to Bangkok with me. Aunty Mai and I can help you find more information before you fly home. Not much else you can do right now.'

Reluctantly, he figured his surrogate uncle was right. 'I'll need to collect an emergency passport in Phuket. Maybe the Embassy team there will have more information.'

'Let's go then.' Aek ushered him to an SUV parked at the bottom of the ramp.

They stopped at a small rural hospital on the drive through verdant tropical forests. There were no foreigners, and many staff had been diverted to bigger hospitals as part of the recovery effort. As they turned west into Phang-Nga province, great limestone boulders dotted the landscape, emblazoned with emerald trees. After the relative normality of Krabi town, the scenery offered an unfamiliar backdrop of calm against the chaos.

Aek said, 'Almost at Phuket already.'

As they crossed the bridge onto the island, Monty stared out to sea on the right, heart pounding and sweat beading on his forehead, despite the harsh aircon.

Beaches on either side of the narrow channel were strewn with driftwood and broken boats. And then onto the busy dual carriageway cutting through the centre of the island for thirty miles, with the day-to-day carrying on as usual. His head spun from the rapid scene changes from normality to devastation and back.

Getting a temporary passport at a makeshift embassy office in a converted furniture shop was straightforward. However, there were no new leads on Alan's whereabouts, so they headed for the airport.

Monty pulled his phone from his backpack and punched in a message to Hatty. *I've started my journey home. In Bangkok tonight before flight home tomorrow. Desperate to see you. xx*

Her reply pinged back straight away. *I'm so happy you made me cry. Can't wait to see you, my darling. I love you so so much. xx*

The two men wandered into Phuket's main airport terminal. Monty carried a small rucksack that was too big for the sum total of his possessions: some basic clothing and toiletries, his document folder and phone, everything purchased in Krabi. He had around one hundred pounds worth of Thai baht in a money belt around his waist, which would be more than he'd need before returning home.

Outside, taxis were loading up with travellers from a recently arrived flight. Most were non-Thais, in clothing ill-suited to a beachside retreat. There was no buzz of excitement, just serious faces and sombre eyes, often red. A legion searching for loved ones lost.

Those who had been on holiday had left in the preceding four days, some on commercial airliners, others in military transport planes, and many in coffins.

Monty removed the folder from his rucksack, and pinned a missing person sheet on a large noticeboard near check-in.

'I think I may have taken that photo, Monty,' Aek said, with a mournful smile.

Tears flooded Monty's eyes and his body shook as he sobbed, oblivious to anyone around. 'I just want to find him.'

The thump of the aircraft landing made Monty start and he stared into the darkness and orange lights of Heathrow. His ankle throbbed and his feet were swollen, making it hard to pull on trainers. As he stepped onto the cold exit walkway, he realised that he wasn't dressed for an English winter. He gazed at everything wide-eyed, from the bright tourism posters to the toilet signs, as if seeing them for the first time.

Worried that he might not be allowed into his own country, he waited in the snaking queue at passport control, his emergency travel document gripped tightly in his hand. Early morning rush hour at Europe's busiest airport. He looked at the different travellers mostly chatting excitedly or calming their kids. Several had noticeable injuries or difficulty with movement, and to those who caught his eye he nodded.

Then suddenly he was face to face with an immigration officer.

She looked at his stamped sheet of paper before considering him, concern etched in her eyes. 'Welcome home, Mr Wiles.'

He forced back the tears and said, 'Thank you.'

As he walked through customs, he was lifted up by the prospect of seeing Hatty, yet anxious about how she'd feel about him in his diminished form. Strangely, he imagined her still wearing the green dress from the staff party.

And, finally, there she was in the crowd. In jeans and a winter coat, her auburn hair tied back. The most beautiful woman he'd ever known. The love of his life. His hope. His slender link to a now unfamiliar past.

She smiled, wiping both eyes with her fingertips, then rushed towards him, arms outstretched, her handbag and a large carrier bag in the crook of one arm.

Instinctively, he wrapped his arms around her waist and lifted her off the ground, suspending her mid-air, untroubled by his ankle.

She cupped his face and kissed him, her emerald eyes wet, her fragrance so familiar and so comforting. Their tears merged into a single stream.

'I love you so much, Hatty, I'm sorry . . . ' He could barely utter the words through tremors that rippled his face.

She shook her head vigorously, her cheeks flushed crimson. 'I love you with all my heart, Montgomery Wiles, and don't ever say sorry again. You've been through hell, but I'll take care of you now.'

Once she'd persuaded him to put her down, Hatty took his hand and they walked towards the car park. 'Are you happy to stay at mine? I want to look after you, but if you prefer I can take you back to your place.'

He became short of breath and sweated. 'I just want to be with you right now.'

CHAPTER 20

2 January 2004

Monty thrashed and kicked his free leg in a bid to release his foot from the grip of steel and concrete.

Alan came to help, but was dragged away, air bubbles bursting from his gaping mouth.

Monty twisted and screamed as his foot broke free. And then he woke on a scorching roof, coughing up the stinking contents of his lungs. There, a body-sized bag. He unzipped it, and Alan glared out, wide-eyed—

Gasping, Monty sat up in bed, heart thundering against his ribs. He felt the soft bedsheets and looked around the unfamiliar darkened space, trembling.

But then there was Hatty, hugging him. 'Monty, it's okay. I'm here. You're in my apartment.' She flicked on a night light and wiped sweaty hairs from his forehead.

He stared at her, disoriented. 'What time is it?'

'Two in the morning, darling.'

'Oh. Sorry. Terrible dream.'

'You're safe with me. I'll take care of you.'

He took a large gulp of water and got up for the loo. When he returned, Hatty pulled the duvet over them, before hugging him close. He rolled onto his side, nestled into her arms and cried quietly for several minutes. Her embrace was familiar and reassuring, the soft curves of her hips, the silky warmth of her face against his and the faint myrrh of her perfume from the day before.

Hatty was now a solitary shaft of light in the muddy shattered kaleidoscope of his mind.

She clasped his hand and held it to her. 'Ssh, my love. I'll always be here for you.'

When Monty awoke, Hatty had gone, and he missed her grievously. He flicked on a bedside light and checked the clock; already past ten in the morning. Sitting up, he noticed a white dressing gown folded on the duvet beside him, so pulled it on and left the room.

The lounge was bright with French doors that led to a balcony and views across the Thames. An Ercol sofa and chairs grouped around a wool rug in the centre of the room. Books neatly lined shelves. Artwork hung in wall spaces. Classical jazz played softly. It was very 'Hatty'.

And there was his gorgeous girlfriend, on the sofa, hair tied back, in a long-sleeved t-shirt with faded jeans, reading a magazine. She looked up, padded across the room and kissed him softly on the cheek, wrapping him in her arms. 'Hello, sleepyhead. Would you like some coffee and breakfast?'

'Yes, please.' He held on, her feel, her fragrance, her warmth recharging emotional batteries that had run flat. Eventually he let go and followed her into a kitchen, fitted with modern equipment and dark marble worktops. Anxious about invading her space, he stood at the entrance and watched.

'You fell asleep before dinner last night; you must be starving. Would you like waffles? I made up some batter. I've got filter coffee on the go but can make you an espresso or cappuccino if you want?' She gestured to an Italian coffee maker on the counter.

'Oh, waffles would be nice, thank you. Anything convenient. And I'd love a filter coffee, please.'

She turned and walked to him, looking into his eyes and cupping his face in her hands. 'Just feel at home, okay? No need for please and thank yous.'

He slipped his arms around her waist. 'I'm sorry. Last night was probably not how you imagined our first night curled up together.'

'Ssh, I can't even tell you how happy I was to have you home with me.'

'What did I ever do to deserve you?'

She touched his nose. 'The simple lovely things. Now, you can stay here if you like or relax on the sofa. I've got the weekend *Financial Times*, or you can watch some telly.'

He preferred to stand and watch, coffee mug in hand, as she made waffles and chatted about things they could do later in the day. It was impossible to focus on anything beyond the here-and-now and being around Hatty was his sanity life-raft on stormy seas.

'Breakfast is served.' Holding an earthenware plate in one hand and a small jug in the other she kissed him softly on the cheek as she walked to her small dining table by the window.

He followed stiffly, sat and admired the fluffy waffles with blueberries and raspberries on the side. Pouring maple syrup liberally from the jug he smiled up at Hatty who sat next to him, unable to take her eyes off of him. 'These are the best waffles I've ever had, thank you so much.'

She rubbed his hand, half-smiling, cheeks flushed. 'You just enjoy them.'

The waffles were delicious, and he hadn't savoured food so much since he left hospital. He polished them off before emptying his coffee cup.

'Let me refill that for you.' Hatty got up and he followed her into the kitchen.

Even a few yards distance felt too much. 'Hey—' he touched her shoulder and she turned to him with a smile '—thanks for being you.'

'Stop it.' She threw her arms around him.

He kissed her forehead and rubbed away tears with his thumb. Magical wisps of auburn framed her face, honeyed skin dusted with cinnamon. 'Did I ever tell you how I adore your freckles?'

She breathed sharply, her smile like the perfect sunrise. 'Of all the compliments, Montgomery Wiles, I'll take that one as a first.' She kissed the tip of his nose and wandered to her sideboard, pulling out a gift-wrapped package. 'I know you probably don't feel like Christmas now, but I got you this before you went away.'

Tearing off the wrapping to reveal a new digital camera, he studied the information on the box carefully. He'd left his old camera in his bedroom on the day everything changed.

'It's the latest one, with really high megapixels whatever that means,' she said.

She'd obviously put a lot of thought into this and as he'd got her a photo album for Christmas it kind of made sense. And he didn't want to hurt her feelings after the care she'd gone to. 'Honestly, sweetheart,' he said, hastily brushing the image of his hotel bedroom aside, "it's perfect.'

The aroma of pizzaiola sauce and 'nduja sausage in the dining area was rich and sumptuous. Having collected clothes from Monty's house in Greenwich, they'd stopped for dinner at a favourite local family-run Italian restaurant. Over wood-fired pizza and a bottle of Valpolicella, Hatty chatted about life and he was happy to listen, struggling for conversation.

They'd chosen to eat early as he wasn't ready to bump into locals he knew and have the stress of everyone's sympathy. His life was a tangle of anxiety, confusion and doubt as it was, and he loved her for not making a big deal of his situation. She knew him better than anyone else, except perhaps Alan. He winced.

In the taxi home, his phone buzzed.

'Hey, Monty, it's me, Serwah. Just phoning to ask how you are getting on?'

He released Hatty's hand. 'Hello, kiddo. I'm back in London. What are you up to?'

'I'm volunteering up the coast. And, good news! I found my friend Lakshmi and she's okay!'

A thin smile spread across his face. *Missing people were still being found alive a week after the tsunami.* 'Brilliant. How'd you find her?'

'It's a long story. Actually not that long, but very expensive if I make this a long call.'

He heard her chuckle at the end of the line and another small fragment of light appeared in his subconscious. 'Hearing from you is priceless.'

'So any news about your dad?'

'The Embassy said that the online photos are causing lots of misunderstandings, so I've hit a bit of a roadblock.' He rubbed the back of his neck. 'I'm glad to be at home with Hatty though.'

Hatty squeezed his hand.

Monty closed his eyes, his mind whirring over options about Alan's whereabouts. 'There are practical things I need to get sorted out here, like a new passport and stuff. I'll probably fly back to continue the search when everything is sorted.'

'Are you sure that's a good idea, brother?'

'We'll see. Can't think that far ahead right now.'

After the call, Monty stared out the window at the blizzard of bright lights in Central London, his thoughts in southern Thailand.

Hatty stroked his arm, gently. 'Everything okay?'

He turned and smiled, taking her warm hand again in his. 'Yeah, sorry. That was just someone I met in Thailand. She lost contact with her friend after the tsunami and has just found her.'

'That's good news. How did you meet?'

'She was in the same hospital as me and we—' the Chinese temple flashed into his mind again and his nerves jangled '—well, we went through the same ordeal and were forced together by circumstance.'

'I'm glad you were able to meet someone nice.' She paused. 'And you said something about going back to Thailand?'

There was an almost imperceptible edge to Hatty's voice that, had they not been close for so long, he mightn't have noticed. He fiddled with the pack of cigarettes in his pocket, wondering how many more minutes the taxi would take.

'I have to, sweetheart. Dad's still out there somewhere.'

CHAPTER 21

3 January 2005

Staring at himself in the mirror, Monty assessed his bandaged bicep and the scratches on his face and body, which were fading. He brushed his teeth and wandered into Hatty's room, dressed only in boxers.

Bedside lamps created a warm glow. Sitting at the edge of her bed, Hatty brushed out her silky hair. What little make-up she wore had been removed and her skin was flawless and radiant. His darling Hatty didn't need make-up to be the most beautiful woman in his world. A simple pearl camisole and matching shorts displayed her elegant figure and long legs.

Looking up with a big smile, she said, 'Feeling refreshed?'

'I am. Still look a state though.' He grinned sheepishly, before sitting on the bed beside her, and kissing the top of her head. A surge of warmth coursed through him.

She kissed his shoulder ever so gently and considered the dressing. 'I'll go to the chemist tomorrow and get a new bandage.'

He met her gaze, saw her anguish, and worried whether he deserved to be so cared for. 'You've been so wonderful.'

Her eyes never left his, emeraldine like the purest undiscovered rockpool fed by warm Andaman waters, his personal sanctuary from torment. She shuffled closer and brushed his lips tenderly with hers.

Closing his eyes, he responded to her kiss, his mouth opening, their tongues dancing. His fears evaporated and he cupped her face, his fingertips delicately caressing her ears and tracing a line along her jaw. Desperate to commit every beautiful detail of her to memory in case of separation.

'I'm so glad you're safe,' her voice trembled. She stood and turned to sit on his lap, facing him. Brushing stray hairs from his brow, her eyes bore into his.

'Thank you for saving me,' he whispered.

Slowly she took his wrists in her hands and placed them on her collarbone, pushing them across her skin, freeing the lace straps of her camisole from her shoulders.

He gazed at the cotton fabric, as it fell away over her breasts, before being consumed again by her eyes, hotter than any thermal spring.

'I'll never want anyone else but you.' He pressed his lips hungrily against hers, consumed by desire for his soul mate.

Wrapping her legs around his torso, she tugged the camisole over her head, the fabric ruffling her hair as she pulled it away. Her bottom rubbed against him as she moved, sending forks of heat through the base of his stomach, his breath deepening to an animal growl.

She closed and opened her eyes slowly, tickling his abdomen with her fingernails.

Joy played across her face as he traced his fingers over the shallow rails of her ribs and onto her hips, running his hands under the elastic of her shorts.

'You're my guardian angel,' he muttered.

'Here to rescue you.' Her hair glowed in the soft light like a perfect sunset.

An image of a ginger-haired woman at the beach flashed into his mind. A dazzling smile frozen forever. Ice surged through his veins, and his breathing quickened. He clamped down on this jaw, trying to arrest the terminal ebb of his vitality as his body slackened. Scrunching his eyes, his hands balled into fists.

Hatty rested her cheek on his shoulder.

'I'm really sorry,' he croaked.

'Shh, it's okay. You're safe with me. I'll always protect you.' She took his hand and kissed his knuckles one by one. 'We can get through this together.'

4 January 2005

'Do you think you'd be up for popping into the bank this morning?' Hatty asked, over breakfast. 'Everyone has been asking after you non-stop.'

In her work clothes, she was pretty as a picture, her hair worn up, silver cufflinks at the sleeves of her cream blouse and a pencil skirt that accentuated her hips. Her make-up was understated, her porcelain skin perfect. For a flicker, his pride burnt through the anxiety.

Then in an instant, his heartbeat kicked up as he thought about a tidal wave of well-intended sympathy at the office. 'I don't have a suit here, so they'll have to take me as they find me. As long as I can go in with you, I suppose I'll be alright.'

She kissed him lightly on the cheek. 'Of course you can come with me, silly. And if it's too much, I'll bring you back, okay?'

They walked out into a cold winter's morning. Hatty hailed a black taxi, steam puffing from her mouth. Under a powder-blue sky, the Tower of London looked pristine as they trundled across Tower Bridge before heading east towards Canary Wharf.

Within an hour, Monty's head throbbed and his mouth was bone dry. Everyone wanted to talk to him, hug him, offer high-fives and generally throw painful bucketloads of earnest bonhomie and relief over him.

Bob, the VP, offered a stiff half-hug. 'You look like a character from the bloody *Blair Witch Project*.'

For the first time that day, Monty grinned. 'I'm trying to look more and more like you, Bob, so I can one day be a dried out miserable VP too.'

He smiled and clapped him on the shoulder. 'Good to see you back, lad. Now bugger off and don't come back until you are rested up and ready.' He then looked at Hatty, his gaze steady. 'And thanks for looking out for him.'

'Shall I come back with you?' Hatty asked as Monty turned to make his escape.

'No, that's okay, lovely. I'll get a cab and chill out until you get home.' He smiled. 'Hey, let me make dinner tonight. Would be nice to do something normal.'

'That would be lovely. Thank you.' She kissed him on the lips, with no heed to the horde of colleagues watching on.

Breathing in her fragrance, blessed by her presence, the throbbing eased.

A fancy delicatessen occupied a small unit nearby and Monty spent an unpressured few minutes selecting ingredients for dinner. Grabbing a large bottle of mineral water, he noticed the alcohol shelf. After an emotional tussle, he looked around to see if anyone was watching and grabbed a bottle of whisky, guilt creeping up his back like a hot itch.

Wearing silver trunks, a young blond boy walked by Monty as he sat by the pool. A giant wave rose up in slow motion and crashed down upon them. He clung to the boy as they tumbled over and over beneath the torrent, slamming against solid blocks and sharp edges.

The boy stared into his eyes. A man and woman swept past, waving frantically as they were carried away.

Then the searing pain along his arm. His grip weakened and the boy was torn from his embrace, gazing at him, bubbles emitting from his mouth.

He thrashed and strained every sinew to rescue Hendrick but every effort sucked fetid water in his lungs.

'No, no, I don't want to . . . ' he gasped and opened his eyes, dazed and confused.

'Hey,' Hatty whispered, 'you're safe and here with me.' He lay on the sofa, his head in her lap.

Monty breathed in rasps while she stroked his hair.

With a full stomach he'd fallen asleep on the sofa after dinner. He'd made a lasagne from scratch, which she had gushed about, as if it was the most delicious thing she'd ever tasted. It undoubtedly wasn't. But the comforting normality of a meal with the woman he loved was healing.

And now he was back in hell, tormented by hideous dreams that wouldn't leave him alone. He stood and pulled the cork on the Scotch he'd bought earlier. 'I need a drink.'

The annoying thing was that he'd held back from the whisky all day. But with his hands shaking, he really needed it now as he slid open the French door and stepped onto the balcony.

'Spoke to the Foreign Office after I dropped you off earlier. There was a mix up with the paperwork which explains why the body I had to endure seeing in Krabi wasn't Dad. Not their fault but getting information is near impossible.' He took a drag from his cigarette and blew a thick cloud of smoke into the night sky.

Hatty stroked his hand. 'They have been taking flak in the newspapers about their tsunami response. I guess they are trying their best.'

'Seems a bit left hand, right hand to me, frankly.'

'I'm just glad to have you back home, darling.'

'Me too. Don't know how I'd get through without you, my love. And thanks for not minding too much.' He waved his right hand. 'With the smoking and all.'

She rubbed his knee. 'Will you think about doing something for me, once you're more settled?'

He stroked her hand with his thumb. 'Yes, of course.'

'Maybe get an appointment at the doctor's surgery? I'm worried about your stress. They might be able to help.'

'Okay, sweetheart.' He yawned and stubbed his cigarette out, guilt and anxiety crashing in immediately.

CHAPTER 22

6 January 2005

Wind rustled softly through trees around the cemetery as Monty placed a clutch of flowers on the polished plinth. *I miss you, Mum. I promise I'll bring Dad back to you as soon as I can.*

He stood and hugged Hatty. 'I told my mum about you when she got sick as it really lifted her spirits.'

She smiled and put a gloved hand on his cheek. 'I bet she was an amazing mam.'

Wrapped in winter coats, they walked hand in hand to the car.

Hatty threaded through the narrow lanes of the postcard English village with its ancient oaks and flint-fronted houses. Within minutes, the car crunched onto the gravel drive of the eighteenth-century thatched farmhouse.

Monty's thoughts drifted to that wonderful summer barbecue six months before with Alan and Hatty chatting gaily in the family garden.

A woman in plain clothes and a uniformed officer stood beside a police car in the road.

He groaned. 'Our visitors have arrived.'

'Hello, are you Monty Wiles?' the woman asked as she approached.

'Yep, that's me.'

She reached out and shook his hand. 'Nice to meet you, Monty. I'm Sandeep Chowdry. This is Constable Dodds, a forensics officer at Winchester police station.' She turned to Hatty with a warm smile.

'This is my girlfriend, Harriet,' Monty introduced.

'It's really nice to meet you, Harriet. Shall we go inside, as it's cold today, isn't it?'

Monty ushered the officers into the lounge.

Sandeep wore a smart black suit, her dark hair tied back neatly and worn up, her tone calm and respectful. 'Okay, Monty, as I mentioned on the phone, I'm a family liaison officer with the Hampshire Constabulary. But just call me Sandeep, not Sergeant Chowdry. My role is to make sure you're informed about any developments in your dad's case. Does that all make sense so far? I know it's a lot to take in.'

'Yes, thank you, it's fine.' His replies were curt, his patience thin.

'Good. So, I know the Foreign Office has told you the identification of the deceased has been complicated. Right now, another family has lodged a claim for the body that you initially saw online, which you said appeared different to the body you saw at the temporary mortuary. I'm afraid this means we now need to follow a process called disaster victim identification. Is that all clear so far?'

He nodded. 'How long's that going to take?'

'I'm going to be completely honest and say I don't know how long the process will take, and I can't promise it will be finalised by a certain date. But given the number of people killed, it may take some months, I'm sorry. However, I'll do all I can to make this as straightforward for you as I can. And, importantly, everything about the case will be strictly confidential. Is that all clear?'

He grunted, his mind numb.

'Now if it's okay with you, Constable Dodds will need to spend time in your dad's room taking hair and fingerprint samples that we can use in the investigation.'

Hatty's breath was soft on his shoulder. She was curled on her side in bed, under the soft caress of the duvet.

Through the dim glow of a night light, Monty stared at the delicate lashes, against her cheeks, and adorably unruly auburn strands on the pillow. She *was* his only anchor against the crashing anxiety that threatened to sink him each day. Yet at 3 a.m., he had been tossing and turning since midnight.

He slid out of bed and padded into the hall.

With the blinds open, a full moon threw ghoulish shadows across the lounge. He sat at the dining table and flipped open his laptop.

Having no ordered plan, he scrolled for news about missing tsunami victims. Most of the articles majored on the dead or the reunited, but not the missing.

His eyes hurt and a pinch in his bladder reminded him that he should have gone to the toilet an hour ago. After some minutes he exhaled sharply, tiptoed into the toilet and relieved himself without flushing, to spare the noise. He grabbed his cigarettes from the sideboard, gingerly poured himself a whisky and stepped back onto the balcony.

The fiery heat of the whisky did nothing to moderate the bitter breeze that sliced through his pyjamas. Frustration weighed like an iron yoke around his neck, and he hunched over to take long drags from his cigarette, staring blankly across the Thames. *Well, if that ghastly photograph wasn't Dad, perhaps he's still alive somewhere? Alone, badly injured, waiting to be found. Scared, probably. Gosh, he must be worried witless.* He shivered uncontrollably, his hand shaking every time he put the cigarette between his lips. However hard he stared, he could discern no hopeful clues about Dad in the acrid clouds of smoke he blew into the cold night sky.

A light came on, and he tossed his cigarette over the balcony with a start. Wrapping her nightgown around herself, Hatty wandered into the lounge, squinting.

He stepped inside sheepishly, sliding the French door shut. His ankle throbbed from the cold, so he sat heavily on the sofa.

'Are you okay, darling? It's four-thirty in the morning.'

'Yeah, sorry. I was up searching stuff on the internet.'

She perched next to him, placing a hand on his knee. 'Can I get you something? Cup of tea or milk maybe, to help you sleep?'

'That's okay, Hats. I'll try and get some more sleep for a bit. I just need to book a flight back to Thailand.'

Concern was etched across her forehead. 'Are you sure that's the right thing to do? The police and Foreign Office are trying their best to find people who are still missing.'

'Sorry, but I think the lot of them are clueless.'

'I know.'

He breathed out heavily through his nose. 'Look, I've got to go back, at least for a while. There must be more concrete information on Dad's whereabouts, something I can do. I'll ask Bob to let me have another week off.'

'I just think you might be better off here until we hear something concrete.'

He stood, desperate for the cold solitude of the balcony and the numbing comfort of his reawakened nicotine addiction. 'Please don't, Hats. It's not like I want to.'

CHAPTER 23

11 January 2005

A Gurkha guard checked Monty's passport at the ornate iron gate. Halfway along a tree-lined drive sat a bronze statue of Queen Victoria in a circle of grass mown like a cricket pitch.

Nick Evans waited inside, dressed in a suit and yellow tie.

'Nick, good to see you again.' Monty extended his hand as he passed onto the manicured grounds of the British embassy in Bangkok, sweat soaking his smart shirt.

'Good to see you too, Monty. How was your flight?'

'Strange to be honest. The last time I flew to Thailand, I was with Dad.'

They walked past the statue and around a curved path to the portico of a colonial-style mansion.

'I'm really sorry about the difficulties you've faced in the search for your father.'

'I understand how incredibly complicated it must be, but the system doesn't seem to help.'

'Do come on through.'

A butler in a white tropical uniform stood at the door to the British Ambassador's Residence. With a *wai*, he ushered them into a polished teak corridor lined with artwork.

Monty followed Nick into a reception room on the left, taking in the piano and lounge furniture, paintings, and what appeared to be Thai and

British ceramics in teak display cabinets. The upper-class décor felt far removed from the suffering of ordinary people, who had lost everything in the tsunami. Yet Nick seemed okay. The diplomat had replied with surprising equanimity to Monty's angry text message and had offered to meet.

'Would you like tea or a cold drink? I can recommend the lime soda.' Nick sat in an armchair at one end of a coffee table. He smiled. 'David, the ambassador, is happy for me to have meetings here when he is otherwise engaged. Sorry he wasn't available to see you himself.'

Monty sat on a deeply cushioned sofa. 'I can imagine he's busy. And a lime soda sounds nice, please. How long have you been back in Bangkok?'

'Just got back yesterday. My first break since Boxing Day. Going back the day after tomorrow. A team is finally flying out from London to set up a proper office.'

'Shouldn't you be having time off?'

He chuckled darkly. 'Now that's an interesting idea.'

The butler reappeared, placing tall, chilled glasses and a jug of cloudy lime soda on the coffee table, and poured a drink for each man.

'I'm glad we had a chance to meet again. I was obviously sad to hear about the difficulties you've faced.'

'Look, I understand how hard you must be working. But as you can imagine it's tough.'

Nick placed his glass of lime soda on the coffee table before looking Monty steadily in the eye. 'Do you have anyone at home to help you? Wife, girlfriend?'

'Girlfriend, Hatty.'

'Can I ask how Hatty has coped through all this?'

'She's been amazing. Really, I'm so lucky.' He thought back to two days prior at Heathrow, Hatty struggling to hold back tears.

'Good.'

He grunted. 'How about you, Nick? Family out here? Or girlfriend?'

'I was with a lovely girl just before the tsunami. We met through work. She's a recruitment consultant, and I was looking for a new economist through her company.'

'And you asked her out?'

'I tried, and she kept me at arm's length for a long time. Smart girl. Went to Chulalongkorn University, Thailand's equivalent to Oxford. Then one Sunday morning, she took me to a noodle bar in the quiet backstreets near the Grand Palace. After that, we went on daytime excursions to temples, local food places and hipster coffee shops that tourists would never get to see.' He exhaled heavily.

'Sounds old-fashioned romantic. I mean, in a good way.' *All those fun trips and lunchtime get-togethers with Hatty helped build the emotional foundations for our love.*

'It was the best. We got closer. I met her friends, then her family. It was all headed in one direction, but . . .' he trailed off.

'What happened?'

Nick stared briefly into space. 'The tsunami happened. I used to date a university student. She was a sweet girl but, with hindsight, too immature for me. Her family is from Phuket.'

Monty's heart accelerated. 'Was she caught up in it?'

'I was looking through body photographs. I saw a face shot, and it was the mirror image of my ex. Swear to God. My heart leapt into my mouth. I thought, maybe she went to Phuket after we broke up. I don't know. I phoned, sent text messages. No reply.'

His mind flashed to the hospital lobby in Krabi and that horrendous photograph he thought was Dad. 'So is she dead?'

'No. I discovered just yesterday that she'd been safe in Bangkok all along.'

'Wow.'

He held Monty's gaze, unblinking. 'The point is, it really messed my mind, so I understand in a tiny way what you are going through. People are desperate to find their loved ones. They see a photo, it looks remarkably similar, and that's it. In my case, it was a girl I'd dated for less than a year. Even so, I still haven't got past the anxiety of not knowing.'

After their talk, as they wandered back down the landscaped drive, Nick asked. 'So, you're flying south this afternoon?'

He sighed and thought about retracing his steps to the disaster zone. 'I have to keep searching while uncertainty remains about what happened to Dad.'

'You should meet the British police team down there. They'll give you the most up to date picture.' He paused. 'Although, I have to be completely honest and say I'm not sure it will take you much further forward.'

Monty turned to him. 'Well, maybe. But I'm not ready to give up while there's still a slither of hope. Anyway, thanks for all your help.'

The diplomat shook his hand. 'Take care of yourself down there, Monty. And don't stay away from Hatty for long. For the sake of your mental health, you need her more than you need to be here right now.'

CHAPTER 24

12 January 2005

The taxi crossed Sarasin bridge from Phuket and plunged into the jutting limestone landscape of Phang-Nga province. Monty drifted in and out of sleep but woke with a start as the car slowed.

'Thai Prince die near here,' the driver said, pointing to the right.

He leant forwards between the front seats and peered ahead. Off to the right, beached a full kilometre inland, a grey patrol boat with 813 painted white on the bow. 'Jesus,' he breathed.

Stretching into the distance, the road was dirty, debris piled on the verges. Occasionally, skeletons of derelict buildings appeared way off to the left through trees stripped of undergrowth. The swathe of destruction continued uninterrupted for forty minutes.

Eventually, the taxi pulled over, and he stepped out. Parked at the roadside, police and military utility vehicles, minibuses, and TV trucks, with helicopters sat on white circles in a field.

In the heat, the nauseating stench of death was overpowering.

'Monty!'

He turned to see Serwah walking briskly towards him, tugging white overalls off her shoulders and tying them at her waist.

'I'm going to hug you, but I warn you, I'm really sweaty. Sorry, you got here a bit earlier than I expected, and I was running late.' She tiptoed and wrapped her arms around him, pressing her damp face to his.

The back of her spaghetti strap top was soaked but her embrace was calming, though the knuckles of her spine suggested she'd got thinner. 'God, I'm pleased to see you, kiddo.'

'Me too, brother. Come on, I'll take you to meet my friends.' She led him to a *songthaew* pickup taxi, and said a few words in basic Thai to the driver before they jumped in the back.

'You speak Thai now?'

'Just a few phrases. Like directions and give me a beer and *Phad Thai*, please.' She grinned.

He gripped the overhead handrail as the pickup accelerated.

'Do you have any more news on your dad?' Serwah shouted through the din of wind and traffic.

'No—' he groaned heavily '—I just spoke to the British police in Phuket, and we are no farther forward. But I guess there's a small chance that no news might mean good news.'

'I'm so sorry, Monty.'

'How long do you think you'll stay up here?' he asked, taking in the hustle and bustle of the small provincial town.

'Probably another week, if I can stand it that long. I need to get back to my university. As much as I want to help, I don't think it would be sensible.'

'How come?'

She shivered. 'You'll find out.'

He grunted.

'How about you? How does Hatty feel about you coming back?'

'Worry, to be honest, though it's not her fault. I'll just stay here for a day, see if I can find out anything, then head back.' He reached into his pocket, only to find his mobile phone out of charge. *Dammit.*

'Make sure you do, okay?' The vehicle drew to a halt by a park, populated with a rainbow assembly of tents, and Serwah hopped onto the tarmac. 'This is us.'

A wall was plastered with bright paintings about peace and hope, with pictures of the missing.

Monty fished the buff folder from his rucksack, adding Alan's missing person notice to the collection.

Young people milled around in groups, cooking at fire pits, drinking, or playing music, like a ghoulish Glastonbury. 'I'm probably the oldest person here.'

'Don't be silly. You'll fit right in.'

'Serwah,' someone called.

She waved back. 'Here we are.'

A slim guy in surf wear and smartly trimmed hair stood under the dappled shade of low trees. He stepped up to hug Serwah then took Monty's hand, pumping it enthusiastically. 'It's my guess that you are Monty? If so, then I am Bert, short for Adalbert,' he said in a German accent.

'Bert is my special buddy in camp, always looking out for me and the others,' Serwah said with a beaming smile. 'Oh, there she is.'

A young woman in purple dungarees hugged Serwah and contemplated the new arrival. She was petite and shorter than her friend, with delicate features and long black hair tied into a thick braid.

'And this is my darling Lakshmi, who I told you about.'

13 January 2005

The stench told Monty they were close. Despite the roar of the exhaust pipe and din of rush hour, the people in the back of the *songthaew* pick-up were silent, lost in thought. At 9 a.m. the temperature was already nudging thirty.

Having arrived, they found a vacant patch of grass and donned hooded coveralls and surgical masks.

'Are you absolutely sure you want to do this, Monty? I'm worried about you.' Serwah asked, big eyes framed by her hood and mask.

Over breakfast, she had pleaded with him to return to Hatty, but he'd dug his heels in. He didn't want to shirk what others were doing and find another reason to feel inadequate. And maybe a good deed here might pay him back with a clue about Alan's whereabouts.

'I'll see how I go, and if it gets too much, I'll leave and meet you at the camp later.' Sweat had already soaked his t-shirt and tremors shook his hands.

Serwah and Lakshmi wandered off to gather dental data at a site where the dead cared not about distinctions of race or religion.

'So, Monty, you are stuck with me for the day,' Bert said.

They walked through the triangular temple gate. Officials milled around, some in police and military drill, a larger number in bodysuits. Volunteers walked by carrying a sagging body bag.

Darkened corpses lay all around in squares marked out by smoking dry ice. It was an otherworldly place where souls lingered in an ill-tempered queue between death and their final resting place.

National flags fluttered in a humid breeze beneath the trees and between refrigerated shipping containers. A Union flag lifted Monty's spirits, but briefly.

'We're over here. We can work as a pair, okay?'

Volunteers worked calmly at tables in a shaded area.

'Yeah, sure. Just tell me what to do.' Monty pulled on thin latex gloves and adjusted his mask.

'So, you need this clipboard, pen and evidence bags. We retrieve any valuable possessions, put them in a bag, write down the details on the form, okay?'

He studied the form then nodded. 'Got it.'

At an unattended table, Bert unzipped a bag and bent to inspect the cadaver inside. Soon, he handed Monty a grimy watch with a thick leather strap.

Wiping the watch face with a rag, Monty studied the gold Roman numerals against an ivory background. The leather strap has a crocodile-skin pattern, just like the new strap he'd bought for Alan. Tears flooded his eyes, blurring his vision until he wiped them with the back of his free hand. Turning to Bert, he peered into the bag to see wisps of grey hair, and shuddered.

'And a ring.'

Without looking back, Bert handed him a gold wedding band. After he'd wiped it, Monty whistled through his teeth. *Dad's ring was thicker than this and didn't have any pattern.*

'Okay, next bag,' Bert announced.

They settled into a routine, methodically collecting, recording, and storing the victims' personal possessions. After a while, Bert stood back and exhaled sharply.

'You alright, Bert?' Monty's mouth was dry with thirst, acid bile stinging his throat.

'Sorry. Would you mind if we swapped for a while?'

Monty slapped his new friend on the shoulder, and they changed places. Then as he unzipped the next bag, he gagged. The shrunken figure of a child in a filthy swimming costume that was once pink. Skinny legs bent up to her body, A long mat of tangled hair obscured her face. She gripped a pink toothbrush in her hand. His mind wandered to Alan and Daisy organising his travel bag with his favourite teddies, and a wash bag with a blue toothbrush and bubble bath.

Then his stomach convulsed and he staggered hurriedly to a tree which he leant against to spew onto the dry grass in a torrent. There was a reassuring slap on his shoulder, and Bert passed him a bottle of water. 'Sorry, mate, you okay?'

Cold water tumbled over Monty's head and he relished its cleansing and sanctifying power. The wash area consisted of breeze block cubicles, open to the sky, with a water vat and plastic scoop in one corner. He scrubbed his hair with a bar of soap, rubbing the suds over his face and neck for a long time, breathing in its carbolic scent. When he'd washed, he refilled the vat for the next person, dried, and pulled on boardshorts.

Back at the tent, Bert sat in a camping chair and, without getting up, handed Monty a beer from a plastic cooler.

'So, Monty, how do you feel?'

'Better for being clean.' He rubbed his nose with the back of his hand, although the scent of death still clung to the tiny hairs inside.

'You did well today.'

He grimaced. 'Thanks. I figure someone somewhere must be looking for those poor souls, just like I'm searching for Dad.'

A cloud of sadness darkened Bert's face. He reached out with his bottle and clinked it against Monty's. 'Yep. I lost contact with two of my university mates and haven't seen or heard from them yet.'

'I'm really sorry.' Monty reached for his rucksack, withdrawing a bottle of whisky, and a couple of plastic cups. 'Might need something a bit stiffer. Join me in one?'

The German considered him, before replying. 'Okay then. Just one though. Don't think I can do this work with a hangover.'

He poured two fingers for each of them, handing a cup to Bert before downing his in one stinging draft. 'So, what's next for you when this is all done?' he asked, refilling his cup and lighting a cigarette.

'Go back to Berlin. Finish my Masters. Actually, I applied already to do a PhD at Oxford University.'

The warmth of the whisky and the cloud of smoke in his lungs were like sedatives, and he relaxed into the chair. 'That's really great. I can show you around London.'

'Thank you. I want to visit Birmingham too, where Serwah studies.'

You're sweet on her. 'She'd love that. I've never been to Birmingham. If you go, I'll bring my girlfriend, and we can all have lunch.' With his phone still flat, had hadn't called Hatty for over a day, and anxiety crawled over his skin like an inflamed rash. He splashed more whisky into his cup.

When Monty woke at dawn in his stuffy tent, his mouth was cottony, dry saliva caking at the corners. He drank his last remaining drips of water before opening the tent and blinking against the early morning rays. Hands trembling hands, he lit a cigarette, more comforting than breakfast.

'Hey,' Serwah whispered and stepped the few yards across from her tent, her face a picture of concern. 'You alright? We're worried about you.'

Was he alright? Right now, his thoughts and emotions bounced up and down on a rubber band. 'I've probably felt better.'

Bert appeared with a camping mug of coffee and a greasy paper bag. 'I got you a drink and some Thai donuts.'

'Cheers.' Monty grabbed the bag and sunk his teeth into a donut and his stomach churned from the assault of fried food. But he dipped the next in a small pot of green custard, finding the milky sweetness settling.

Serwah touched his knee. 'Bert and I think you really need to go home. We're worried about you.'

'Trying to get rid of me already?' he grumped.

'It's not that,' Bert continued, 'it's just that we've had a bit of training with bodies, and it's already hard enough for us to deal with it. Being here will make you feel worse.'

He closed his eyes, a headache spreading across his forehead. He fished his phone out of his bag. 'Do you know any place where I can charge this? I really need to call Hatty.'

'There's an internet café just five minutes from the entrance to the campsite. They'll let you charge your phone there if you are checking emails,' she replied. 'Please call her!'

CHAPTER 25

14 January 2005

'God, where have you been, Monty? I've been crazy with worry,' Hatty echoed down the line. Anxious, hurt.

The internet café was full of western volunteers. He closed his eyes, and replied softly. 'I'm sorry, Hats, my phone died, and I've only just been able to recharge it.'

'Where are you and what are you doing?'

'I'm up the coast from Phuket. I met my friend here—' he paused and rubbed his temple '—where the bodies are being processed.'

'What friend is that?' Her tone was inquisitorial.

Ice ran through his veins. 'Just a friend I met after the tsunami. Serwah. I told you about her.'

There was a long pause, and a sniffle. 'The Foreign Office has finally sent a big team to Phuket to look. Do you think you should come home until they have news?'

He was unable to focus, feeling told off and under pressure that he just didn't need. 'Err, yeah, probably. I'll fly back to Bangkok tonight, then hopefully home tomorrow evening.'

15 January 2005

Having showered, Monty arranged the small collection of personal effects in his rucksack.

'Before you go, I've got something for you,' Aek said from the door to the beautifully appointed bedroom.

'Okay, Uncle Aek.'

He'd insisted Monty stay with him and Mai in Bangkok before flying home. 'Your dad and I used to drink Chinese tea together. Let's start a new tradition, you and me.'

A comfortable lounge occupied the mezzanine level of the modern townhouse by the Chao Praya river. Aek fixed espresso-sized cups of tea and placed them on the coffee table, before relaxing into an armchair.

Monty sat in a cushioned sofa, surrounded by Aek and Mai's family photos and sipped the unsweetened tea, which had a powerful, pure flavour. The jolt revived his senses. 'This is really good.'

'*Pe* Alan's favourite.' He grabbed an album from a shelf and placed it on the coffee table. 'That's for you. Keep it.'

An enlarged photo of Alan and Daisy decorated the leather cover. Tears welled in his eyes as he stared at it then quietly turned the pages. It contained a lifetime of photographs of his parents with their beloved Thai friends. The first was a black and white shot of the four in sixties fashions posing on Westminster Bridge, Big Ben in the background.

'I was younger than you in that photo. Our final year at university. We were the only Thai people and everything was cold and alien to us in London. But your mum and dad were so kind and made us feel welcome and at home.'

'They really loved you, like family.' His voice cracked.

Aek's smooth features creased into a wistful smile. 'I still remember when *Pe* Daisy phoned to tell us she was pregnant. Aunty Mai was five months' pregnant with Nat at that time, and it was so lovely to hear them talking excitedly about being mammas.'

Monty rubbed his eyes with the back of his hand.

'Your parents were proud of you, Monty, very proud,' Aek continued. 'They would tell us about how well you were doing, at school, at university, at the bank, and we would do the same about Nat.'

'That means a lot.'

Aek stared at him like a headmaster. 'Your mum and dad would be worried about you now.'

Hairs rose on the back of his neck. 'What do you mean?'

He reached into a bag at the end of the sofa and removed an empty whisky bottle, which he placed on the coffee table. 'They would be worried about your health.'

They must have found it while tidying up my room. He'd struggled all day not smoking. Now, his closest family friend saw through him, like he was a teenager again, caught by his dad with a can of Carlsberg Special Brew in his room. He felt ashamed but also annoyed at being called out. 'It's just a difficult time, that's all.'

Aek put a hand on his. 'I know, and I can't even understand how difficult. And I don't want to make you feel more sad.'

He stared at the coffee table, blinking back shame. 'I just want to find Dad.'

Aek came across and sat beside him. '*Pe* Alan is dead, Monty. That is so difficult to imagine right now, and it breaks my heart to say it because it feels so unkind. I know you don't have confirmation. But you need to accept that *Pe* Alan is gone and pray for his soul.'

Tears splashed the glass cover of the coffee table as Monty wept, his head lolling forwards. He'd give anything right now for a long draft of whisky and the giddiness of smoking one cigarette after the other but now even *that* was denied him. He had become a hostage both to addiction and to kindness. He *knew* his parents would hate to see him this way, but *they* were no longer here.

After a while he balled his fist and said, 'I wish I could do something positive to remember my parents by.'

'Let me and Aunty Mai help you,' his uncle replied.

The next day, Hatty was waiting in arrivals, her face drawn. She wrapped an arm around his neck and kissed him on the cheek. 'It's nice to have you back.'

Monty rubbed her back distractedly. 'Thanks.'

'How was your flight?'

Staring through the crowds of people towards the exit sign he felt around in his pocket for his cigarettes. 'Ugh, not great, to be honest.' He was light-headed, his body unsure of the correct time. He hadn't slept on the twelve-hour flight. Three coffees before landing had left him artificially alert, despite his senses otherwise fogged by alcohol.

'Let's get you home.'

Rain fell heavily, the lights of other cars an amorphous glow. His jaw muscles ached from grinding his teeth, and he stared out the window blankly.

At Hatty's apartment, he took himself to bed with a bottle of water, tossing and turning, yet unable to drift off. The terminal stop button pressed on his search for his beloved father and best friend. His restless curiosity replaced with emptiness that pulsed toxic fumes of inadequacy throughout his soul.

Sometime around midday, Hatty appeared at the bedroom door. 'Was wondering if you'd like a spot of lunch?'

'Sure, okay.' He got out of bed stiffly and pulled on the jeans and t-shirt he'd worn on the plane.

In the lounge, Hatty had laid out the table with fresh baguettes and all manner of cheeses and cold cuts. She stood at his side as he sat, running her hand over his shoulder. 'You like the deli by the office, so I thought this would make a good lunch.'

'Thanks.' He sliced the end of the loaf off, cut it down the middle and spread it thick with butter, before layering on brie and jambon. His mouth was arid, and the crust scratched his throat, making him cough. He took a sip of water and lay the sandwich on his plate.

After a few minutes of heavy silence, Hatty said, 'I was wondering if you'd like to get out this afternoon and have a walk along the Thames? Nice way to catch some fresh air.'

'Maybe,' he replied. 'Still pretty knackered though, so might go back to bed.' He knew she was trying to help but he didn't want to be managed.

She placed her hand on his.

It sat there inert and heavy like a warm handcuff, shackling him with good intention.

'Did you find out anything useful in Thailand,' she asked, quietly.

Closing his eyes he breathed slowly in a vain effort to temper his heart. 'Not especially.' Rising from the table, he kissed her cheek and lay his hand briefly on her shoulder before walking to the bedroom.

CHAPTER 26

19 January 2005

A young Thai girl in a pink swimsuit skipped into the bathroom, and fetched up her glittery brush to clean her teeth. She turned and smiled, her face radiant, her eyes hollow black pits. 'Come on, come on, let's go to the beach.'

Gasping for breath, Monty sat up dazed in the darkened room. His watch said it was two-thirty in the afternoon. Monday. Three days had felt like purgatory. Stepping out of bed, he walked to the window, pulling the curtains to one side, to reveal St Paul's cathedral under a gunmetal sky.

Knowing he had no clean clothes, he shuffled through Hatty's drawers and wardrobe to find a small selection of his things, but nothing he wanted. Suddenly, he desperately needed to escape this beautifully furnished cell. To drink and to smoke without anyone – especially Hatty – seeing.

Hastily, he tugged his clothes and shoes on, gathered up his toiletries from the en suite and placed them in his rucksack.

In the lounge, Hatty sat on the sofa, her back to him, reading and listening to music.

Instinctively, she turned her head, her eyes rimmed red, before standing. 'Everything okay, darling?'

'Yeah, I'm okay. Look, I just need to go back to my place for a bit and sort out some stuff, if that's okay?'

Her shoulders slackened. 'Yes, sure, okay. Shall I drive you in the car?'

Glancing at the door, he replied. 'No, that's okay, Hats. I'll just get a cab or something.'

She hugged him, her chest moving in shallow rapid sobs. 'Stay here, let me help you, love.'

He shrugged out of the embrace and stood, his arms limp, desperate to escape the jail of her generosity.

'You've been amazing, Hats,' he said, wanting vaguely to make it easier on her.

'What will do you at home?' Her voice quavered.

'I've got a lot of paperwork to work through. About Dad.' His voice hardened, irritation and a desire to escape kicking in.

'Oh, okay.' Defeat softened her tone. 'Will you come into the office tomorrow?'

He whistled through his lips. 'I'll see how I feel.' He kissed the top of her head, before turning, opening her door, and pushing it behind him with a soft click.

Walking into the chill January air, he pulled his jacket snug around his throat, his steps lighter, an intolerable weight lifted from his shoulders. Depression is a one-player game, after all. He wandered for ten minutes, avoiding eye contact with other passers-by and occasionally ducking into a secluded spot for a cigarette, where he wouldn't be seen.

Eventually, he spotted an off-licence where he bought a couple of bottles of whisky, several bottles of wine, two cartons of cigarettes, and a large selection of crisps and refrigerated pies. He'd sooner not have to leave his house again until he felt ready and hoped this would be enough for a couple of days.

21 January 2005

The knocking was insistent. *Shit, go away.* He stared emptily at the horses racing along an anonymous green furlong somewhere in England on the TV. His eyes traced a line up to his mantlepiece and the framed photo of his parents that was mounted on the expensive wallpaper above it. He flopped his arm off the sofa to grab his pack of cigarettes. Almost empty. On the coffee table, four grimy tumblers, an almost-empty bottle of Scotch, an overflowing ashtray, and a chipped jug of water.

Bloody hell, where's my lighter? Without getting up, he felt around the hardwood floor, his fingers brushing through empty food wrappers, until he touched the smooth plastic cartridge and grabbed it.

The knocking intruded again. 'I don't want anything,' he shouted.

There was a pause, then a sharp rapping on his window. He looked up, but his curtains were closed, to prevent eavesdropping on his misery. *Dammit.* He got up, his lower back aching, and walked to the Victorian bay, pulling back the curtain a crack.

Hatty stared back at him, her face stony. 'Let me in,' she shouted.

He blew out his cheeks and surveyed the bombsite of his lounge. Various bits of used clothes and underwear on his IKEA armchair in one corner, hardly a patch of empty flooring, and paperwork scattered beneath his sofa.

He rubbed his cheek, feeling the thick stubble, and walked out of the lounge, dressed only in tracksuit bottoms. His tiled hallway was five yards of relative normality and neatness in comparison, but he never lingered there.

Opening the door, Hatty stood ramrod straight, hair tied back, her overcoat neatly pinched at her waist, gloved hands balled in fists.

She stared at him, her emerald eyes unblinking and not leaving his, shaking her head slightly. 'Can I come in, please?'

He swept his arm along the hall and she walked in briskly.

She overtook him, sending alarm bells clanging in his head.

'Let me get you a cup of tea.' He rushed after her, but not quick enough to divert her away from the lounge. Body shaking, he stood in the hall, like a child caught red-handed and burning with shame.

Hatty reappeared. 'Is this what you've been doing for two days, while I've been phoning you non-stop with no answer? Drinking and smoking yourself to death?'

'I don't know what you want me to say.'

'Two weeks ago you said you loved me, today you don't know what to say.' She stared at him.

I've always loved you. 'I did. I mean . . .' He stared up at the ceiling, cringing inside. 'I'm sorry.'

'You shouldn't have gone back to Thailand. I don't know why you did. I'm worried sick about your health, Monty. I really love you, can't you see?'

'You're the best,' he whispered, biting the corner of his finger.

'You can't keep disappearing on me. Why did you have to switch off your phone in Thailand? I was near going out of my mind then. What were you doing this with friend of yours?' Her anger now filled the blanks of his extended silence with her concerns.

'Huh? My friend Serwah?'

'Yes!'

Irritation flared inside of him. 'My phone ran out of charge, that's all. Why are you bringing up Serwah? My relationship with her isn't what you think.'

'Well, you've given me a lot of time to think as you've disappeared for the past two weeks, save a brief appearance at my flat when you didn't talk to me much either.'

His voice hardened. 'I go to Thailand for a week to search for *my dad* and you think I've been up to no good with someone I just met. You disappeared to New York for the best part of two years.'

'That's different,' she yelled. 'We discussed my career at every step and you said you were supportive.'

'And I meant it. But this is about trust. You've never really got past the idea that I might somehow be another cheating wanker like Andrew,' he spat the words out.

'Now you are just being mean.' Tears flowed down her face.

Without hearing her words, volcanic rage erupted out of him and he bellowed. 'I have never cheated on you and I never would. You were everything to me, okay. EVERYTHING!' He punched the wall, a sharp pain shooting through his fist.

'And you are everything to me, Monty,' she sobbed. 'Why won't you let me help you?'

His shoulders slumped. He stared at the only woman he'd ever truly loved, filled with self-loathing, yet unable to explain how her kindness felt like a noose. 'I don't know.'

Wiping her eyes she stared at him for a few moments before whispering, 'I love you.' Turning on her heels she walked heavily down the hall and he watched as the panelled door clicked behind her.

'I love you too,' he croaked. For the next thirty minutes he sat in the lounge, head in his hands, fingernails tearing through his scalp, crying like the lost child he was.

CHAPTER 27

27 March 2005

Commuters in expensive suits spilled out of the broad glass-canopied entrance to Canary Wharf Tube station like pinstriped pennies from a one-arm bandit.

Monty wore shades to moderate the spring sunshine. Four hours of sleep had left him with a dull headache. Whisky, Winstons, and wanking until the early hours made up his near-daily routine. What was left of his spare time he spent at a mixed martial arts gym, taking his anger out on punchbags and increasingly reluctant sparring partners. The shaved face was a sticking plaster, maintaining a veneer of normality. But he barely had the juice to go through another day at the bank.

His life was buried in an open-ended forensic pending tray; a bureaucratic netherworld between mortality and whatever fate had in store for his dad. And the real kicker was that Hatty was now his '*friend*'.

His *friend*! He'd almost prefer it if she had shut him out of her life. Then he could have remained in his miserable sorrow hollow, alone though free from suffocating pity. Or at least, tried to. Instead, she'd been so desperately, heartbreakingly Hatty. Kind Hatty. Perfect, efficient Hatty. He'd phoned her in tears to say sorry, she'd apologised, although he didn't for the life of him know why.

Now, *his* Hatty was in the middle of his life once more for meals and chats on the phone whenever he felt more crap than normal. She'd helped him set up a fundraiser for Thailand, always amazing and supportive. His guardian angel. Girlfriend in name only, if that. Like a mirage, she seemed within reach, but he didn't have the strength to lay his vulnerability at her feet.

Red and green numbers tumbled down his screen like a waterfall. He bought and sold, sold and bought, making more money for the already rich. It was vacuous, though he did okay. Not riding the wave, but decent enough.

Animated voices distracted him from across the trading room.

'The Trentmeister General is back, wahay.'

In a thousand-pound suit, Trent Morgan towered over men in shirtsleeves.

Monty blocked out the banter, but the clamour grew as the American processed towards him.

'Have you seen Hatty since you've been back, Quentin Trentino?' a voiced asked.

'Nah man. She keeps blowing me off. And not in a good way.'

Raucous laughter erupted.

He stared blankly at his screen.

'Hey, Monty. You don't mind, do ya?' Trent was close now.

'Sorry, what?'

'Word on the street is that you and Hatty aren't dating no more. Mind if I dive into the pink pool and swim around some?'

A molten gout of fury bubbled up inside. Standing and turning square to the American he said, 'You know what, Trent?'

'What's up?'

'I hate swimming.' Jaw clenching, energy surging through the muscles of his shoulders and neck, Monty smashed his forehead against Trent's nose.

The American staggered back, blood spilling down his chin and over his suit. He clutched his face. 'Jeez, man.'

Monty grabbed Trent's shoulders and kneed him hard in the crotch.

Howling like an angry bear, Trent doubled over.

Traders stood up from their cubicles and stared.

Tapping a pen against his fingertips, Vice President Bob's attention focused squarely on Monty, his voice steely. 'That was quite the show you put on there, lad.'

He had it coming. 'Sorry. Is he going to press charges?'

'He's got every right to. You broke his damn nose. But I've told him to move on. Eyewitnesses have said he was winding you up. Forget about it.'

Monty fidgeted in the seat. 'You've done me a favour there, Bob. Thank you.'

The hard-boiled Scottish banker stared back. 'I don't know what you are doing here, Monty. You're my best trader, but you're barely keeping up with the new kids.'

Hairs rose on his neck. 'Are you letting me go? I've been through a tough time, you know that.'

'I do know that. And if I were any other VP in this business, you'd be out on your arse right now. Unlike them, I happen to give a shit about what happened to you.'

He stared at his expensive shoes. 'So, what are you saying? Pick up my game? I'm struggling to get through each day as it is.'

'I did my time in Iraq in nineteen ninety-one with the Royal Scots Dragoons. I saw death there, a whole lot of it. Maybe not like you just saw in Thailand, but bad enough for a lifetime. Whether you're in a suit or in sandy desert drill, it doesn't matter. A couple of the men from my company survived Iraq but didn't survive what came next.'

The words hit Monty like high-velocity rounds to the chest. He rapped his hard leather heels repetitively against the legs of the chair.

Bob stared at him, unblinking. 'You remind me of one of them.'

Cornered, Monty spluttered, 'I'm lost, Bob.'

'You're not lost, laddy, you're depressed. Seriously. Lots of people want to help you, not least Hatty.'

'I just seem to push her away.' His jaw trembled.

The middle-aged banker glanced at the framed photo of his wife. 'And yet, she's not run away from you at a hundred miles an hour like some people would.'

'I'm just a massive burden.'

He sighed. 'Stop assuming the limits of that young lady's kindness, before it's too late.'

'Open to advice on how,' Monty whispered.

'Just take some time off. See your doctor. Do something different for a while. Sort your dad's estate out – I know that's been tough. I'll keep you on salary for a wee while.'

'But I don't know what to do.'

'Do something that makes you feel good about yourself and gives you a positive outlet. Hatty's helped you raise money for good causes, so go and find one. Get a kaftan, join some Save the Whale campaign, and buy vegan shoes, if you want.'

Tears welled. 'I owe you big time.'

'You don't owe me anything. Just focus on yourself and embrace those trying to help you.' The Scot stood and hugged Monty awkwardly, clapping him on the shoulder. 'Now bugger off and I'll see your ugly face when you're back. Just keep yourself out of trouble and be sure to stay close with that lass of yours, Hatty.'

Birmingham, England

Monty killed the ignition and stepped out. The university campus teemed with students bouncing between its sundry red-brick buildings.

'Monty,' Serwah squealed.

He turned and she ran at him, hair in big bunches, in matching jacket and shorts with thick tights.

She flung her arms around his neck. 'Oh, God, it's so good to see you again.'

He laughed, for the first time in forever. 'It's good to see you too, kiddo. How have you been?'

She pulled away and pointed at the sleek car at the kerbside. 'Wait, before I answer that, can you explain why you've come for lunch in a new Mercedes?'

'Ugh, thought if I drove it would ensure I didn't drink at lunchtime.'

'The question was more Mercedes than method of travel?'

'The devil pays well.' He frowned. 'Anyway, I'm selling it. Not going to need it where I'm going.'

'There are probably better things to do with your money anyway. Like tackling world poverty, disease and racism, for starters.' She flashed him a pearly smile and took his hand. 'Come on, let's get lunch.'

A stone's throw from the university, they entered a world of Mughal décor suffused with the inviting aroma of Indian spices, evoking thoughts of a grand durbah in Delhi.

'If you come to Birmingham, you've got to have a Balti.' Serwah ripped off a piece of buttery naan, dipping it in a steaming ochre pool of deliciousness.

'Oh, my, this tastes so good.' Monty tucked in with gusto and for a brief while set his cares aside.

'So, you left your job at the bank?' she asked.

'Yeah. Sort of. I've been put on paid leave of absence I've been suffering with—' he coughed '—you know.'

'Depression? It's okay to admit it.'

He continued, 'Being in the UK isn't working for me. I thought I'd go back and spend some time in Thailand. Hatty was a gem in helping me raise money for charity. Not sure what yet but I've got relatives, well, kind of close family friends, in Thailand who can help me figure something out . . .'

'But how does Hatty feel about that?' She studied him.

'She's not happy, though I'm not sure what I can do. I haven't been the easiest person since all this happened.' He waved his hand as if to illustrate the 'this'. 'We've drifted apart. I mean, she has been completely amazing. But still, it's been hard on her.'

'I bet she's desperate to understand how she can help you.'

'She is, although I've not been great at talking about stuff, causing all sorts of misunderstanding.'

'Like what, for example?'

'Like she suspects I was having some sort of *thing* with you in Thailand.'

'No way?' Serwah squealed. 'Did you explain to her about me, though?'

'Not really. I just told her we were just friends and there was nothing between us.'

'Like *that's* going to help.' She snorted. 'You men are so rubbish at stuff like this. Shall I give her a call? Tell her that we helped each other out, are like family, and that I don't fancy you anyway?'

He buried his head in his hands. 'That sounds completely horrendous. Anyway, we're still in touch, so . . . '

'It's just so sad.' Serwah dabbed her face with a napkin. 'Hatty's your penguin.'

'What's that supposed to mean?'

'Penguins find a mate and stay with them forever.'

He grimaced. 'Yeah. Well, right now I'm the only person flopping around on their belly trying to propel myself forwards.'

'That's a bit unfair though. I bet she's had a terrible time this past few months. Okay, she didn't go through what you did, but that doesn't mean she's not hurting. Just try to open up and talk to her. Not talking seldom helps.'

He was sweating and his back itched. 'Anyway, have you spoken to Bert lately?'

'Changing the subject!' A beaming smile lit her face. 'I speak to Bert several times a week.'

'I see.' Monty exaggerated his voice. 'And is he still planning on studying at Oxford?'

'As a matter of fact, he is.'

'He's sweet on you, you know that, right?'

She looked at him sideways. 'Yeah, I know it.'

His eyes narrowed as his mind drifted back to the body site in Takua Pa. 'Did Bert ever locate his friends?'

'No, they're still unaccounted for.'

Poor sod. He grunted.

'Anyway, Bert is helping their parents organise a trip to Thailand at some point. They just want to go there, you know?'

'Yes, I understand.'

'How long do you think you'll stay in Thailand?'

'Not sure what my plans are but yes, we'll have to meet up if I'm still there. Be nice to see Bert again.' *I should email him. See how he's getting on.*

Silence fell and they focused on their food, comfortable with each other's silence. Eventually, he looked at Serwah, who had a remarkably cheerful visage despite everything she'd experienced. Rocking from side to side, and straightening both arms against the side of his body, he said, 'So, you and Bert, eh?'

'Is this some sort of dodgy penguin impression?'

He chuckled. 'Might be.'

'Oh, stop it.'

'Hey, I've had an idea. Could you help me choose a gift?'

Hatty insisted on driving him to Heathrow.

He'd tried to refuse, but she wouldn't take no for an answer.

At the security gate, she asked. 'Your flight gets in tomorrow afternoon, then?'

'Yeah, that's right.'

She looked down at her feet. 'You'll get in touch if you need anything, right?'

'Of course I will, Hats.' Her face was drawn, she had no make-up, and her auburn hair was in a tight ponytail, but she'd never looked more beautiful. Yet there she was, out of reach, and he was leaving.

Wringing her hands she said, 'You don't have to go away, you know? You could stay, and I'd try harder to help you.'

'I'm sorry. I'm only making a mess of everything here. Look, I got something for you.' He withdrew a rectangular parcel from his rucksack.

'What is it?'

'Open it.'

'Don't you need to get to your plane?'

'Please.'

Pushing a finger through a gap in the wrapping, she teased apart the paper and opened the box slowly, studying its contents in silence.

'It's a penguin.' The locket was rendered in gold and studded with small emeralds.

'I can see that.'

He shrugged and stared at the gift. 'Someone told me that penguins find their soulmates and stay with them their whole lives.'

'But you're flying to Thailand.' Her voice was flat.

'I just thought that if you ever wear it, it'll connect you to me, wherever I am.'

She put it in her handbag, wiped her face with her glove and smiled weakly. 'Go on then, or you'll miss your flight.'

'Come here and give me a hug.'

She reached around his waist and squeezed him tightly, not letting go. 'You'll come back again one day, won't you?'

He gently pulled her away, looked into her glistening green eyes, and kissed her forehead. 'I hope so.'

Passing the security barrier, he turned to wave, but his penguin was gone.

CHAPTER 28

April 2005

With a ding, the fasten seatbelt sign illuminated and Monty clicked the metal belt buckle together. Instinctively, he glanced to his right as if expecting to see Dad. Instead, Uncle Aek read a book, while Aunty Mai gazed out the window. As the aircraft banked, the emeraldine Andaman appeared below, dotted with glaucous green islands and boats like lozenges. Muddy smudges had replaced previously manicured fingernails of golden beach.

Another ding sounded when the plane came to a halt. With tourism having dried up, the aircraft was half-empty. He followed Aek and Mai into the terminal at Krabi airport, dressed in knee-length shorts and a t-shirt with a military-style rucksack over his shoulders. He'd packed for several days, though he had no clue how long he'd stay. One hour was still too long for concrete plans.

A woman in uniform approached, and *wai*'d respectfully to Mai.

'Someone from the local government come to help us today,' Aek explained, following his wife and her new companion towards the exit.

Monty dozed in the back of the minibus. He'd hit the booze on the flight out from London and, with the combined effect of the jet lag, was dog-tired. Occasionally, he'd open his eyes with a start, to stare out the window.

Leaving the bustle of the town, they drove through verdant palm groves and small villages, passing an occasional mosque or Buddhist temple. Dogs lounged in the shade of roadside stalls laden with tropical fruit, colourful fabrics and clothing. After half an hour, they pulled off the road by a café, with Johnnie Walker and Coca-Cola signs, and gaudy plastic furniture.

Mai turned to him. 'So we are going to a fishing village. Their infant school was destroyed, and we want to help them build a new one.'

Monty nodded. The money Hatty had helped him raise would go towards the cost of the build. *Hatty.* He wondered whether or when he might see her beautiful face again.

'As *Pe* Daisy and *Pe* Alan were teachers, we thought the project would be a nice way to honour them.'

His attention snapped back into place. *I never stop thinking of them.* 'They would be really happy about that, Aunty Mai.'

The narrow strip of road turned to dirt, and they bumped and bounced over every rut.

Soon, they crested a hill, tin rooves sloping down to a sparkling Andaman that stretched to the far horizon.

The minibus drew to a halt by another vehicle.

Aek popped the boot to retrieved carrier bags filled with fresh fruit.

'Can I help you carry those?' Monty reached out a hand.

'Thank you. You're younger and stronger than me.' Aek smiled.

A pleasant breeze took the edge off the blistering heat as they followed a narrow track down the hill, hemmed by stilted houses with an occasional vendor selling supplies and food. Older men and women sat in shaded verandas watching the world. Children ran here and there, in tatty shorts or sarongs, and a miscellany of t-shirts.

A group of boys kicked around a wicker ball, laughing and shouting. Reaching into his bag, Monty pulled out the camera Hatty had given him and took a few snaps.

One of the more confident kids came over and stared wide-eyed at the hi-definition coloured image. So, Monty took another photo which elicited giggles, and soon other boys joined in the fun.

When he looked up, Aek and Mai had gone, so he continued alone towards the sea, his heartrate quickening. Approaching the beach, a dystopian scene of chaos and destruction unfolded. Buildings were washed away, leaving messy spaces littered with debris and splintered stilts. Men and women of all ages bent to the task of re-building.

Towards the sea, wooded inlets to mangroves, where previously prawns and crab were the prized catch, were clogged with silt.

He walked to the pile of broken fishing boats among a detritus of baskets and tangled nets. The hulls had been stripped of the car engines with long propellor shafts. Back towards the village, a tide mark drew a dirty line between destructions and normality.

Leaning against an upturned vessel, he lit a cigarette with shaking hands then held the open pack towards a nearby fisherman, with leathery-skin and grubby cut-off jeans.

The man took a cigarette and lit it, sweeping his arm across the expanse of beach and talking in quick-fire Thai, between drags.

Monty discerned the words '*very bad*' and '*boats damaged*' but little else. After a while he found himself alone with the gentle and troubling sound of the sea, so he walked back towards the village.

A small girl watched his approach from the rough wooden step of a stilted house, big-eyed and solemn. She wasn't playing with the other kids.

Dressed in a clean sarong and a faded yellow t-shirt, he figured she must be five or six.

He knelt at a small distance, took a bottle of water from his rucksack, and held it out.

She shook her head and folded her arms.

He took a drink, then fished into his rucksack again, pulled out a banana, inspected it carefully, and glanced at the girl. 'Banana.' He smiled.

She started at him, then with eyes like dark-brown almonds, returned her gaze to the banana.

He frowned. '*Phuut Thai mai dai khrap.*' I can't speak Thai.

'*Gluay kha.*' Her voice quavered, then she looked at him, puzzled.

'*Glooday,*' he replied in an exaggerated voice.

She giggled before growing serious. '*Mai, kha.*' No. '*Gluay*!'

He peeled the banana and held it out.

She studied him nervously, before taking it in her tiny hand and munching on it.

An excited squeal burst his reverie, and he looked up the hill at a young boy chasing a ball.

The girl with the banana returned his smile when he waved goodbye, dimples punctuating her blushing cheeks.

Wandering past the boy, his attention snagged on a woman swabbing the arm of another on the veranda of a house.

Dressed in leggings and a flower print t-shirt, her hair in a ponytail, there was something familiar about her, but he couldn't figure out what.

Her head tilted, before she turned to stare at him.

It was definitely her. '*Khun* Fah?' he asked uncertainly, with a *wai*.

'*Kha*,' she replied, taking a step closer, her eyebrows puzzling at the strange *farang*. '*Khun* Monty?'

'Yes.' He didn't know what to say.

'I don't understand.'

'Oh—' he paused and gestured up the hill '—I came here with my friends, Thai friends.'

'The people from Bangkok?'

He nodded.

'Excuse me a moment.' She turned to her patient and finished dressing her arm, talking softly in Thai.

Once finished, she walked down the steps.

'*Khun mae!*' Mum! The boy playing ball ran to her, flinging his arms around her legs, before studying the strange *farang*.

Fah stroked the boy's back. '*Khun* Monty, this is my son Moo.'

Having only met in the hospital, it had never occurred to him to think about her having a normal, family life. Dropping to his haunches, he smiled at her son. 'Are you Moo the cow?'

'Pig!' he replied in English with a toothy grin.

'Moooo.' Monty made a cow noise.

The boy burst into giggles. 'Oink, oink!'

'What made you come back to Thailand?' Fah enquired.

'I'm searching for my dad.'

She frowned.

'My friends suggested we come here to help, as I believe the school was destroyed.'

'Yes.'

'Anyway, it's nice to see you.'

'Thank you. I volunteer here some days, give medical help to people. It's my honour.'

Aek reappeared, and *wai*'d Fah, before looking at Monty. 'Meeting new people already?'

'Not new people. Fah saved my life when I was in hospital.'

'Oh?' He looked at the nurse and spoke respectfully in Thai, occasionally glancing at Monty.

It seemed to put her at more ease.

'*Pe* Somchai, the village elder, has invited you to eat with him. *Khun* Fah, please join us,' Aek offered.

She demurred, pointing towards Moo.

Removing his shoes, Monty climbed the short steps into the building which was larger, befitting a village chief, with three rooms. The wooden floor was clean, and rugs had been laid in the centre of the wide veranda. Two women bustled around woks on a hot primus stove. A wiry man with wrinkled skin and a sarong waved for him to sit, so he took a place beside Aunty Mai.

Steaming dishes of vegetables and seafood curries were placed on the rugs with a large bowl of rice, plastic plates, cutlery, and cups of water.

Monty felt guilty, realising this was more food than many villagers would see in a day. '*Khob Khun mak khrap*, *Pe* Somchai.' Thank you very much, *Pe Somchai*.

Somchai's unblinking gaze never left him, except when he spoke, in which case he directed his remarks via Mai, as the translator.

'*Pe* Somchai explained that thirty people were killed. It could have been more but many were out at sea and some ran up the hill.'

Monty nodded. 'Please tell *Pe* Somchai how impressed I was by his village. Everyone is working so hard to rebuild it.'

The village head nodded approvingly, before replying.

Mai interpreted, '*Pe* Somchai asked why you came back to Thailand?'

He sighed heavily. 'I wanted to do something good as so many Thai people helped me.'

'*Pe* Somchai says you are welcome to visit Ban Puu anytime.'

An idea flashed in Monty's mind. 'I'd like that. Could I perhaps stay in the village for a while. I wouldn't ask for anything or cause problems.'

Aek turned to Monty and asked. 'What will you do if you stay here, Monty?'

His shoulders slumped. 'I don't know. It just seems a quiet, peaceful place. Maybe I just want to be somewhere different and—' reaching for Thai, he picked on the name of the Thai king's palace two hours from Bangkok '*glai gangwon*': far away from troubles.

'You know Thai too well, *Nong* Monty.' His uncle chuckled. 'But there is no palace life here. They don't have electricity, and no one speaks English.'

'I can improve my Thai,' he replied, flatly.

'*Pe* Aek,' Mai intoned softly, 'maybe it will be nice for Monty to see what's happening with the school.'

Somchai studied the *farang* impassively before saying, 'We have no spare houses or food.'

'I can live in the hotel to start with and come to help in the village if *Pe* Somchai thinks it would be useful?' he replied, plaintively.

The old man nodded as Mai conveyed the words.

Fah loaded bags into the boot of her car as Monty returned up the hill following the meal.

After an exchange of *wai*'s, Mai settled into friendly conversation with her. 'Please help *Khun* Monty if you can, as we are returning to Bangkok. He is a dear friend to us.'

Fah studied him sceptically, before asking, 'do you like Thai food?'

Aek and Mai dropped him at a hotel in the centre of Krabi on their way to the airport. Having showered, he lay on the soft bed, calmer than he'd felt in some time, and slept for a couple of hours.

When he woke, he grabbed his phone, and connected a long-distance call.

'Hello, Monty, is that you?'

'Hello, Hats. Yes. Just wanted to let you know I'm in Krabi now.'

'Oh, I'm glad to hear that. Where are you staying?' Her voice was even, betraying no hint of emotion.

'In a hotel tonight, then I plan to spend a few days in a village, down the coast.'

There was a pause. 'What are you planning to do there?'

'My family friends are supporting the rebuilding of a school there and I'll use the money we raised to support that . . . '

'Did the money reach Thailand yet?'

At twenty thousand pounds, it was a hefty sum, and Hatty was being typically rigorous. But he scratched his fingers through his scalp, suddenly anxious about the transactional direction of the conversation.

'Yes, Aunty Mai confirmed that the monies have been safely deposited in Bangkok.'

She breathed heavily and silence filled the five-thousand-mile space between them. 'Will you call me every week, so I know you are okay?'

'Yes, of course.'

'And try to go easy on the drinking?'

He closed his eyes and rubbed his temple. 'I'll try.'

CHAPTER 29

April 2005

An aroma of roasted pork and dried fish imbued the humid air. Tables and food carts were laid out around a central square of the night market. Hawkers called out to prospective customers, mostly Thais.

Monty spotted Fah in a pink summer dress, with another lady in green. He knew instinctively that she would not meet a *farang* man on her own, to avoid giving the wrong impression. And that inviting him to dinner was only out of respect to Aek and Mai, to avoid losing face by inhospitality. The friend peeled off to browse the market.

'Hello, nice to see you!' He pressed his hands together in a *wai*.

Fah responded in kind. 'Hello, *Khun* Monty. How are you, *kha*?'

'I'm okay, thanks. I almost didn't recognise you.' Everything about her was neatly put together, including the bobby pins that held every loose hair at bay and her understated make-up. Her features were delicate, her eyes like almonds.

She smiled. 'Is this compliment?'

'Ha, yes, I suppose.' He lowered his eyes. 'How are you?'

'I am fine. You like Thai food, right?'

'Love it.'

She led him to a food stall where enormous woks billowed clouds of steam, pushing away his hand when he tried to pay for their order.

Occupying an empty table, Fah poured them water from a jug and handed him a Chinese spoon and fork.

He tucked into bright-green beans with a shrimp sauce that made his eyes water. 'Wow, that's spicy.'

'It is called *sataw*. Do you like it?'

'I've never tasted anything like it. It's bitter but kind of addictive.'

'It's very popular here.' They set about their food in silence, before she continued. 'So, *Khun* Monty, what made you come back to Thailand?'

He sat back and considered how best to respond. 'I didn't feel happy staying in London, knowing my dad might be here somewhere.'

'Do you have other family in England now?'

He paused, unsure how Hatty would want him to refer to her, after everything that happened. 'No immediate family. A girlfriend. Well, Harriet is her full name – Hatty for short.'

Fah's face brightened. 'Hatty is a beautiful name. Have you been together long?'

'We've been close for almost three years.'

'But you didn't get married yet?'

'It's a long story. But maybe one day.' He laughed nervously. 'I mean, I hope so, but you never know.'

'Don't you love her?'

'I love her more than anyone else in the world.'

Fah wrinkled her brow and spooned some soup out of her bowl, whereupon they fell into silence again and finished the various local specialties.

'Do you want something sweet? I be right back, okay?' Without awaiting a response, she rose and wandered off. After a few minutes, she returned with Styrofoam bowls of a dark jelly and shards of ice in coconut milk.

'Thanks.' Monty gingerly picked through the ice-cold dessert.

'How long do you think you will stay here, *kha*?'

He scratched his fingertips through his hair. 'I honestly don't know, at this stage.'

'So, you think your dad might still be alive?'

He breathed heavily. 'I think he is probably dead. But I don't want to give up hope.'

'I see. So, you are searching for him, right?'

'Well, not exactly. The police are doing that.'

'Thai culture is not the same as *farang* culture.'

'What do you mean?'

'It is difficult to explain in English.'

His shoulders slumped. 'I should learn to speak better Thai.'

Her eyes narrowed, like she was grappling with everything he'd said. 'Don't stay for too long searching for something you may never find.'

'Oh, it's a bit more complicated than that.'

'Life is complicated.' She shook her head.

'I'm sorry, I feel like I've offended you in some way.'

'No, you did not. I am pleased you returned to Thailand. Anyway, it is late and I must work tomorrow.' She rose and proceeded out of the food market, Monty following.

Hawkers, shoppers and motorbike taxi-drivers hustled around the busy entrance. Fah paused and turned to him, the faintest hint of sadness in her expression.

'A woman at the village told me you were being kind to the child, *Nong* Oi, right?'

'Oh, yes.' His heart warmed at the recollection of the little girl. '*Nong* Oi.'

'Her mummy and daddy were both killed by the wave. And yet she is a good, kind girl every day. Rather than searching, *Khun* Monty, just try to do good things every day, then maybe happiness will come back to you.'

Fah brought her hands to her chin, turned on her heels and walked away. Her colleague reappeared. They hopped in a taxi and were gone.

Monty watched them drive off, hot tears burning his face.

Part III

LIVING

Hatty and Monty

CHAPTER 30

Hatty
June 2005

'Excuse me, Hatty, you have a visitor downstairs in reception.' Barry angled his beaming, rotund face and shoulders through the open door to her office.

Smiling, she looked up at her personal assistant. 'And I thought I had an afternoon free of meetings, for a change?'

'I thought that too, Hatty, but apparently this is something personal. I offered to go down, but they insisted on seeing you. Something about Thailand and your friend Monty.'

Fiddling with her fingernails, she glanced at the family photographs on her wall. Among them, in a glass frame, Monty wrapped his arm around her bare shoulders dressed as Fred Flintstone. She shook her head. *Perhaps the deepest love cannot withstand life's sharpest blows?*

'I really think this is an important one, Hatty,' his voice softened.

While she still hadn't got used to having a personal assistant, she'd hit the jackpot with Barry. She knew he was fiercely protective of her feelings and would have thought carefully about this. Groaning, she got up from her desk. 'Ugh. If you insist.'

'I'll come down for emotional support if you want, but I think you're good.'

As the lift whished swiftly down, she stared at the poster advertising a different bank's US investment portfolio in subprime mortgages. *Surely someone must see that ill-considered house of cards will come crashing down one day?* A bright ding announced her arrival on the ground floor.

Sunbeams slanted through towering glass walls at reception which was quiet save for a lone visitor sat upright on a sofa. Strikingly pretty with high cheekbones, her skin a rich ebony, her black hair in thick spirals that tumbled onto her shoulders. She wore a simple white blouse and calf-length jeans with flat sandals.

The woman looked up, her face splitting into a smile. 'Hatty?'

Hatty barely had time to nod before she found herself wrapped up in a hug by a stranger. Yet she knew instinctively who this was. The person who had set her nerves jangling after her broken boyfriend returned from Thailand. Gently extracting herself, she asked, 'And I think you must be Serwah?'

'Yes, that would be me. You're so beautiful, just as Monty described you.'

Despite her reserve, she couldn't help but be flattered. 'Gosh, that's incredibly kind of you to say, thank you. Do you fancy a coffee or tea? The café here's nice.'

They followed the rich aroma of robusta beans and buttery pastries to a pastiche of Rome, with jaunty Italian music, Carrera marble and red-and-white-check table cloths.

'This place looks cute,' Serwah enthused.

Hatty pointed at the glass display cabinet and its piles of biscotti and pastries. 'You should try a *fiocco de neve*. They're honestly to die for.'

With their lattes and snow dusted choux pastries they sat at a secluded table.

Reaching across, Serwah took Hatty's hands, and looked at her with kind, intelligent eyes. 'I'm sorry, I've wanted to visit you for ages but was caught up with my studies until recently. I'm so pleased to meet you finally, after everything that happened,' she shrugged, 'you know, on Boxing Day. Monty's like the big brother that I never had.'

'I'm pleased to see you looking so well after that ordeal.' With a wrinkle of her nose, she asked, 'I think Monty may have said you were a dentist?'

'I am now. Just finished my finals last week.' She wiped her wrist across her forehead in an exaggerated manner, and chuckled. 'Have only just recovered from the stress. My boyfriend is taking me for a tour of Germany for four weeks from Saturday.'

She has a boyfriend. 'Did you meet your boyfriend at university?'

'No, in Thailand, you know, after . . . ' Serwah studied her carefully. 'I'm guessing Monty didn't tell you much about it, did he?'

Hatty stared at her untouched *fiocco* and clenched her jaw, before she whispered, 'Honestly, not that much.'

She sighed. 'I worried that he might not have.'

For the next twenty minutes, Serwah told Hatty everything. Her traumatic first meeting with Monty. How he had rescued her from the bar. His ill-advised return to Thailand.

Hatty took the final sip of her latte, before placing the cup back into its saucer with a porcelain clink. 'I just wish he'd told me all of this, you know? Everything he's done since then makes a bit more sense. But at the time he just closed himself completely and—' her voice trembled '—it wasn't like it happened suddenly. I watched him turn away in slow motion, my heart screaming out, but unable to prevent it.'

'None of this is your fault, Hatty.'

'But there must be something I could have done to make him feel better at the time?'

'The thing is, I don't think you can make anyone feel better after such a devastating ordeal. Just being there, being supportive and loving can help the person know they are not alone. And you did that. Monty told me you were totally amazing.' She paused to take another sip of latte as if composing her thoughts. 'Even though you could only see Monty's brokenness at the time, your kindness saved things from getting worse for him.'

'I loved him and helped him as much as I could and yet he still left.'

'I know. But you need to keep reminding yourself that you couldn't have done any more, and that what you did, you did through love.' Distractedly, Serwah touched a silver cross on a necklace at her throat. 'One of the first things Monty told me was that you were the love of his life.'

'He told you that?' Now Hatty touched the delicate penguin that she wore around her neck each day.

'He did. And I was with Monty when he bought you that pendant, you know?'

'You were? He told me that penguins find their perfect mate and stay together forever. Yet he didn't stay.'

'He didn't leave because he stopped loving you. He left because he was unwell and didn't know how to cope.'

Hatty reached across, took both Serwah's hands in hers, held her gaze and said, 'Thank you for everything you did to help my, well . . . '

'Your boyfriend.' Serwah finished the sentence for her.

Tears welled in her eyes again. 'How can that be so when he's there and I'm here?'

'I know you've suffered so much during this time as well. But I really believe your love for each other is strong enough to survive this.'

'Strong enough to last for how long though? One year? Five years?'

'Don't think about the timeframe, just believe and never lose hope.'

'But I *can't* put my life on hold forever. What if I meet someone else?'

'Then let your heart tell you what feels right.'

She sniffed. 'Gosh, do you want another coffee? Think I need one.'

Serwah stood. 'I'll get them as you got the first round. Actually, fancy sharing another of those *fioccos* with me?'

'Would love to.' Hatty picked at her fingernails again and decided she was overdue a manicure. She'd never stopped loving Monty. But she felt like a failure whenever she remembered wanting so badly to help him but watching him drift away. Maybe she could write to him more often and talk about every-day stuff, not just practical things. There might be things he wanted her to send him from London that he couldn't get there. She had no idea what his life was like now.

CHAPTER 31

Monty
July 2005

Laughing and cracking jokes, fishermen unloaded the day's catch from gaudily painted boats. Waves washed white spume around their ankles before retreating down the beach. An ozone aroma of fish filled the air.

Monty sat on dry sand, hands clasped around his knees. The beauteous sea retained a magnetic and terrifying allure.

'Tell me the story again,' Oi pleaded in Thai.

He turned and smiled at the orphan girl in the new sarong and flowery t-shirt he'd bought her. Her glossy black hair was cut into a blunt bob, a big white clip keeping the fringe from her round face. He broke the top off a black fruit and passed it to her. 'First, you have to tell me the name of this in English.'

'*Mangosteen*,' she said, before picking out a white segment and munching on it.

'Very good. *Mangosteen*.' He ruffled her hair.

Wide eyed, he lowered his voice to a whisper. 'In the land where I'm from, many oceans from here, I have a guardian angel. Do you know her name?'

'*Thep* Hatty. Is she beautiful?'

'Yes! In my whole life I have never, ever seen an angel quite so beautiful as *Thep* Hatty. Her hair is like the perfect sunset, softer than the silken robes of gods, fragrant like the rarest orchids.'

'I didn't know there were *farang* gods too.' She wrinkled her eyebrows, before popping another mangosteen segment into her mouth.

'We have one God but lots of angels. But none of the angels are as magical as *Thep* Hatty. When I'm scared or sad, she enters my dreams to protect me from unkind spirits.'

'And her eyes?'

'Her eyes are green, like the purest coral sea.'

'And the dance, tell me about the dance!' She clapped her hands and her voice rose two octaves.

'You'll find her among magical dancers in brilliant white costumes, who spin gracefully on tiptoes like bamboo in the wind.'

Oi stood, pinched her thumbs and forefingers, and straightened her skinny arms out to one side, before, bending at the knees and twirling her hands in circles. Angling her neck, her almond eyes followed the graceful movement of her hands with studied concentration as she swept her arms across her body in the style of classical Thai dance.

Monty's chest swelled and he clicked off some photographs. When she finished he clapped, '*oh-ho, geng sut yord na khrap* – oh that was really amazing.'

'Am I a good enough dancer for *Thep* Hatty?' she asked nervously.

'You are the very best and cutest dancer I ever saw.' He knelt in front of her. 'But do you know what?'

'What?' Her face puzzled.

'You are also *jakateee*!' He grabbed her gently and tickled her ribs with his fingertips, as she squirmed and squealed.

She was soon breathless and her cheeks pink from the fun of it. They rose and padded, barefoot, across the beach, Monty carrying their sandals. Admiring the new stilted houses, he took in the green sweep of the hillside, which day by day looked less like a disaster zone.

Oi took his hand. 'You must miss *Thep* Hatty a lot?'

He thought of Hatty's hand in his and sighed heavily. 'I miss her every day and every night. But, she is always in my heart. And if I was not here I would miss you too much.'

'I'd miss you too, *kha*,' she replied, glancing up at him.

Women hurried back and forth, carrying baskets overflowing with fish. Some smiled or called out, and he returned their greeting. It was humid, with the wet season imminent.

Height aside, Monty resembled the fishermen, in knee-length baggy trousers, loose long sleeves, and sandals. His face was chestnut brown though he kept his hair short, with the help of a woman in the village.

'Oh, ho, look at the handsome man coming to see *Pe* Tik,' a portly woman in bright sarong and t-shirt called from the veranda of a pink stilted house near the beach. Oi climbed the steps to join her.

'Hello, *Pe* Tik. You look extremely beautiful today.' Monty grinned and bowed his head to his fingertips.

'Sweet mouth!' Bursting into lusty peals of laughter, she bent to stroke Oi's cheeks and sniff her hair. Leaning over the veranda to display her bosom, she called down. 'Did you want some rice soup? I made your favourite.'

'No, I don't want to inconvenience you, *Pe* Tik.' He went through the routine of putting up a fight to avoid appearing to take advantage of the hospitality offered.

She frowned and waved her hand at him. 'Come in, come in. You're getting skinny and you'll never get a wife looking like that *na*.'

Leaving the sandals on the step, he sat cross-legged on the veranda.

In football kit with a wicker ball under his arm, Tik's fifteen-year-old son Ton offered Monty a deep *wai* before slapping his hand in a low-five.

'Don't be too long, you have schoolwork to do,' Tik called after him. 'Oi, sit down, child, you need to eat something to fatten you up.'

Oi sat cross-legged beside Monty as Tik plonked bowls of steaming, aromatic rice soup on the mat. A freshly cracked egg floated on the surface, and assorted condiments and dried fish were set down.

Monty spooned a little vinegar, fish sauce, sugar, chilli and peanuts into Oi's dish, her favourite combination. She slurped at the hot porridge noisily and he smiled, remembering how he ate Ready Brek as a child.

Content after a delicious breakfast, he gathered up their bowls and rinsed them out. 'Shall we do some work now, *Nong* Oi, before the others come?'

'*Kha*,' she replied, before disappearing into the sleeping room and returning with a maths exercise book and pencil.

She settled herself on the floor and they looked through her work. Her maths was excellent for a six-year-old and he pointed out just one small error, explaining the solution patiently.

Before long, five boys and three girls appeared at the top step, *wai*-ing before Monty summoned them to join in.

From teaching *Nong* Oi, he had quickly caught the attention of Somchai, the headman, and because of that now ran a maths and English class most mornings.

Monty hadn't intended to stay in the village for long, after his first visit with Aek and Mai. But helping Oi had given him a purpose and something to focus on.

Losing both her parents at the age of six put Monty's own experience into some perspective. Quiet and solemn for much of the time, her sweet smile often broke through when they were together. And she increasingly played with the other kids.

There had been no further developments in his dad's case, so day-to-day life in a fishing village occupied most of his attention. Aside from the vast emotional cavern created by his separation from Hatty, he felt relatively settled, which was an improvement.

At the top of the village, Monty had paid some men to help him build a house. The simple village diet and hard physical labour had melted away the sluggishness and fat, not to mention sharpening his Thai skills.

The house was identical to others in the village, painted a ruddy brown and with a large veranda. A satellite dish crouched on the roof, through which he connected with the outside world.

Having returned from a trip into Krabi, he checked his emails, clicking on a message from Hatty. Their relationship had become transactional, and they spoke less on the phone these days, but their correspondence provided a thin emotional lifeline.

At the low rumble of a vehicle, he snapped his laptop shut and walked to the end of the veranda.

A white Landcruiser appeared through the trees and pulled up next to his pickup.

Somchai and some of elders formed a greeting party, so Monty pulled on his sandals and wandered down to join them.

A woman in flowing linen trousers and a white silk blouse stepped out, accompanied by two Thai women in United Nations polo shirts. Her shoulder-length hair was dark and glossy, and she wore expensive sunglasses.

She *wai*'d politely to Somchai and the elders while her Thai colleagues helped make the formal introductions. Her gaze then fell quizzically on Monty.

'Hi, my name is Monty. *Pe* Somchai thought it might be helpful for me to join as I speak English and some Thai.'

She extended her right hand. 'Hello, I'm Genevieve Rochat from UNICEF in Bangkok. These are my colleagues from the UN regional office in southern Thailand.'

The two Thais pressed their hands together and he returned the greeting.

Somchai led the group down towards the sea, turning right towards a site where building was in progress. Foundations were laid; the smaller wing of the L-shaped structure was already complete. To the side, kids kicked a wicker ball over a badminton net.

A circle of plastic chairs was laid out under the shade of a tree. Over syrupy sweet coffee, *Pe* Somchai explained the work that had been done in the village since the tsunami.

Genevieve and her colleagues then laid out what UNICEF could do to help with education for children up to age six.

'So, are you French?' Monty asked, as he spooned fried rice onto Genevieve's plate.

'No, I'm Swiss,' she replied with a smile, the warm sea breeze ruffling her hair. 'And you? I take it you are not Thai?'

Looking up from his plate, he studied her before gazing across the bay at the fishing boats bobbing on the water. 'I'm English. Before this year, I was working in banking. I figured I could be more useful helping people here, who have nothing.'

Genevieve considered him with eyes bluer than an Alpine sky. 'You were affected by the tsunami?'

'Yes. My dad and I were caught up in it. Sadly, Dad's still missing.'

She reached across and patted his forearm. 'I am very sorry to hear that. You know, there are a lot of people like you in Thailand now. Everyone helping, but also searching.'

'I'm not sure how much I'm helping, to be honest, but the people in Ban Puu have helped me a lot.'

She took a sip of water and pushed her empty plate to one side. 'The food here is amazing by the way.'

'I'm glad you like it.' The street-food vendor looked identical to the other stilted houses but had seating on the veranda, with the living room converted to a kitchen.

'So, now you are helping with this school and, my colleagues tell me, running a small class. Do you have experience working in education?'

'No, not really. I'm teaching a group of nine kids. I can't exactly say it was planned, though.' His mind drifted to helping his mum decorate her classroom like a Roman piazza and an idea for an activity sparked in his mind.

'But you spend a lot of time with one of the children, no, a little girl?' Her question carried the faintest air of interrogation.

'Yes, although, just to be clear she lives with a guardian in the village, *Pe* Tik. I saw many too many dead children after the tsunami. Then I met this little orphan girl here, and I'm kind of an orphan now; we just seemed to bond.'

She nodded. 'That's kind and I hope you understand my reason for asking about this.'

By late-afternoon, as the UN team was packing up, Genevieve sought out Monty again. 'Thank you for lunch. What you're doing here is worthwhile and I'm sure it is helping you to heal as well.'

'To be honest, it's the least I could do after all the help this village has given me.'

'I know, but still, I see so many volunteers like you. It's always difficult as Thai people don't want foreigners telling them what to do. Anyway, good luck with everything.'

'Thanks. *Pe* Somchai, the headman, seems to have his head screwed on and I'm just ready to help if they want me to.'

'Excellent. So, you will mostly see my colleagues after today, but I will pop in sometimes to see how you're getting on.' She held his gaze for a moment longer than formality would require and he caught the scent of her expensive perfume. 'As you can imagine, it's a busy time right now.'

'I really can. Have a good flight back to Bangkok.' He waved as the car disappeared back into the trees before returning to his veranda. His bedroom was stuffy from the midday heat, so he settled in his hammock to skim emails.

His phone buzzed and he picked up straight away. 'Monty speaking.'

'Ah, Monty, thanks for taking my call, it's Sandeep from Hampshire police.'

He scraped the fingers of his spare hand down the stubble on his cheek. 'Oh, hi Sandeep. Good to hear from you.'

Her normally upbeat voice carried an edge. 'I'm sorry this process is taking so long but I'm afraid I've got some difficult news.'

Every racing beat of his heart throbbed in his temples. 'Go on?'

'I'm sorry, Monty, but the body photograph you initially saw online in December has now been positively identified as a Finnish citizen. I just wanted to let you know.'

He'd pretty much given up on that line of inquiry, but it was now officially closed so the news came as a hammer blow.

Looking around for his cigarettes, he asked, 'What does this mean about Dad's case?'

'It means we continue to wait. The Identification Centre is identifying lots of victims each day. I know that won't be of comfort to you right now. Just don't lose hope, okay?'

Tears streamed down his cheeks. 'Okay.'

Darkness had fallen and in the preceding three hours he'd only stepped off his hammock to grab the bottle of Thai liquor from his room, and his remaining pack of cigarettes. Staring up, he struggled to focus on the wooden boards of his roof as they disappeared into the black of night. The bottle, still clutched in his hand, was half-empty and he took another sloshing gulp, which burned in the back of his mouth. Through the alcoholic fog, he counted his remaining three cigarettes and lit one, figuring that he needed at least two for breakfast. Annoyed by the sudden rationing of his addiction, he lay, sobbing quietly, until finally overcome by sleep.

CHAPTER 32

Hatty
July 2005

Barry looked up from his desk as Hatty entered, his large frame wrapped in a pink shirt with a cerise silk tie. 'So how was the women's networking event?'

'It was really nice, thanks. Got talking to a lovely VP from Scotia bank who gave me ideas and offered to mentor me. Oh, and they were handing out these fancy Filofaxes – thought you'd like one.' She reached into her bag and placed a purple leather organiser on the desk in front of him.

'Ooh, you do treat me so well, Hatty.' He grinned. 'So are you in a camomile or coffee mood, now you are back?'

'I think camomile would be just perfect, thank you.' She perched her handbag on the end of his desk and picked up the thin stack of papers in the 'Hatty' tray.

'I'll bring it right in. Oh—' his face straightened '—there's a gift in your office as well.'

At one end of her desk, an enormous bouquet of lilies that filled the room with a glorious scent. For a brief moment, her heart soared on the hope that Monty had organised them for her impending birthday. A small blue card was taped to the cellophane wrap, and she turned it in her fingers.

Hey babe. I'm just back in London and thought you might like these. Trent

'Oh.' Her heart sank.

Barry placed a bone China cup and saucer on her desk, a design he'd sweetly chosen just for her. 'There's your camomile.'

'Oh, you're the best.' She stroked his arm. 'Hey, did Trent mention my birthday by chance?'

'Of course he didn't. He's clueless and even I could find you a more suitable man than Trent Morgan.'

She grinned. 'Do you *have* any straight guy friends, Barry?'

'Precisely my point.' He pouted before stepping back into his office to pick up a call, replying in his brightest tone. 'Hello, this is Harriet Campbell's office, Barry speaking, how can I help you?'

Hatty glanced at the bouquet, before slumping into her chair and leafing through the thin stack of mail, between sips of tea. Several birthday cards in heavy parchment envelopes, which she set aside for the weekend. Then a big smile when she opened the latest event brochure for the Royal Opera House. Spinning round to take in the view from her window she admired the sun glimmering off the skyscrapers around Canary Wharf.

Having slipped the brochure and personal mail in her bag, she grabbed her jacket and headed out.

'Barry, I am going to leave exactly on time for once and so are you, as we have had a spectacularly successful spring and summer. I'll find a peaceful spot to enjoy my brochure and contemplate which ballet to see next.'

'Ooh, look at you. Well, I've got a blind date in Soho, otherwise I'd join you.'

At six o'clock, Hatty stepped off a jam-packed train at Westminster Tube station and studied the colourful posters for West End musicals as the escalator trundled up to street level. *I must get Martha down for a girls' night.*

Parliament Square was packed with tourists around Big Ben, but the crowds thinned as she skirted the Treasury building and walked into the verdant expanse of St James's Park. Whenever she visited, her mind flew to her first night at the ballet with Monty, when they had strolled the Mall late at night, so at ease with each other.

At the quieter end of the park, by Buckingham Palace, she found an empty bench with an expansive view over the pond which teemed with ducks, geese and the occasional pelican. Slipping the brochure from her bag, she spent a while lost in the new season schedule.

'Sorry to interrupt you, Miss.'

She looked up in response to the comforting sound of a Geordie accent. Stood at a polite distance, the owner of the voice was tall with a crew cut and a navy polo tucked neatly into khaki jeans, a thick belt circling his trim waist. He bore some sort of logo on his bicep with a desert camo rucksack slung over one muscular shoulder.

'What makes you think I'm a "Miss"?' she replied, airily.

'I didn't mean to cause offence.' He pointed at her hand. 'You don't have a ring on your finger.'

'I could be a "Ms"?' She lifted an eyebrow.

'Ah. Look, I'm sorry to have disturbed you,' he turned to leave.

'Haway man, I'm just joking with you.'

He turned back. 'You from the north-east?'

'I am, aye. Where you from?'

'Byker.'

'Bit rough that, mind.'

He didn't bite at her sarcasm, remaining at ease. 'It's not all that bad. How's about you?'

'Gateshead.'

'You can hardly talk then, eh?' Small crow's feet edged his unblinking brown eyes, which twinkled somewhat.

She smiled. 'I'm Hatty. And yes, it is "Miss".'

'Pleased to meet you.' He nodded. 'William, though people call me Billy.'

'I've got a dog called Billie.'

'Have you, now? Well, after Byker, at least that's a positive tick in the box for me then.'

She laughed. 'Anyway, Billy from Byker, did you want something?'

'Aye, I just wanted to ask where you got that brochure from?'

'For the Royal Opera House?'

He raised an eyebrow now. 'Did you have another brochure?'

She narrowed her eyes, unable to stop herself flirting. 'Billy from Byker who likes Ballet?'

'Strange though it sounds,' his eyes held hers, then he shrugged. 'Anyways, what's wrong with that? Nice to see stunning, elegant women and listen to gorgeous music once in a while, that's all.'

'Like to ogle the ladies, then, Billy?'

'I'm a man aren't I?' Completely unflappable, though his expression softened a touch. 'It's just where I worked, imagining the quiet serenity and beauty of a theatre gave me something to look forward to.'

He'd certainly got that right. The theatre had so often been her source of comfort, including now. 'Aye, well, I can agree with you there. Where have you been working then?'

'Iraq.'

Oh my God, he's in the military and I've been ragging him. 'I'm so sorry. How was that?'

'It had its moments,' he replied evenly.

'How long you been back?'

'Just flew in this morning. Changed into civvies and thought I'd have a look around London for a couple of days.'

'Oh, my goodness. Here, take it.' She held out the glossy brochure, shaking it, mortified to her core. 'You deserve it after what you've been through.'

'Nah, you keep it. But can I have a quick shufty, then I'll be on my way?'

'A quick shufty?' she asked, artfully.

He shook his head, with a light smile. 'You're a right joker you, aren't you, Miss?'

She grinned. 'Sorry. Look, soldier Billy, have you eaten anything since you landed in civvy street?'

He turned his wrist to stare at a chunky sports watch. 'Not yet.'

'Come on, I'm going to treat you to food. It's the least I can do for a fellow Geordie.'

They found a table at a Thai restaurant just off Trafalgar Square which Hatty had visited often, whenever missing Monty got too much.

Billy was content for her to order a selection of things, and the waiter soon brought tall glasses of beer.

He lifted his glass and chinked the rim against hers. 'Well, thanks for the invitation, Hatty. And here's to my first beer in six months!'

'Wow. How did a boy from Byker manage to stay off the bevvy for six months?'

He chuckled. 'It was alreet. None of the lads could drink anyways, so why should I be bothered?'

She figured he must be in his early thirties, so maybe a few years older than her, yet the experience of war hadn't aged him. He had handsome features with a strong nose, beneath thick eyebrows. A canny lad from Tyneside. In peak physical condition but battle fit – not gym fit – with barely an ounce of fat on him. 'What regiment are you in?'

'The Light Dragoons.' He pointed to the tattoo on his bicep. '"Death or Glory". How's about you? What does Hatty from Gateshead do in London?'

'Well, I certainly don't have an exciting motto like *that* in my job description. I'm in banking, in the City of London. Pretty boring really, graduate entry and been there ever since, making my way up the slippery ladder.'

He nodded appreciatively, pursing his attractive lips. 'Not boring at all. It's impressive. I bet your folks back home must be proud of you, mind.'

'Yeah, I guess. What rank are you in the Army, if I can ask?'

'I'm an RSM, sorry, a Regimental Sergeant Major.'

Hatty brushed her hair behind her ear and leaned forward. 'Wow, that's really senior. How long have you been in?'

'It's just a combination of hard work and Buggins' turn, really. Have done eighteen years now, four more until I hit my twenty-two and can retire.'

'You really don't look old enough to retire.'

Almost imperceptibly, his eyes clouded over for an instant before resuming their calm focus. 'Soldiering's a young person's business. Joined aged sixteen. Just a kid then, to be fair.'

Thirty four. So, seven years. Not a huge difference. She reached across and patted his forearm which was firm to the touch, and warm. 'Well, thank you for your service to our country. So, back for a few months, then off to fight again?'

'Nah, that's probably it for me when it comes to deployments. Done Iraq twice now, not to mention Bosnia, and am moving into an easy posting as an Instructor as RMAS. I might sooner to go back and fight with the lads, though.' He chuckled.

She raised her hands theatrically. 'RMAS?'

He grinned. 'Sorry, Royal Military Academy Sandhurst, where all the posh Ruperts train to be Britain's finest army officers.'

'Okay, so war hero and top instructor.'

'Not sure about the hero. Believe me, wars are won by teams, not individuals. But yeah, I suppose it's a good opportunity.'

The waitress brought their dishes which practically covered a table for four.

She smiled at him. 'I hope you're hungry!'

'I am, cheers, and thank you.' He lifted his beer glass, clinked hers again, and took another sip. Despite having been deprived booze for six months, he wasn't chugging it back. Everything was carefully controlled and disciplined, which was extremely alluring. 'How's about you? How long have you been in banking?'

'Gosh, it'll be six years at the weekend, so positively a baby compared to you. Started on my twenty first birthday, if you can believe that?' Despite his experience, he didn't need to talk about himself all the time and appeared genuinely interested in what she had to say.

He smiled. 'You've done really well for yourself. So, as it's almost your birthday, you'll not have to mind if I pay for this meal, I hope?'

'You really don't have to.'

'I know. But I've had nowt to spend my money on for six months, so it's no bother. So, have you big birthday plans for the weekend?'

She held his gaze, the air between them smouldering. 'Not especially.'

As she stepped into her riverside apartment block, Hatty's steps were light as a feather and unburdened. Gosh, what a surprise the evening had been. There was nothing cocky or showy about William, despite everything he must have been through. Quite different from the blokes at the bank.

It wasn't that she wanted anything romantically with anyone right at this moment. She'd explained how she was figuring out her relationship with Monty and he'd been completely understanding. He knew life was complicated. Having married young, his ex-wife had cheated on him while he was overseas on tour, so he'd stayed single and focused on his career in recent years. They hadn't had kids.

Right now he was easy company and just so refreshingly nice, and uncomplicated. And normal!

After their meal, they'd wandered theatreland and on the spur of the moment, bought last minute tickets to see *Phantom of the Opera* tomorrow. Hatty was just going with the flow, enjoying herself and not overanalysing things. This was just *something*.

In the porchway, she unlocked her mailbox and withdrew the small stack of envelopes from inside, before taking the stairs.

As the door to her flat clunked shut she kicked off her shoes, hung her jacket on the coatrack and dumped her bag on the sofa.

Padding across to her kitchen, she placed the mail on the side and fished out the bottle of rosé from her fridge, before pouring a glass. Turning for the lounge, she caught herself and grabbed the mail. Mostly business and junk mail. But at the bottom, a larger, buff envelope with an airmail sticker in one corner.

Intrigued, she took a sip of the delicate, dry yet fruity wine and stared at the familiar lettering, her heartbeat picking up. This one wouldn't wait until her birthday.

She set her drink down and sat on the sofa, the distant memory of Monty's head in her lap pulsing warmth through her chest. With her fingernail, she prised open the flap and pulled out a thick card of roughly made papyrus. On the front, a stick-drawn figure with crudely rendered copper hair and big green eyes on a round face, with a wiggly smile and a triangular green dress. And childish writing in Thai script. A smile spread across her face and she sighed. *What have you been up to now, Montgomery Wiles*?

Inside, in his familiar scratchy, schoolboy script, the message.

Dear Hatty,

I think the likeness is remarkable, though a drawing of this artistic merit is beyond my meagre talents. While I'm not sure if you like the Picasso school, this image touched an emotional chord in me. Anyway, just wanted to wish you a happy birthday. In whatever you do, I hope, at the very least, you unleash your remarkable smile on the world around you. It makes everything better.

Yours, always,

Monty xx

She shook her head. In whatever *he* was doing, this silly, troublesome man, could resuscitate bubbles of joy in her, however she might try to suppress them. Or try to forget what had befallen. Opening the card a fraction, she set it on her coffee table, pushing back the pain of missing him, then frowned, William's handsome face coming back to her mind.

CHAPTER 33

Monty
July 2005

Monty woke at the sound of a child screaming and staggered onto his veranda, his head aching, his mouth caked and dry.

He ran down his steps, 'What's going on?'

'Where have you been?' Tik yelled.

By a rusty pickup, a man held Oi roughly by the arm, brandishing a knife.

The ruffian shouted. 'Don't come closer or I'll hurt the girl.'

'Look, I'll give you money. I have lots of money. More money than you can get from selling this little girl. Okay, *Pe*?' Monty lowered his eyes, addressing to the man as his senior.

'How much money does this *farang* joker have?'

'Oh, he has lots of money, honest. Let the girl go, please,' *Pe* Tik implored.

'*Pe* Tik, in my sleeping room there's a rucksack and in the top pocket there's a money belt. Please bring that to me.'

She hurried away.

'Just stay calm, and you'll soon have lots of money, *Pe*,' he reassured, cowering.

From his straggly appearance, the man appeared more angry bully than experienced criminal. A small cog in a bigger racket, cruising around villages, hoping to get lucky.

When Tik returned, Monty pulled out ten crisp hundred-dollar bills, and held them up. 'There's a thousand dollars here. Let the girl free and you can have it all.'

A thousand was much more than a people trafficker would usually receive for abducting a child and selling her into the sex trade. But if he left today with Oi, he'd be back for more, dragging bigger cogs with him.

'Put the money on the grass, then step away from it.' The man commanded.

Monty stepped back, hands in the air, ten yards separating them. 'Bring the girl to the money, let her go then take it and leave.'

Stooping, the man picked up the notes with one hand, then released Oi who ran bawling to Tik.

Despite the residual alcohol in his system, Monty was hyper-alert, his hangover suppressed by the adrenaline flooding his veins. Relaxing his shoulders, he closed the gap quickly, hands loose at his sides.

After a moment of shock, the man gripped the knife underhand and swung his arm.

But Monty had practised this move many times and his movements were instinctive. Whipping his right knee up to the side, he swung his leg in a wide crescent. His foot slapped the man's wrist, sending the knife spinning. Landing, he smashed his fingers into the voice box, causing the man to crumple, gasping for air.

Then all he could recall was a blur of punching the prone figure while in floods of tears, until the gentle but insistent grab of men's hands on his arms. And the stinging pain.

As the police piled the cuffed-man into the back of their pickup, Fah's car appeared through the tree-line. Still in her nurse's uniform, she greeted them with a *wai* and glanced across to Monty who had returned to his veranda.

When the police left, she walked up his wooden steps, staring at his lower leg, which he'd rested on his table to reduce the blood flow. 'I will bandage it for you. Please lay on your stomach.'

He winced at the cold sting as she cleaned his wound.

'The policeman said that Oi came to your house, but the door was closed and she thought you went away.' Her words were cold and clipped.

'I was in my room, sleeping.'

'She was frightened so she went to your truck, and this man saw her.'

There was perfunctory rip as she tore open a dressing pack and pressed something soft on his leg before securing it with tape. 'Finish.'

'Thank you.' He slumped in his chair and grabbed a bottle of water from the table.

She turned and gathered up her medical accessories.

'Is everything okay, *Khun* Fah?'

Turning back, she asked, 'How old are you, *Khun* Monty?'

'Almost twenty-seven. Why?'

'Almost twenty-seven? I *am* twenty-seven. So that means I am *Pe* and you are *Nong*, right?'

Having studiously kept him at arm's length since his arrival, she was now establishing herself as the senior in their social hierarchy.

'Err, yes, *Pe* Fah.'

'So you are like my younger brother, and *Nong* Oi could be our younger relative too, right?'

'I suppose.'

Her cheeks flushed red, her voice harsh. 'Would you abandon your young relative like you did with Oi?'

'Actually, I don't have family anymore.'

'And Oi has no family, *na kha*. But she is a *child*!' Her emphasis on the word child was cutting. 'You can't meet her every day at the same time then not show up without letting her know. Did your family do this when you were little?'

He hung his head. 'No, of course not. Look, I know it's my fault, but I had some bad news last night.'

'What bad news, *kha*?'

'About my dad's case. The investigation has hit a dead end and now I don't know when I'll find him. Or even if—'

'I'm sorry about your dad and I respect him. But he is dead and now we are lucky that Oi is not too. You should not have come here if you were going to cause problems. We do *not* need your money. We do *not* need your help.'

'That's not completely fair.'

'Life is not fair.' She spat out the words, her hands balled into fists. 'All we can control is our actions. If you want easier life, just go back to England.' She turned on her heel and marched off the veranda.

The open spirit bottle was still on the floor where he dropped it in the night. Having lit his final cigarette, he gagged at the foul taste and stubbed it out. He poured the remaining spirit away then threw the bottle in the bin. After a wash and change of clothes, he boiled water and made strong coffee. *Jesus, what a mess.* He punched Hatty's number into his phone but it went straight to voicemail. *What the heck am I even doing here?*

He walked down the hill and found Oi sat on the step of Tik's house. Taking a seat, he handed her a banana.

'Banana,' she whispered.

'I'm very sorry, *Nong* Oi. I was very bad this morning and I made you feel scared.'

She shuffled up beside him. 'I miss my *Por* and *Mae*.'

He put his arm around her shoulder and gave her a gentle squeeze. 'I know you do. I bet your *Por* and *Mae* were such good and kind people, and loved you so much.'

'*Kha*,' she whispered.

'I'll pray to them and ask their forgiveness that I was a bad person today and made you sad, okay? Maybe their spirits can help me be a better person.'

'You are not bad person, *kha*.' She moved closer to him still and the two orphans looked down towards the fishing boats on the beach. 'You just miss your *Por* and *Mae*.'

A warm tear rolled down his cheek.

Pe Tik appeared, glowering from the top of the steps. 'Hey you two, I made some chicken. Come and eat it before all my hard work is ruined.'

Standing at the rail of his veranda, Monty watched headlights approach. Soon, Fah's son Moo came running up his steps clutching a pomelo.

'Hello little Pig, how are you?'

'I am good. Mama told me to give you this.' He held out the round fruit.

'Ooh, my favourite, do you want some?'

'No, thanks, I don't like it.'

He laughed, spotting Fah approach in a summer dress and sandals.

She wai'd. 'Hello, *Nong* Monty. Does your injury hurt?'

'No, it's okay.' He replied, on edge.

Holding out a white carrier bag, she smiled. 'I brought you some *sataw* from the market in Krabi. You remember it?'

'Of course! Would you like to eat some with me? Can I get you some water or lime soda to drink?'

'No, it's okay. We already had dinner.'

Moo's Nanny appeared and played with him in the corner.

'Please, take a seat.'

She occupied a chair opposite him at his table. 'I'm sorry for being unkind to you earlier,' she said in English.

'It's okay, *Pe* Fah. I deserved it.'

'*Nong* Monty, do you know the Thai word *jairorn*?'

He stared at her. 'You mean impatient?'

'Yes, kind of impatient. But the literal meaning is that your heart is hot and you can't control your emotion.'

His skin itched as he sweated. 'Are you telling me off about this morning again?'

'No, no. That's not what I mean, *kha*. I mean that I am *jairorn* as well. Sometimes I do wrong things. But my husband, he was *jaiyen*, so he cooled my spirit.'

It was the first time she'd ever mentioned her husband and he was gratified, though anxious about where the conversation might lead.

'Your husband sounds like a good man.'

'My husband was an officer of the Royal Thai police. He was killed two years ago.'

He gasped and was transported straight back to the beach on Boxing Day, panicking about Alan's whereabouts. 'Oh, my goodness. I'm so sorry. How?'

Fah's brow wrinkled and her cheeks flushed. 'In the south of Thailand. It was a bomb, *kha*.'

Must be tough with a young kid. 'You and Moo must miss him a lot.'

She wiped her eye. 'We miss him and think of him every day. So, I understand you, *Nong* Monty. You miss your dad and want to find him. But, this is your Christian culture, *kha*. Thai people are Buddhist, and we pay our respect to the souls of people we love, even after they are dead.'

'Different way of paying respect but I think just as sad in both cultures, right?'

'Right, *kha*. But you see, my husband's spirit is still with me and with Moo, and he helps us both be more patient. Be less *jairorn*. I believe your father's spirit is still here.'

Monty put his head in both his hands and ruffled his hair. 'Sorry, *Pe* Fah, I am not sure I understand what you are trying to tell me.'

She pressed her fingertips together beneath her chin. 'I think your father's spirit will find peace, if you can find peace in your heart.'

He was at a loss, but then realisation struck. 'You think I need a cooler heart to bring me balance?'

'Exactly. Someone who calms your soul, like an angel maybe, with magical hair.' For the first time since they'd met, Fah grinned.

The Following Day

Heart beating like it might burst through his chest, Monty came to a halt by Tik's house. Barely a quarter of the way up the hill, he had doubled over and rested his hands above his knees, panting hard. *I'm so out of shape*. Breath caught, he continued to walk up the hill, stopping briefly to kick around a wicker ball with a group of kids at the school.

At his house, he eased off his running shoes and took a lime soda from the fridge, the post-run endorphins lifting his mood. As was his daily custom, he grabbed the Flintstone photo, kissed Hatty's smiling face, and shook his head. *I'm sorry, my love.*

Having freshened up, he sat at his table, pen in hand, and started to write. When he eventually finished, his floor was littered with thick balls of discarded parchment. With tear-soaked fingertips, he moistened the flap of the envelope, and sealed the letter inside.

CHAPTER 34

Hatty
August 2005

Hatty stared transfixed at the buff envelope on her coffee table. 'I'm just worried it's going to be something bad.' Monty sending her that lovely birthday card had made sense, but he'd never written to her out of the blue like this. She'd been getting used to their separation, but a letter might announce the admission of a breakup she had denied since he left. She would be heartbroken. Would this be the irrevocable moment when her faded dreams of a life together would dissolve to nothing?

Martha, beside her on the sofa, patted her knee. 'And looking at it all night is going to take the worry away, is it?'

'It might have sat there for weeks if you hadn't come down to visit.' She wrung her hands and stared at their recent, glossy coat of red nail varnish, chosen to match the colour of the Light Dragoon's No.1 service cap.

William had invited her to his regimental homecoming parade and had looked so handsome in his dress uniform, umpteen medals across his broad chest, barking commands to his men as they marched in time. Yet he had an easy manner and quiet authority with them, as he introduced her, including to the senior officers, making her feel thoroughly welcome in his unfamiliar world. A relationship with him would be so much less complicated.

Leaning forward, Martha placed her wine glass down and fetched up the envelope. 'If you like, I'll read it, and if it's horrible I'll chuck it in the bin. How does that sound?'

'Not much better,' Hatty swirled her glass repetitively. 'But go on, then.'

'I reckon William must have some tough mates if you need Monty duffing up.'

'Billy's not like that at all. He knows about Monty and isn't pressuring me to go further just now.'

Martha tore open the flap and carefully unfolded the sheets inside, before reading the letter in silence. Which was odd, as Martha was not the silent type.

Hatty rose and wandered into the kitchen, opened the door to a storage unit above the hob, and pulled out a half-eaten Toblerone, that she'd saved for an emergency.

When she returned, Martha was rubbing her eyes with the backs of her hands, and her neck and cheeks were scarlet. 'I'm going to need bloody glasses like Dad at this rate.'

Deflated, Hatty slumped onto the sofa beside her, snapped off a triangle of praline chocolate and held it out. 'Here. Always helps me.'

'I'll swap you.' Her sister held out the letter.

Hatty took it, and moved to the armchair she liked to read in. Past eight o'clock, the dusk illuminated the parchment between her fingers.

My Dearest Hatty,

Letter writing is an old-fashioned art, but as you like ballet, I hope you'll indulge me this once.

There are many things I wish I'd said to you before I moved to Thailand.

Sorry is the first thing to say. I will always feel shame at the hurt I caused you.

I can't easily explain the places I went to in my mind. But I want you to know that your love rescued me. The fear of never seeing you made me run from the wave. When I wasn't sure if the next breath would be my last, your angelic smile appeared, fortifying me. Your care helped me resist the temptation of death's unforgiving embrace.

Though we are apart, I rejoice that you live. Like a Titian sunrise, your distant light helps me get up and confront each new day with hope.

While all I see today are footprints pressed into the sand by other people, you will always be the circle in my sand.

Every time I close my eyes, I am reminded of each step we shared from that magical moment you touched my heart, and I knew that I could love no one but you, kind, cautious, smart, sassy and utterly gorgeous, Hatty.

I take comfort in knowing that the last words I said to my dad were 'I love you'. Wherever your footsteps lead you, and howsoever old we may be, I pray our paths may cross again one day. And that, if but once, you let me tell you again that I love you, lest those words be my last.

Always yours,
Monty xx

Quietly, Hatty lay the letter on her coffee table and put her head in her hands. Then she rose, pulled back her French door, and sat on a wicker garden chair outside. Surrounded by terracotta pots bursting with summer flowers in pinks and purples, she stared at the dome of St Paul's cathedral, illuminated amber by the setting sun. Her narrowed eyes flitted constantly across the urban sprawl around that place of worship, as she could not for the life of her focus on a single thought or feeling. Then she was aware of the heat in her cheeks, so scrunched her eyes in a bid to deny the sensation. But she couldn't, and the tears rolled down her face. Slowly at first, until the pent up lava of emotion inside erupted in a hot flood that left her chest aching from the sobs.

'I just don't understand,' she whispered, her head in Martha's lap on the sofa. 'Why he'd go away then write such beautiful things.'

'Maybe he had no choice.' She stroked Hatty's hair.

'But everyone has a choice.'

'Maybe in normal circumstances, everyone has a choice. But depression is devastating, and life can tip us upside down when we didn't expect it.'

That made sense to her. Although she still felt a failure for not being able to help him. She sniffed. 'I don't really understand why he sent the letter anyway. It was like a goodbye.'

'If it was, then it was the most beautiful breakup note I've ever seen.' She stretched over Hatty's prone form and fetched up her glass of wine, taking a sip.

Hatty sat up, and straightened the fabric of her blouse, before looking hard at her sister. 'What do you think it was, then?'

'I just think,' Martha's voice cracked, 'he loves you more than anything in this world, Harriet Campbell, and maybe thinks you've given up on him.'

Her voice rose two octaves above her sister's. 'Why would he think I gave up on him? He left. I did all I could to help him.'

Martha held her hands up, wine glass still balanced between thumb and forefinger. 'Hatty, he lives five thousand miles away in a fishing village. He's had a lot of time to think, he's been really down, and he'll probably figure – correctly as it happens – that you are doing brilliantly well and moving on nicely at work and in your personal life.'

'Why do men have to be so complicated?' She doubled over as she blurted this, pummelling the sofa cushion with her fists.

Martha rubbed her back and said softly. 'Best thing you could do would be to jump on a plane and go see him. At least you could talk face to face, even if it's for the last time.'

CHAPTER 35

Monty
September 2005

Gentle lilting music wafted on a warm sea breeze. Musicians played wooden pipes, the stringed *khim* and a boat-shaped *ranard* xylophone on a low stage by the newly opened school. *Pe* Somchai sat centre stage in his finest village attire. Aunty Mai was beside him together with Municipal officials from Krabi and the local police and military chiefs.

Monty hunched in a plastic chair among the villagers, tall enough to get a good view of proceedings without craning his neck. He spotted the back of Genevieve's head, sat at the front, dark hair held up in a claw clip, revealing her long, alabaster neck.

Dressed in bright silk sarongs, with thick gold necklaces and jewelled bangles at their wrists, eight girls danced on the square of earth betwixt stage and audience. Arms straight, they bent their fingers back and twirled their hands in circular movements in time with the slow rhythm of the music. Bending at the knees, they tilted their heads gently from side to side, orchids in their hair, serene smiles on their faces.

Gosh, she looks so sweet today. He waved at Oi who beamed back, her cheeks blushing with the touch of rouge applied by *Pe* Tik. A swell of pride erupted within him, and he snapped a couple of photos.

'Was I good?' Oi squealed as she tottered towards him in her little heels after the performance.

'You were the most amazing dancer I ever saw.' Kneeling, he sniffed her warm cheek and gently touched her neck.

She wrapped her arms around him and giggled. 'The other girls were good too.'

'Ah, but you were the best.'

Aunty Mai approached, elegant in a crimson silk dress and formal black shoes. 'So this is your little friend Uncle Aek has told me about?'

He stood, and *wai*'d. 'Aunty Mai, this is *Nong* Oi.'

Wide-eyed, Oi pressed her hands together high against her face in a sign of the deepest respect.

'You look very pretty, *Nong* Oi,' Mai said to her lightly. 'You did so well today.'

He felt Oi's cheek again which was hot. 'I should take her back to *Pe* Tik, I think she has a slight fever.'

'It's okay, I'll come with you, *Nong* Monty. It would be nice to talk before I go back to Bangkok.'

'Will you carry me, I'm tired?' Oi said.

'Carry you?' he replied with exaggerated surprise. 'I'm very tired so maybe you can carry me!'

She made the cute snorting sounds he adored when she giggled.

'Oh, alright then, but I can't give you a piggy back with that sarong.' He lofted her onto one shoulder and wrapped his arm over her legs for support, while she held his head and twiddled with his ears.

Having dropped her off, he walked slowly up the hill with Aunty Mai. All around, villagers gathered in clumps around a dancer or musicians, chatting happily.

'*Nong* Oi really loves you,' Mai offered, calmly.

'I love her too. She's helped me put my life in perspective.'

'I asked my friends in Bangkok about adoption, as you requested. They say it isn't straight forward and can take at least one year, but it might be possible.'

'So, some hope then.'

'Yes, some.' She nodded. 'Your mum liked to say that you can't have a day off until children are eighteen, and after that you are on call twenty-four hours. Is this what you really want?'

He chuckled. 'I had amazing parents and want so much to give Oi that love and stability as she grows up. Should I tell her I'm thinking of this?'

'I think first find out some information and maybe talk to the relevant people.'

A narrow shaft of light appeared in his mind. *Hope.* Then his thoughts drifted to Hatty in England. *Sacrifice.*

Monty placed a spoonful of steamed rice in the centre of Genevieve's plate, before ladling sour prawn curry over the top with a chunk of thick *cha-om* omelette.

'You're turning into a Thai gentleman,' she gazed at him across the table with a view of the sea, where they often had lunch during her working visits.

'I suppose after six months I've got used to the Thai way of doing things.' In some ways, Genevieve evoked his past life. She was in her late twenties, expensively dressed, attractive and urbane. As a representative of UNICEF, she was well paid and sophisticated, exactly the sort of woman he used to date.

'So, what are your plans now the school is open?'

Thinking back to his conversation with Mai, he pondered the question. 'For the time being I plan to stay here, at least until the New Year, while I look into adoption.'

She smiled, her lip gloss glimmering in the sun. 'I think you'd make an amazing father actually. Though it seems you are not yet ready to leave Ban Puu.'

'There's practically everything I need to survive here for now.' He paused. *Everything except Hatty.* 'But yeah. I plan to return to a more normal life one day.'

Holding his gaze with her deep-blue eyes, she said, 'When you come back through Bangkok, you can maybe have a shave, put on some normal clothes and take me for dinner.'

Taking a heavy breath, his brow wrinkled. 'It would be nice to see you in again in Bangkok. Being completely honest, though, I'm still hopelessly in love with someone in England.'

Reaching forward, she squeezed his hand, the softness of her touch arousing feelings he hadn't experienced since his world fell apart. 'Do you think the hurt will fade one day?'

Monty shook his head slowly. 'I can't promise that it will.'

The air was boiling with humidity and Oi's temperature had developed into a mild fever since the show. She lay on the veranda with her head in his lap and he gently wiped a wet flannel across her forehead before settling her down to sleep with Tik.

As he wandered up the hill, the heavens emptied on the village soaking him to the skin. At the house, he changed into dry boxers, brushed his teeth and listened to the downpour hammering his tin roof as he sought sleep. It took him a while to settle, worried as he was about Oi's health.

Then, abruptly, he was dragged out of sleep by a loud banging on the door. He checked his watch. *Almost dawn.* 'Who is it?' he called.

'*Nong* Monty, it *Pe* Tik.' The sound of the voice was muffled by the door.

After pulling on a t-shirt, he opened the door.

'It's *Nong* Oi. She's in pain and is crying a lot.'

Suppressing the rising anxiety, he slipped on running shoes and ran down the hill.

He heard the crying before he bounded up the steps onto Tik's veranda., a stricken Oi, curled on her mat in a foetal position, her face twisted in pain. He knelt beside her and put his hand on her neck which was feverish.

'I should take her to hospital now,' he said to Tik.

'Call *Nong* Fah, she'll be able to help.'

Oi's sweaty face rested against his shoulder as he carried her up the steep hill,. With her still in his arms, he dialled Fah's number.

'Hello, *Nong* Monty. What's up, *kha*? It's very early,' she replied.

'It's *Nong* Oi. She has a fever, a sore stomach and has been sick. Can I bring her to the hospital?'

'Where is her stomach hurting, do you know?'

'I think at the bottom.'

'Maybe appendix. I can phone Krabi hospital to tell them you are coming. It might be strange for them that a *farang* brings a Thai girl.'

Having gathered water, his wallet and passport, he laid Oi gently on the rear seat of his pickup, whispering, 'You'll be okay, sweetheart, I've got you.'

Soon, he turned left onto the main highway and after twenty minutes was carrying her up the ramp into Krabi hospital, almost nine months after he checked out.

Mercifully, Fah had called ahead, and after he'd filled out various forms, and pre-paid for an emergency appendectomy, Oi was wheeled in for surgery.

During the interminable wait, he wandered across to the 7-Eleven where he'd bought cigarettes and beer after the tsunami. He took in the rows of tobacco and alcohol products, but instead opted for a bottle of cold green tea and a hot dog. From a small selection of toys, he chose a teddy with gingery brown fur. So many of the girls' toys were pink, which made him wince. *I think she'd like this one.*

Several hours later, a nurse ushered him into a private room.

Waves of relief flooded over him, upon seeing Oi, propped up, though still groggy from the anaesthetic. She looked tiny in the enormous white bed and he drew up a chair, taking her little hand in his.

'Hello, *Nong* Oi. I brought someone to see you.' He held out the teddy.

She tucked it under her arm and smiled weakly, before snuggling into the pillow. 'Thank you, *kha*.'

'What should we call her?'

'Hatty.'

'Oh.' A lump rose in his throat. 'That's a nice name.'

Worry creased her face. 'Will I be on my own here?'

He looked at the camp bed laid out in the room. 'No, sweetheart. I'll be with you the whole time.'

After she fell asleep, he slipped off his trainers and lay back on the bed, staring at the ceiling and trying not to dwell on the last time he'd been in this hospital.

He dozed, until the buzzing of his phone brought him up with a start.

'*Sawas-dee khrap,*' he answered quietly in Thai. 'This is Monty Wiles.'

'Have you turned into a Thai person now?' Hatty's teasing voice breezed lightly down the line.

The hairs rose on the back of his neck, and he sat up cross-legged, running his free hand through his hair. 'Er, hi Hatty. How are you?'

'I'm okay, thanks. I was more worried about you. Is everything okay over there?'

He glanced at Oi who had opened her eyes and watched him closely. 'Yep, it's mostly fine, I think. Why do you ask?'

'It's just I received a letter from you in which you say lots of lovely things. You haven't been taking wacky baccy or any other banned substance, I hope?'

'You know that I've never taken drugs. And there's a death penalty for drug offences in Thailand. Were you just phoning to taunt me, or . . . ?'

'Quite the opposite, actually,' she said, mysteriously. 'Anyway, thanks for the letter, it was the loveliest letter I ever received from a man. It was the only letter. But still.'

He could visualise her smile at the end of the line and it warmed his heart. 'Well, I suppose I had a rare and non-drug-or-alcohol-induced moment of clarity.'

'That makes me happy too. Anyway, I phoned to wish you a happy birthday.'

'It's my birthday today?'

She laughed lightly. 'Have you lost track of the days over there?'

Scratching his hair and glancing at Oi, he said, 'Err, probably.'

'There was something I wanted to mention, just to see how you'd feel about it.'

His heart thumped against his ribcage, tightening his chest. 'Yep, okay. Go ahead.'

'I have a business trip to Singapore in a couple of weeks. Well—' She paused again '—I wanted to ask how you'd feel about me coming to visit Ban Puu?'

Anxiety and elation clashed in his mind like cymbals. 'I'd like that. Of course, I'd more than like that.'

'As much as anything, it would be good if we could have a proper talk, face to face.'

His back itched as he broke out into a nervous sweat. A talk might mean good things or, possibly, horrible things. And the reality of the basic conditions of the village came crashing in on him. 'Will you stay in Krabi town though?'

'I was hoping to stay in Ban Puu.'

'It's pretty basic you know. No air-conditioning, barely any electricity. No fancy restaurants.'

'I'm choosing not to be offended by that comment. If you can cope, then I'm confident I can.'

'Sorry. It would be great to see you again. Sleeping in a wooden shed will definitely be a new experience.'

'Well, if this year has taught me anything, it's been to try new things.'

He smiled and rubbed his temple hard with his fingertip, Oi focusing on him from her bed, Hatty the teddy under her arm. 'Yep. So many new things.'

CHAPTER 36

Hatty
October 2005

'Welcome to the Raffles Hotel, madame,' a towering Sikh doorman said, his white turban pristine, his frock coat braided and a black cummerbund around his waist.

'Thank you,' Hatty replied with a smile, shaking off her wet umbrella and placing it in a wicker stand. A tropical downpour had done little to clear the oppressive heat and she was glad to feel the cool of Singapore's most iconic hotel. The fragrance of lilies filled the colonnaded reception, a string quartet playing, which faded into the background as she followed the concierge's polite directions to where she wanted to go.

Her heels clicked rhythmically against the white and black tiles as she walked into the cocktail lounge, which was uncrowded early on a Monday evening.

Sat at the bar, Connie turned and waved, before springing out of her stool. Looking fabulous, as always, in a flowy blue dress, her short hair in a round afro that framed her sharp features, she walked, arms outstretched, towards Hatty. 'There's my girl!'

Hatty fell into the taller woman's embrace, joy overflowing at the reunion with her best friend from work. 'Gosh, I've missed you. Can't tell you how happy I am to see you again.'

'And me, you, baby. Welcome to Singapore!' She held Hatty at arm's length for a moment, admiring. 'Look at you in that pretty little gold dress as well, with your hair all short and sassy.'

She stroked the bob of hair at her ears and smiled. 'Thought I needed to go with a shorter cut for a change, as it always works so well for you'.

'Mmm, hmm, the boys round here are gonna be in trouble tonight when they see you!'

Hatty perched on a bar stool next to her friend, their knees bumping.

'Can I get you a drink, madame,' the barman, dressed in a white shirt and black waistcoat asked, with the clipped consonants of the Singapore accent.

'I think I'll have a Singapore sling like my darling friend here,' she replied with a smile.

'And get me another please, sugar,' Connie added.

'Coming right up,' he replied with a polite smile.

Hatty took in the decorative splendour of the bar with its low teak roof, high arched windows and heart-shaped punkah fans that swished lazily back and forth. 'This place is every bit as nice as I'd heard.'

'My apartment is just ten minutes' walk, so I come all the time. Shame you're only passing through, otherwise I could really show you the town.'

'Shame indeed. Although while I've got you I want to find out what you've been up to. Lots of people tell me what a brilliant job you've done since you came here.'

'You know it. Hey, what can I say, working here is fantastic. People are hard-working but know how to have fun. And Singapore is like paradise, so clean yet so exotic.'

'A bit like me?' Hatty grinned.

'Dang right.'

'Your drinks.' The barman placed two long goblets on the bar, filled with ice and a rich pink cocktail of gin, cherry brandy, grenadine and juice.

Hatty took a sip through the straw and savoured its fruity punch. 'Well, that makes a good first impression.'

For the next while they settled into gay chatter, eating peanuts from a hessian bag on the countertop and dropping the shells on the floor, a Long Bar tradition. Within an hour they'd caught up on the insignificances of life since their brief reunion over dinner in London in the summer. The bar buzzed with the inflow of guests, normally in smart attire. From time to time, men would approach to strike up conversation with the beautiful women, but Connie skilfully batted away their attentions with a winning smile that didn't leave them deflated.

'So, you flying to Thailand the day after tomorrow?' she asked.

Hatty fiddled with a peanut shell and threw it on the floor. 'That's right. Ripping off the plaster!'

'How'd you feel about seeing him again?'

She ran her finger around the base of her cocktail glass. *How to answer that one?* Her last recollection of Monty was through floods of tears at the departure gate at Heathrow, with him monosyllabic and closed off. 'It's important for me to see Monty. He was . . . he is a big part of my life and, in one way or another, always will be.'

Connie studied her closely. 'Does he know you've found someone else?'

'I'm still just friends with Billy right now, but no.' She thought about the dress she'd bought for next week's Regimental ball and how Billy would look in full mess dress. And how she might not be able to resist dragging him into her room if things carried on between them as they had.

'So this is kind of make or break, right?'

'Yes, I guess it is. I honestly don't know what to expect. And maybe that's okay, because I won't have any big expectations from it.' She took another sip of her cocktail.

'So, just tell me again, how long have you known Monty?'

She gazed across the crowded bar and all the people settled into familiar chatter while she did the calculation. 'Well, just over three years since we really connected, I suppose.'

A cheeky grin spread across her friend's lips, accentuating her high cheekbones and sparkling through her caramel eyes. 'And you two ain't *ever . . . ?*'

'No. The timing has never been right. I was in New York for all that time and now he's in Thailand.'

'Now Monty's sending you beautiful letters from his fishing village, right?'

Like a droplet of tropical rain, the tear slid down one cheek and she dabbed it with a napkin. 'Well, he just sent the one.' Albeit the most heart-breaking, touching letter she had ever read.

'He loves you Hatty, and you love him too.'

'I do love him . . . I'm just . . . '

'Scared?'

'Yes, alright then, I'm scared,' she stuttered.

Connie leant forward and took her friend's hands in silence for a while and stared off into space. 'You know, I told you about a good friend of mine, who lost the love of her life in the World Trade Centre on 9-11?' Her words echoed like they'd been dragged up from deep in her soul.

Hatty squeezed her hand and said softly, 'Your friend Shanice? Yes, that was so heartbreaking.'

'You know Shanice would do anything to have him back again. Anything. Even if he was broken up, lost a leg, in a wheelchair, in a coma, she don't care.' She squeezed Hatty's hand in return. 'You get to see Monty again. He wants to see you, you want to see him. Nothing else, all the difficult times you been through, none of that don't matter.'

She dwelled on their countless incredible times together and how much those memories had carried her through this year. 'You're right.'

Connie sat back in her chair and grinned. 'Sure I'm right. And, I'm just saying, but you got to get naughty with *one* of them hot English dudes soon, or I'm going to move in and steal one. Hell, that Monty is just a one hour plane ride from here, so use it or lose it, honey.'

Hatty almost spat her cocktail out from laughing. 'You know, funny thing is, the two of you would make an amazing couple. You're both just such beautiful people, inside and out.'

'Now, ain't that the truth?'

CHAPTER 37

Monty
October 2005

Dawn crept over the hillside casting shadows from the stilted houses like squares of night-time hiding from the sun. Monty walked up from the food vendor's hut, a bulging carrier bag in one hand.

Oi watched him from the top step of Tik's house.

'Are you ready then?' he called.

She grinned and waved. 'Yes, *kha*.'

'I'm still cooking so I'll wait for them here,' Tik called, a strong aroma of garlic and galangal wafting off her wok.

Oi fell in beside him, in knee-length shorts and her school polo. After her discharge from the hospital, she'd recovered quickly and was doing really well with her studies.

At Monty's house, they took a seat on the bottom step. He pulled out a pack of fried *pa thong ko* donuts, dipping one into a container of green pandan custard, and passed it to her. 'Your favourite.'

'Thank you.' She finished munching on the first morsel and asked, 'are we going to see the big planes today?'

'After you finish school. Are you excited to meet another *farang*?'

'A bit scared.'

He laughed and stroked her hair. 'She's really nice, I promise. Nicer than me.'

'She's an angel.'

'Well, that's how I think of her, yes.' He coughed lightly. 'But when you meet her she'll seem like a normal person. Just the most beautiful person you ever saw.'

Her eyes were like saucers and she shuffled up beside him as she munched on another piece of donut. 'Okay, *kha*.'

From the treeline, shaven-headed men in orange robes walked gracefully and barefoot towards the village. Each carried a silver bowl wrapped in a cloth shoulder bag.

Monty knelt and Oi stood beside him, their hands pressed together in a *wai*.

Each monk took turns to remove the silver lid of their bowl, so he and Oi could place bags of food and a bottle of water inside. A small blessing was offered before the holy men walked on towards the neighbouring house, where the next family waited patiently to give alms.

The Buddhist simplicity of letting go of attachment had helped him find a day-to-day balance in this place he now called home. And if one day he did adopt this intelligent, sweet young girl, it was really important to him that she hold on to her culture.

The car slowed to a halt in the main car park at Phuket Airport, whereupon Monty stepped out before opening the rear door.

Oi hopped onto the tarmac, Hatty the teddy clutched tightly to her chest.

'Do you want to leave Hatty in the car, so she doesn't get lost?'

'I'm a bit scared.'

'Okay, well, I'm sure she'll show you there's nothing to worry about.' He took Oi by the hand, hoping she didn't major on the teddy when its human namesake arrived.

It occurred to him, what a novel experience going to an airport must be for her. He recalled Alan driving him to the airport perimeter road at Heathrow. They could sit for hours with a flask of tea and a couple of bags of crisps, watching the planes take off and land, calling out the names of the airlines. A Singapore Airlines 737 taxied up to the terminal building and he shuddered.

The arrivals board confirmed what he already knew; Hatty was here now. His palms were sweating. He'd never expected his past and present lives to collide like this. She was the love of his life, had been since that first moment in the canteen. Yet here he was with a girl he loved like a daughter who Hatty had never met, didn't even know about.

'I need to go *chee*,' Oi said, snapping him out of his reverie.

'Oh, okay. Come on then. We'll have to use the men's room.' Looking around, he ushered Oi into the gents' and stood guard outside of the cubicle. When she'd finished, he lifted her on his knee so she could reach the basin to wash her hands.

She was awestruck by the hand-dryer and giggled loudly when Monty turned the nozzle towards his face and let the air ruffle his cheeks and hair.

Then, unable to delay longer, he led Oi by the hand back into the waiting throng, every nerve on edge.

CHAPTER 38

Hatty
October 2005

After a micro-blast of tropical heat Hatty stepped into the air-conditioned chill of the terminal. *Another step closer.* Wandering briskly through arrivals she arrived at the immigration desk before the queue. The officer, medal ribbons across the left pocket of her brown shirt, smiled as she handed Hatty's passport back. 'Welcome to Thailand!'

With everything she needed in a carry-on, she avoided a nervous wait at the baggage carousels. Staring at the glass exit doors, her breath quickened like she was poised on the edge of the striking circle on a hockey pitch, waiting for the ball. Briefly closing her eyes, she inhaled deeply. *Here goes then.* The doors swished open, ushering her into a noisy throng of waiting relatives and taxi drivers hawking for custom, held at bay by a chrome rail.

She looked right: nothing. Then, turning left, she gasped, straining against the urge to burst into floods of tears before a stronger wave of emotion broke through. She giggled. And then she smiled, broader and more joyful than before all that had befallen this year. Perhaps, the only time she had truly smiled with her body and soul since Christmas Day, when Monty phoned her from Thailand, before everything changed.

'What kind of almighty trouble have you created for yourself now, Montgomery Wiles?' she whispered. Of all the crazy situations she thought he might have got into in Thailand, *this* had never crossed her mind. She waved brightly.

Monty, tanned and toned, dressed in knee-length denim shorts and a faded blue tee, waved back. Beside him, holding his hand, a little girl with long black hair, clutching a teddy, noteworthy for its auburn fur.

She walked briskly towards them, sunlight lancing through the windows, beside herself with relief laced with intrigue.

'Hatty, it's lovely to see you.' He leant in stiffly and kissed her on both cheeks. No more City cologne, just the warm familiar scent of him that had always been there, which subliminally she had missed beyond words.

'It's nice to see you too, Monty. I almost didn't recognise you.' She ran her free arm around his back, which was warm and slightly damp from the heat outside. The touch of his kiss lingered on her cheek as she stared into his deep-blue eyes, looking at her the way he had from the first moment they met. Then she took in his messy hair and sun-tanned features. He looked different and yet, in the most important ways, just the same. Dropping onto her haunches, she looked at the little girl, in her smart chino shorts and sky-blue school polo and stroked the auburn bear with her fingertip. 'Hello, sweetie, what's your name then?'

The girl stared back, seemingly star-struck. 'Hatty.'

She laughed lightly. 'Hatty's my name.'

The girl looked up at Monty for help and he said something to her in Thai.

Her eyes returned to Hatty's. 'Oi, *kha*.'

'Nice to meet you, Oi,' she said softly, offering a shallow *wai* which the girl returned, dimples breaking out on her cheeks as she smiled.

'Did you have any suitcases or anything?' Monty asked.

'No. I left my business suitcase in Singapore. This will do for three days.'

'Come on then. Paradise awaits,' he murmured. He took Oi by the hand and grabbed Hatty's carry-on before they all walked towards the exit.

'Teddy name is Hatty,' the little girl said softly, in high-pitched lilting English, looking up at the teddy's namesake with wide almond eyes.

'You named her after me? Oh, that's so sweet.' She ruffled the girl's back with her fingertips.

Oi grinned as they stepped out into the heat.

'Well, this is a surprise,' Hatty said, an eyebrow raised.

'Good surprise or bad surprise?' Monty replied.

Glancing at him sideways, she didn't reply. *A completely unexpected, but not unpleasant surprise.*

'I really like your new hairstyle. Short suits you.'

'Thanks. I needed something new.' She met and held his gaze briefly, before dropping her eyes, to mask the whirlwind of gaiety and confusion inside.

The drive through the lush scenery of Phang Nga province took around two hours.

On arriving at the village, she admired the orangey-brown stilted house at the top of the hill, as Monty placed her carry-on on the veranda. After Hatty the bear, a colour theme was emerging. She pushed the low curtain of auburn hair behind her ear.

He rubbed his hand down one side of his face and said, 'Not exactly Buckingham Palace, but I like it.'

Walking beside Monty down the gravelly track towards the sea, Oi took her hand protectively. From the verandas of near identikit stilted houses, the occasional older person popped up their heads to stare at the unfamiliar *farang*. A group of boys kicking around a wicker wall, stopped to look.

A boy in sandals, tatty shorts and a faded Manchester United football peeled away from the group, ran up to Monty and high-fived him. He glanced nervously at Hatty before falling into conversation with Oi. The children scampered down the hill, framed by the glittering turquoise sea which stretched off to the horizon.

'It's so beautiful,' Hatty enthused, and for the first time that day, Monty's lips tugged into a shallow smile.

On the steps to a pink house, a plump lady with bundled up black hair, in a bright yellow t-shirt and grey sarong, beamed down at Hatty. 'Hello, welcome, lady,' she said, pressing her fingertips together in a *wai*.

'This is *Pe* Tik, Oi's guardian.' He said something in Thai to the lady, who responded to him in quickfire fashion.

Tik waved to coax Hatty up her wooden steps.

'*Khob Khun kha*.' Hatty pressed her hands beneath her chin and slipped off her sandals,. 'These are for you, from England.' She handed Tik a tin of sweets, shaped like a London double-decker bus, and pulled out various colourful tins for the children.

Tik had prepared a veritable feast, with three curries, two kinds of rice, prawn cakes, fried soft-shell crabs, spicy papaya salad, noodles, fresh fruits, and water.

'It all looks amazing.' She smiled warmly up at Tik. '*Khob Khun kha*.'

Oi positioned herself between Hatty and Monty throughout the meal. Monty played the role of translator, often blushing crimson when Tik said something boisterous. Yet he didn't drive much conversation himself and seemed distracted and on edge.

With dusk falling, and the fierce heat of the day moderating to a warm hug, he stood and lit a storm lantern, which cast them all in a dull glow.

By eight, Hatty was tiring. Just two days into her visit, the jetlag still clouded her senses. As if spotting the clue, Monty rose and stretched his arms to the rafters, before gabbling something in Thai to Tik and offering a *wai*.

Farewells seemed to take a long time, with much *wai*'ing and effusive chatter. Oi came to her side and hugged her leg, before saying sweetly, 'Good night.'

It was dark outside as she walked back up the hill beside Monty in silence, their footsteps crunching the gravel. Many of the houses were blacked out, but shadowy faces watched from those that were illuminated. Sometimes their hips would bump together, or their fingers would brush, sending a tingle up her arm. But after a brief hug at the airport, an invisible wall had remained between them. There was so much she wanted to say, and some things she need to tell him. But not now. Now, Hatty Campbell was happy to be here and to rejoice quietly in Monty's every breath, his every word and touch.

At his house, he disappeared into the darkness of his room which soon shone with the hiss of a lamp, before he emerged, anxiety creasing his tanned face. 'I hope you'll be comfortable enough. I'll sleep right out here on a hammock, so if you need anything, you only need say.'

She threw her arms around his neck and pressed her cheek to his, his powerful heartbeat recharging her emotional batteries. 'Don't you worry a bit about me. This is just perfect, thank you.'

He buried his face into her hair and sniffed it deeply, which was *different* but nonetheless affectionate. 'Sorry, must be a bit strange for you to come here.'

'Stop it. There's nowhere else on this earth I'd sooner be right now.'

He rubbed her shoulder gently. 'I'm glad you came.'

'Me too. So, goodnight then.' She kissed him lightly on the cheek.

His eyes shone at her like harvest moons. 'Night.'

She retreated into the bedroom. Inside, on the tidy square of wooden floor, a thin mattress was dressed with plain sheets and a pillow. Slipping off her chinos and blouse, she lingered at a small table in the corner with a closed laptop, some books – including a well-thumbed copy of *A Town Like Alice*, and a can of deodorant. And, catching herself, she stared at the leopard-print picture frame, picking it up and bringing it close to her face, in the dull light. Frowning, she knelt and fished a tissue from her bag, to polish the glass. Then she stopped herself, when she discerned the shape of Fred's lips in the smudge around Wilma's dazzling smile.

She pulled her cell-phone and fired off a message to Billy.

Arrived in Krabi safe and sound. All good. Will message you when I head home. Hatty x

Daylight filled the small room and a strong aroma of coffee burst through her senses. Pulling a light sarong from her bag, she wrapped it around her body, tying it above her bust, and stepped onto the veranda, to find Monty reading in his hammock.

In an easy movement, he tipped out and stood. 'Did you sleep okay?'

'Gosh, I slept amazingly, thank you. Is that coffee for me?' She glanced at the glass pot on the table.

'It is,' he pulled out a chair for her and poured coffee into an enamel camping mug. 'I got you some different fresh fruits and rice porridge, if that's okay?'

It was more than okay, and she settled down to breakfast, with Monty fussing around her. From a distance, she admired the white topped waves gambolling towards the shore under a cornflower sky. 'Where's little Oi this morning?'

'Oh—' he scratched his fingertips through his hair '—she's at school, but will finish at lunchtime.'

'Ah nice. She thinks the world of you, you know? I can tell.' She smiled.

He cast his eyes down at the table, before meeting her gaze. 'The feeling is mutual. Her parents were killed by the wave, so . . . ' He frowned.

'Oh my gosh, that's so awful, poor little thing.'

'Yeah.' His heel rapped against the leg of the table.

She turned her face to him. 'Thank you for the letter. It was so honest.' She paused. 'And heartbreaking.'

He exhaled heavily through his nose. 'I meant everything, you know. You're the only woman I've ever truly loved.' He wiped his eyes with the back of his hand.

'I'll never stop loving you, Monty. But I felt so empty for so long after you left. Waiting, hoping. Not knowing what to do.'

'Have you found someone else?' His voice was strained.

There was no point sugar coating it. 'I have, sort of. Just very recently.'

He closed his eyes momentarily. 'It's okay, Hatty. I understand. Right now, I'm just happy to see you again and that I could say how sorry I was properly.'

She took his hands in hers and leaned forward to look into his eyes. 'Just to be clear, nothing has happened between me and William. He knows I still have feelings for you and understands I need time. I just wanted to see you again. There's so much we didn't discuss.'

He smiled though his eyes were flat. 'Honestly, it's fine, I get it.'

She shook her head and sighed. That was it, he was closing down again like he used to before, giving up without a fight. 'It's lovely to see how you've got back on your feet here, Monty. What are you planning to do, especially regarding little Oi?'

His eyes searched hers, as if for clues about how she might respond. 'Honestly, I have been looking into the possibility of adopting her. There's no guarantee it will be approved, and it could take a year, so, a long way from a done deal.'

Wow. She remained silent for a while, only because she didn't want to confuse either herself or Monty with what she said next. 'But you want everything to work out though, right?'

'Yes, yes, of course I do.' He frowned. '*Pe* Tik has three children already and has done well by Oi. But I could give her a good life after all she's been through. And I've cleaned up my act.' He paused. 'You know, with the drinking and smoking.'

If only parenting was just about not drinking or smoking. She wasn't sure Monty really understood the enormity of this. In a few years sweet little Oi would start to blossom into a sassy woman. After she got through the emotional rollercoaster of puberty. 'Well, that is definitely positive.'

'I'm sorry, I just. . . '

'Don't be sorry, Monty. For what it's worth, I think you'd be an amazing dad.'

He frowned. 'Thanks.'

They'd put the difficult stuff on the table and had hit a bit of a dead end in the conversation. But there'd be plenty of time before she went home, tomorrow.

Hatty smiled and rubbed his knee. 'Hey, once I've freshened up shall we go into Krabi and buy a few things?'

He smiled. 'Yes, that sounds nice.'

After lunch, Oi emerged from Tik's house, in a yellow swimming costume, with a blue flower on the front.

Hatty had bought it for her and was pleased that it fit. She had changed into the bikini that she purchased in Bournemouth the year before, a sarong around her for the walk to the beach. 'Come on then, sweetie.'

They walked hand in hand, fishermen staring open-mouthed as they unloaded the catch from their painted boats.

Monty shoved his hands deep in his pockets and sat on the sand.

Hatty let her sarong fall to the ground and led Oi into the light surf that foamed at their feet.

It didn't take long for her to be waist-deep, holding the little girl beneath the shoulders as she giggled and kicked her legs. 'Is it fun?' she asked, slowly.

'Yes, yes,' Oi squealed.

Hatty stared at the shore, where Monty sat, his arms wrapped around his knees. After a while, she guided Oi back into the shallows before the two girls walked up the beach towards him.

'You want to try coming in the water?' she asked.

He scratched his hair vigorously. 'I dunno. It's making me anxious enough just watching you two.'

Her heart ached for him. 'Tell you what, Oi might like to be our lifeguard and look out for any danger while we paddle in the water?'

He grimaced, but reluctantly stood and spoke to Oi in Thai, whereupon she sat and watched them attentively.

His hand was damp and clammy when she took it and led him slowly into the sea, still in his shorts and t-shirt. They got to waist deep when his body and arms started to shake and his teeth chattered.

She turned to him. 'I'll keep you safe, don't worry.'

He stepped close to her now, for the first time since their perfunctory embrace at the airport. Goosebumps broke out along the length of his forearm, and he scrunched his eyes tight, cheeks shaking. He gripped her hand tighter and tighter.

'It's okay, I'm here with you,' she whispered.

Like the dam had burst, he flung his arms around her back and buried his face in her neck, his chest shaking violently with every silent sob.

She held him close, stroking his hair gently. 'Shh, it's okay. I won't let anything bad happen to you now,' she whispered, tears streaking down her face.

Standing in the aquamarine sea, they held each other for what seemed an eternity.

Later, having towelled themselves dry, they walked back to Tik's house where they enjoyed another hearty meal. Monty was chatty now, often breaking into laughter when messing around with Oi. He pulled out his camera and took a few photos. Hatty's heart melted at seeing something of the man she had fallen so deeply in love with before everything changed.

With a full stomach and a happy heart, she walked back up the hill beside him.

'Do you want a lime soda?' he asked, reaching into the fridge on his veranda.

'Sure, that would be lovely.'

He popped the cold can on her shoulder, making her squeal indignantly. Yet her fingers lingered on his as she took the drink, and his hand brushed across her shoulder sending a tingle down her spine.

He sat beside her on the top step, their legs pressed together.

Having cracked the can open and taken a cooling sip, she stared down the hill and out to sea. For the first time this year, she felt at a greater peace, yet struggled to fathom the suffering that had taken place here, which Monty had endured. The huge amber sun dipped its round belly in the sea on the horizon, the fierce daytime heat once again softening to a warm embrace. Instinctively she leant into him, and rested her head on his shoulder.

Monty's phone buzzed, dragging him out of the moment and he fetched it from the table. 'Hi, Monty Wiles . . . Oh, hi Sandeep . . . What? When? Oh . . . ' His voice became strained.

She turned to look at him, his head buried in one hand, the phone pressed hard to his ear. Standing, she stepped behind him and gently rubbed his back.

Monty dropped the phone. It hit the floorboards with a report like gunshot.

An official swung open the doors to the refrigerated shipping container, and Hatty gagged as the frozen smell of death breezed out.

'Monty, you do not need to view the body as the positive identification has already been done by forensic analysis, and I would recommend that you don't.' Nick Evans, the British embassy official said quietly.

Monty nodded, his body shaking all over.

Two workmen in hooded suits and masks entered the container and quickly emerged with a sagging black bag, about six foot by three, which they placed carefully on a gurney.

A Thai man in a dark suit emerged from a plain black van, with a folder of paperwork. After a minute or so inspecting the bag and inserting information onto a form, he spoke with Nick. Within ten minutes the process of completing the paperwork for the transfer of the human remains of Alan Wiles to a funeral director organised by his son, Montgomery Wiles had been finalised. Monty remained silent throughout, including when he had to sign anything.

Yet, as the workmen wheeled the gurney towards the dark van, he broke free of Hatty's embrace and ran after them, putting his hand on one end of the bag. 'Dad, I'm so sorry,' he wailed.

The men continued towards the funeral director's vehicle, Monty holding on to the gurney, not letting go, sobbing, until the men were forced to stop. 'I should have warned you Dad, I should have known.

I'm sorry.' He knelt by the gurney and kissed the bag at one end where it bulged slightly. 'Dad, no Dad, it's all my fault.'

Hatty ran to him and hugged him from behind as hard as she could. 'I'm here, darling. You need to let your dad go home to be with your mum, just like you promised her. It's okay, he's at peace now, you found him. Your parents would be proud of you.'

His nose streamed as he stared forlornly, arm outstretched as his hero, mentor and best friend was lifted off of the gurney and placed in the back of the vehicle.

The rear doors slammed shut with a loud clang. As the van pulled away, he slumped to the floor, crying his heart out on the blistering concrete as the tropical sun hammered down.

With strength she didn't realise that she had, Hatty kept it together. What he needed now was kindness and practical help. She sat with him, commandeered an umbrella and bottle of water, so he didn't get heat stroke, and discussed final practicalities with Nick.

It was two days since Monty had received the phone call from the Hampshire police. Besides helping coordinate arrangements with the British embassy, she had helped pack everything Monty needed for the journey home including his passport. She'd ensured Oi was settled with Tik, shielding the little girl from Monty when he was in his worst state and working hard to maintain a sense of normality, so she didn't get scared. Monty would be coming back to Ban Puu soon after a short visit to England. Hatty even promised to visit again in December for Oi's seventh birthday, which ensured a smiling, if teary farewell.

Finally, Hatty persuaded Monty to get up from the floor, took him to his pickup and helped him into the passenger seat.

Walking to the back of the vehicle, she let herself weep briefly before pulling it together. She pulled out her mobile phone and sent a message to Billy. With profuse apology, she wouldn't be able to make the Regimental ball but would call him when she was home.

Then she wiped her eyes, got behind the wheel of Monty's truck and drove them to Phuket Airport to start the long journey home.

CHAPTER 39

Monty
November 2005

The hearse drew to a halt outside the white thatched house in a small village near Winchester. An arrangement of jasmine flowers spelling 'Dad' sat against the polished coffin, an ornate bouquet of lilies and roses on top.

Monty stared out of the window and shivered, alone in his parents' home. Well, almost.

'Time to go, Monty.' Hatty, dressed in a black, calf-length dress, squeezed his knee.

He stood, barely looking at her and they sat in silence for the short drive, the only sound a low thrum from the engine of the funeral limousine.

At the old Norman church, they stepped into the chill late autumn and waited as the pallbearers carefully withdrew the casket and lofted it onto their shoulders.

Together, they processed slowly up the steps, to the stone arch, its oaken doors apart. A vicar greeted them there, a black stole around his white vestments. 'We brought nothing into the world and take nothing out. The Lord giveth and the Lord hath taken away: blessed be the name of the Lord.'

Monty gripped Hatty's hand through the introduction and opening hymns. Then after the reading, he walked to the lectern, staring out at pews packed with mourners, only really aware of her. Clenching his jaw, he glanced at Alan's coffin and took a deep breath.

'Dad would have been delighted that so many people came, in his words, to "cheer him on" at his funeral.' There was a light ripple of laughter.

'My dad, Alan George Wiles, was born in Winchester fifty-nine years ago on a bright September afternoon. Apart from his time at university, he lived in this village his whole life. The only child of George and Helen, he'd meet another only child and his kindred spirit at university, my beloved mum, Daisy. They married six years later in the beautiful church at the village of Eling, where Mum was born.

'While today I mourn, I take some comfort from the reunion in heaven of my parents, a moment Dad awaited with joy, not fear.

'I know with complete certainty that Dad wouldn't want me or anyone here to be sad. He'd want everyone here to live and rejoice as he did each day.

'Dad met every setback and disappointment with a wisecrack. He teased me that keeping him awake at night as a baby cured his desire for more children. I learned later that complications after my birth meant Mum could only bear me.

'Where Mum was the fire, Dad was the ice, and I loved him because he cooled our souls. Every holiday, school event, day trip, all my life, was illuminated by laughter and the glow of my parents' unbreakable love.

'When Mum was diagnosed terminally ill, Dad stayed positive, taking care of her with the same adoration no doubt, as when they were courting. I was in awe of but also terrified by the unconditional sweep of Dad's love.

'It's only now I see that he was enriched by Mum's love not until she departed, but until he died. He was fortified by her memory when she passed and comforted by the certainty of their reunion in death.

'Dad would joke with me: "Monty, son, one day you'll wake up alone in your expensive mansion to confront the devastating reality that you're not Peter Pan after all". For a long time, I never really understood what he meant.

'After Mum died, I'd buy Dad gifts and take him for days out, which he'd enjoy, while saying I shouldn't have gone to the expense. He'd ask what was going on in my life and whether *I* was happy.

'Dad never rejoiced in material possessions. He wasn't driven by ruthless ambition. Armed only with his faith in God, his love for Mum, for me, and his friends, he had it all.

'I was absolutely the luckiest kid alive because I was loved unconditionally every day. Oh, Dad could tell me off, like when I released the handbrake on his car and it rolled into the vicarage wall.' Another ripple of laughter.

'But Dad was there for me at every stage in my life, comforting me when I was sick, cuddling me when I felt sad, cheering me at every turn. When I made mistakes, he wrapped his arm around me and would say "worse things happen at sea, son". As it turns out—' Monty looked up at Hatty, her eyes glistening with tears '—he was right about that too.

'It has taken me ten months to grapple with Dad's death. I can't even begin to describe how difficult this period has been.' His lip trembled and he ground his teeth.

'They say, never meet your heroes, but I grew up with mine. If I can become even half the person, the parent and the husband that my dad was, then that surely will be a far greater memorial than any words I may say to you now.

'Alan Wiles was to me the best man, my best friend.' Tears streamed unabated down his cheeks. 'The best dad I could ever hope for.'

He walked, eyes cast to the floor, to the front pew, and sat beside Hatty who took his hand. The organ started, he heard a shuffling of leather soles on stone as the congregation rose and lifted their voices to the roof in the hymn 'Jerusalem'. Completely unable to compose himself, he eventually rose to his feet and stood hand in hand with Hatty, comforted only by the melody of her voice.

The sun broke through and a soft rustling of the trees was the only sound, as the pallbearers lowered Alan's coffin into the grave, finally to rest alongside his beloved Daisy.

From among the mourners, a young woman with ebony skin and voluminous black hair tied back approached Monty, a taller man with dark hair at her elbow.

Serwah, red-eyed, stood on tiptoes and hugged him. 'That was such a beautiful speech, Monty; your dad would have been so proud of you.'

Bert slapped his shoulder and shook his hand. 'I am very sorry for your loss, Monty.'

'Thanks for coming. It's great to see you both again.'

Serwah peeled off and wandered towards Hatty, who was talking to other guests.

A cloud of gloom darkened his already dreadful day, and he dug his hands into his pockets.

'You okay?' Bert asked, glancing across at the two women.

'Hatty's seeing someone else,' he grumbled.

'Yeah, Serwah told me, sorry.'

'In fairness, it's all my fault. I just shut her out after the tsunami, and I've been a mess ever since. I can't blame her for moving on.'

'Are you really sure she wants to move on? Maybe she's waiting for you to let her back in.'

'Hmph. Anyway, how's life at Oxford treating you?'

'It's good. I like it. It means I can see Serwah at weekends as Birmingham is not so far away by train.'

'So, are you two are now properly an item?' Out the corner of his eye, Serwah was talking animatedly to Hatty, who sometimes nodded her head.

Bert grinned. 'How did you guess?'

For the first time that day, he smiled. 'Call it intuition. Oh, and your smooth Saxony charm and sophistication. Anyway, you make a terrific couple and I'm chuffed for you both.'

'Cheers, mate.'

Monty suddenly remembered. 'Have you heard anything about your friends who were missing?'

Bert shook his head.

Monty hugged him, 'I'm really sorry.'

With over one hundred people at the service, Hatty had organised caterers to lay on a buffet and drinks for the guests who milled around the ground floor of the family home. She moved around the room constantly making sure that everyone had drinks and everything was working.

'I must say, your girlfriend Harriet is quite wonderful. Both your parents would have adored her,' said a woman from the village with paper-thin skin and white hair.

'Thank you, Mrs Wallace.' He gazed wistfully across the room. 'Dad most certainly did.'

He spotted Bob, the bank vice president and wandered across, reaching out his hand. 'Bob, thanks so much for coming today.'

The Scot's handshake was dry and firm, and he considered his protégé with an even gaze. 'I wanted to be here and pay my respects, after everything you and your dad suffered.'

Monty reached into the inside pocket of his jacket and pulled out an envelope. 'Here's my letter of resignation, as we discussed. I appreciate your understanding about this.'

'I'll be sad to see the back of you, although I think you're doing the right thing.'

He noticed Aek and Mai across the lounge and excused himself.

'*Uncle* Aek, *Aunty* Mai, thank you so much for coming all this way.' He pressed his hands together and they returned the greeting.

'It is our honour to pay our respects to our dear friend, *Pe* Alan,' Aek replied.

'There's someone I really want you to meet.' He caught Hatty's eye and she joined him. 'This is my dearest friend, Harriet. Harriet, this is *Pe* Aek and *Pe* Mai.'

Hatty pressed her hands together beneath her chin.

Pe Aek's face broke into a wide smile, and she said, 'Yes, of course we know who this beautiful person is. It's really nice to meet you again, *Khun* Harriet.'

Pe Mai said, 'Thank you for helping *Nong* Monty during this difficult time. If you come to Thailand again, please stay at our house in Bangkok.'

When Serwah and Bert left, they took him to one side on the gravel driveway in a conspiratorial way.

'Oh, my God, Monty, Hatty still loves you so much. Don't give up on her, this other guy is just a fill in. He's not you.' Serwah whispered, gesturing energetically with her hands, tears in her eyes.

When the guests had all gone, he was glad to take off the suit and tie that had become unfamiliar over the past ten months. The day had left him exhausted, and he suggested to Hatty that they get a take-away meal from the Indian restaurant in the next village.

She'd agreed to stay overnight in the guest room as he didn't want to be alone.

By eight o'clock, he was nodding off on the sofa. He kissed Hatty awkwardly on the cheek before retiring to the room that had been his since childhood.

'There it is again, the earthquake. Did you feel it?' Alan asked.

'Yeah, I don't think anyone missed that one.' Monty looked around, 'Anyway, you've met Hatty twice.'

'Harriet, your best friend from the bank? If you had any sense, you'd have settled down with her a long time ago.'

He met the unwavering headmaster's gaze and wanted to say more, a lot more. Wanted to tell him what had transpired at the Christmas party a few days ago – how he and Hatty had progressed from best friends to so much more. That Alan's wish, not to mention his, was finally on the verge of coming true. But he also didn't want to get his dad's hopes up just yet

– not before he felt settled in this new normal with Hatty. 'I'll bring her over for Sunday roast after we get back.'

'I shall look forward to that. But just promise me you won't hurt that lovely young lady's feelings. I'd be cross if you did.'

Monty woke in the darkness, disoriented, and panting. One in the morning and he was crying, unable to stop, the tears soaking his pillow.

The creak of his door made him start, before Hatty pulled the duvet back and slipped into his bed. He lay on his side and felt her body press against him and her arm come around to take his hand.

'Ssh, I'm here now. You cry as much as you want.'

He relaxed instantly, like he'd been shot with a sedative, and fell into a dreamless sleep.

Monty woke before seven, under a duvet warmed immeasurably by Hatty, breathing softly beside him. Though desperate to, he held off kissing her forehead, as he wasn't sure how that would sit. Slipping out of bed, he padded downstairs, stopped in his tracks and stared at the brown envelope on the coffee table.

Turning the slim package over in his hands, he contemplated the Thai lettering and took a deep breath. Pushing a finger under the flap he tore it open and emptied the contents into his palm. Dad's wedding ring and his wristwatch had been cleaned, but the gold and brass were dull, the watchstrap was distressed and the glass face cracked. His thoughts wandered to the body collection site in Takua Pa and he offered a small prayer to whichever volunteer had provided this kindness.

He put the ring onto a finger on his left hand. The ring that his father had worn every day for thirty-three years. He was surprised to find it fit, and the gold was warm. A lump rose in this throat.

Coffee machine refilled and turned on, he opened mail and spent time reading correspondence about bills, legal deeds and other junk.

'Good morning,' Hatty said.

Hurriedly taking the ring off, he turned. She was still in her pyjamas and with no make-up, he adored the cinnamon dusting of freckles over her nose and cheeks. *Just perfect.* 'Oh, morning, Hats. I've got coffee on, but can I get you some breakfast, maybe bacon and eggs, or something like that?'

'You cook me breakfast? Yes, please!'

He busied himself in the kitchen diner, while she perched on a stool at the breakfast bar, sipping coffee. 'I can't believe you're flying back to Thailand today.'

'Yeah, feels so soon. But I'm worried about Oi, to be honest.'

'I bet she's missing you.'

'I've spoken with her a couple of times via Fah, and she seems to be doing okay. But still.' He sighed. 'Are you coming out in December?'

'Yes, of course! I promised Oi I would, and I want to support you at the tsunami anniversary. Plus I'll be able to go to Kanchanaburi to visit my great-uncle in the Commonwealth War Cemetery there.'

Turning, he walked across and placed two plates on the counter, loaded with the full English. 'Enjoy.'

'Oh, my goodness, that looks so nice, thank you. That bacon smells amazing.'

'No probs.' He grimaced. 'Sorry about the crying last night.'

She stroked his forearm. 'Don't be sorry. It was your dad's funeral.'

Monty tucked into his food, before laying his cutlery down and watching Hatty in silence. After a while, he recalled a joyful family memory and drummed his fingers on the counter. 'Hey, in December, would you be okay if I joined you in Kanchanaburi? It's just that I went there a few times with Mum and Dad and loved it. I'd kind of be your tour guide. It's fine if you'd sooner do it alone, though.'

She looked up. 'Don't be silly. Of course, I'd really like that.'

He checked his watch. The last thing he wanted to do was spend the whole day indoors dwelling on the past. He wouldn't see Hatty for another six weeks. These few days had been harrowing, but they had also healed a small piece of his heart. 'My flight isn't until this evening. Do you fancy lunch in Winchester? This trip has been dominated by the funeral and I haven't had much time with you. Plus I want to drop something off for cleaning and repair.' He fingered the brown envelope on the breakfast bar.

'Well, here we are again,' Monty said, at the security gate in Heathrow Terminal 3.

Hatty straightened the collar of his jacket and looked at him. 'Safe travels then. I'll see you in six weeks.'

Stepping from foot to foot, he dug his hands in his pockets briefly, before reaching out to fold her in an awkward hug. Bert and Serwah's encouragement bounced around in his head against leaden slabs of embarrassment at crying for much of the night. 'I'm really sorry about how things have worked out between us this year.'

She ran her hands up his back and kissed him lightly on the cheek. Before looking at him, her eyes sparkling like jewels. 'None of this is your fault, Monty.'

He pulled her deeper into a hug and buried his face in her shoulder. Breathing in the scent of her perfume and committing it to memory. He wondered how he'd get through another six weeks without her. Yet for the first time in as long as he could recall, he realised he had something to look forward to.

On the other side of the metal security arch he paused and looked back to see Hatty still standing there. He smiled, and they exchanged waves before he wandered into departures, the missing her crashing into him like a wave.

CHAPTER 42

Hatty
24 December 2005

Monty stood out in the arrivals hall, smart in beige trousers and an ivory linen polo, his sandy hair recently styled. Upon spotting her, a smile beamed across his tanned face. She'd seldom seen him looking so well, and her heart snagged at knowing he'd healed at some great distance from her.

Groggy from the time change, she fell into his embrace and settled her head against his strong chest.

'How are you feeling after the flight? Tired, I should think.' He gripped her shoulders, looking down at her with concern.

'Ugh, so sleepy.' His familiar cologne, and the comfort of his touch reminded her of the days before everything changed. Their halcyon days when, for a magical moment, she believed their love for each other was invincible. The days before the torment began.

He stroked her cheek. 'I know. But honestly, staying awake is the best medicine for jet lag on the day you arrive, so I have a plan.'

She glanced up at him demurely. 'Not the ballet? It's seven in the morning.'

'Some culture and relaxation! Come on, let's get you to your hotel to fresh up first.' He took her case and led her out the cavernous terminal at Suvarnabhumi Airport into the blasting heat of the car park.

She dozed throughout the drive into Bangkok and was glad of a shower and a quick nap at the hotel after Monty dropped her off. By ten, after a strong coffee, she slipped on a summer dress and, in a blurry state of wakefulness wandered down to reception.

They walked out of the hotel side by side, past a gurgling pond with koi and water lilies and into the tropical heat. She slipped on a wide-brimmed hat against the relentless sun.

Then into the frigid Skytrain over the traffic-jammed streets, sitting beside him, legs pressed, shoulders bumping as they threaded through the shopping district of Siam.

He squeezed her hand and smiled as the train slowed, her signal to follow him off and down the steps at Taksin Bridge.

At the end of a pier thronged with Thai people they boarded a long wooden ferry. A river breeze took the edge off the heat.

He ushered her into a seat, and remained standing. Other people vacated their places for orange-robed monks, the elderly, and children. Her senses were fogged, yet she felt safe in this unfamiliar world with Monty to guide her.

Soon, she gazed out as the boat roared along, cold spray splashing her face as it crashed over the wake of other vessels. The ferry rocked and bashed against rickety piers at each stop as passengers stepped off and others hurriedly jumped on.

After a while, the Temple of Dawn hove into view. The imposing Buddhist stupa, a tower at each corner. Monty took her hand, to steady her as they alighted onto terra firma. He bought bottles of water from a vendor, before they wandered among monks, worshippers, and tourists.

'It's so beautiful here,' she said, marvelling at the ornate coloured mosaics that decorated the whole temple.

'I know, right?' he beamed. 'At some point I'd like to bring Oi up to show her the big city.'

She stroked his arm. 'How's your little lovely coping with you being away for a few days?'

'Oi's doing okay. I speak to her every day and Tik has been wonderful, as always.' His mouth straightened. 'Miss her though.'

This beautiful, smart little girl was now Monty's life, she knew. And she was happy for them both after what they'd endured, though her feelings were bitter-sweet. 'How's the adoption process going?'

He turned and shrugged his shoulders slightly. 'It's going. It all takes time in Thailand, but Aek and Mai have been brilliant. They tell me everything looks promising, and I just need to be patient.'

'And to think it took a six-year-old girl to make you patient, Montgomery Wiles.' She jabbed his arm lightly.

Frowning, he said under his breath, 'It wasn't just her.'

She didn't want him to dwell on the past, so changed the subject. 'So your Aunty Mai and Uncle Aek have insisted I stay at their house the night before I travel home.'

His mood brightened visibly. 'They are both excited about it.'

'Won't they feel put out to have a stranger staying with them?' Truth was, she felt pretty awkward about the arrangement.

He turned to her, his face clouded by sadness. 'They don't think of you as a stranger, Hats, after all we've been through, and all you did to help me. I'm like family to them, so are you.'

After a lunch of pad Thai in a small café behind the temple, they wandered a quiet avenue of smaller temples with sharply raked, tiered rooves, where Monty photographed her. One was empty, so she followed him in, slipping off her trainers. Knowing they'd visit sacred temples, Hatty had followed his advice and ensured her dress had covered shoulders and fell below her knees.

The cool marble floor was a welcome relief from the blistering heat. For a long while, she sat cross-legged on the floor, looking at the golden altar and the beatific Buddha, breathing slowly. Searching for clues but finding none.

She was settled in her Christian faith but nevertheless appreciated the stillness and the opportunity to clear her mind, however briefly. What did faith tell her about a choice between two good men, anyway?

They returned to the pier in silence and boarded a ferry across the river. On the other side, they passed through a cramped, teak alley of shops purveying Buddhist trinkets and tourist tat. Street food stalls threw up aromatic clouds of steam, intensifying the heat further.

'You could set up a side business as a tourist guide, Monty.'

He chuckled. 'I only offer private tours for very exclusive customers. Not entirely sure I'd make a living out of it.'

In her tiredness, the customer reference rankled, as it emphasised the emotional chasm between them.

At the temple of the Reclining Buddha, he ushered her to the back of the compound, and an open-fronted villa. Inside, tens of small Thai women knelt beside visitors on mattresses.

'Thailand's oldest university. Teaching the traditional art of Thai massage. Thought you would appreciate the pick-me-up after your long journey.'

'Gosh, sounds amazing.' She lay on a vacant mattress, adjacent to Monty, and let her masseuse go to work. At first, she found the treatment uncomfortable. Bursts of pain shot through her as her limbs were pulled into various yoga poses, and strong thumbs dug into her knotted muscles. But the next thing she knew, the lady was gently rubbing her back and encouraging her to sit cross-legged – two hours had flown by with her out for the count.

The masseuse finished with a flourish of sharp slaps against her back, and Hatty stretched her arms up high and let out a huge yawn. Turning, Monty was sat upright, his face a picture of relaxation as he looked at her approvingly. 'I reckon you needed that.'

She put her hand to her mouth and yawned again, before taking a sip from her water bottle. 'I think I did too.'

As they stepped out of the pavilion, dusk was falling, the heat reduced to a hug.

'I suggest we get you back to the hotel, have an early dinner and pack you off to bed.'

Having slept for nigh on two hours, Hatty was nonetheless exhausted, her pent-up tension released with every squeeze and stretch. 'I must be the most lightweight tourist ever.' She yawned again.

'Don't be silly. Day one is always the hardest.'

At the crowded kerbside, Monty haggled a decent price with a tuk-tuk driver, before a bone-shaking, noisy race through the back streets of Bangkok. Their bodies clattered together over every bump, until he put a protective arm around her shoulder. She nestled into him and glanced sideways, not wanting to stare as that might make her wistful again.

Dinner in the hotel's Thai restaurant was sumptuous but quiet. She wasn't sure what to expect, coming to Bangkok to meet Monty again. She hadn't expected the enormity of missing him, despite being by his side. And where he had been reserved during her last visit to Thailand, she was annoyed with herself at struggling for conversation.

Their lives were slowly headed in different directions. She hadn't let her relationship with William move beyond friendship before this visit, even though her British friends considered him a definite keeper.

At the door to her room, she looked up at Monty, this scarred yet wonderful man, and her face crumpled. Tiptoeing, she wrapped her arms around his neck. Pressing her face into his shoulder, her eyes scrunched shut and she struggled to stop the tears, her chest shuddering with small sobs.

He rubbed her back, his voice strained by whatever emotional battle was going on in his head that she might never see. 'Hey, what's up?'

Straightening up, she wiped her cheek and smiled at him apologetically. 'I'm sorry, Monty. It's nothing, really. Today has been just amazing.'

He bent at the waist and wrapped her in his big arms, lifting her onto tiptoes. 'It's me who should be sorry. Christmas Day tomorrow and we'll be in the car for ten hours.'

Her frustration became too powerful to contain. 'Monty, I really don't care how long we'll be in the bloody car tomorrow. I wish I could have been here with you last year. Can't you see that? I would have done anything for you not to suffer on your own.'

No reaction, beyond shock on his face.

'I'm sorry.' She kissed his cheek before retiring to her room. Having removed her hot clothing, she lay in bed, tears soaking the pillow until she was cried out and eventually too tired to stay awake.

CHAPTER 43

Monty
Boxing Day, 2005

Monty drove through the mountains then dropped into the craggy limestone scenery of Phang-Nga province before sweeping north to Khao Lak. Hatty was silent. They'd been quiet all day yesterday on the drive down. He hadn't really known what to talk about.

'Oh, my God,' Hatty blurted as they drove past police patrol boat 813, which was freshly painted, the grass around it kept short.

He glanced at it and grunted. Up ahead, he pulled off the road at a junction where a group of Thai police marshalled cars that parked among the trees.

They wandered along a narrow gravel path.

'The undergrowth has grown back, but a year ago you could see through the trees all the way to the sea,' he pointed toward the beach.

'It's hard to imagine what it must have been like, even though I saw the pictures on the news.'

For the first time, the words spilled out. 'Just debris and bodies everywhere. Indescribable. I could hardly breathe and I just hobbled around calling out dad's name. Saw a grey-haired man, but it wasn't Dad, and I was kind of relieved. Hard to explain.'

'I can't even imagine how you coped.'

He sniffed. 'No, me neither.'

They stepped onto pristine golden sands, hundreds of people, Thai and foreign congregated all around.

Hatty slipped her arm around his waist and they stood together quietly for the next little while before the ceremony commenced. Thailand's Prime Minister, dignitaries and diplomats from Bangkok laid wreaths and offered short speeches of remembrance to the thousands who had died in southern Thailand.

He felt stronger with Hatty there to support him, her head rested on his shoulder. 'These parents grabbed me, asked me if I'd seen their son Hendrick. Blond hair, silver swimming trunks.' His chest started to shake, and he sobbed in bursts between each word. 'Then . . . I found his body. Poor kid. He looked so ... terrified, all broken and twisted. And I thought of Dad . . . at school with the new kids. Just like poor Hendrick. Can't imagine . . .' He rubbed his knuckles into his head. 'Just can't imagine . . . how awful that was for them.' His voice was high pitched now. 'I couldn't get it out of my head, I'm so sorry.'

Hatty hugged him so hard, her arms tight around his neck.

'I tried my best, Hats. I know I wasn't good enough.'

She held on and shook her head fiercely.

A tsunami-warning siren sounded, and the coast fell silent, but for the soft lapping of the waves.

'Come on,' he said, taking her hand, and following the crowds towards the sea.

They removed their shoes, stepped into the water hand in hand, and threw fragrant jasmine wreaths into the sea, his thoughts filled with his amazing dad, his wonderful mum and how he missed them both each day.

Hatty pressed her face to his chest.

Trembling, he kissed her hair, warm tears rolling down his nose. Her scent reassured him, and his heart rate tempered. For several minutes they hugged in silence, white spume bursting around their ankles as the waves came and went. He'd spent all his time searching, yet Hatty had always been there.

Monty turned off the road along a dusty tarmac lane towards the sea, flanked by trees. A low skeleton of a building hove into view behind a turning circle of parched grass. To one side, a large pile of debris sat beside an excavator.

Monty parked in front of the building and stared out the window.

'Is this where you stayed?' Hatty asked softly.

He sniffed and pointed at the roof line. 'Yeah. I woke up on top of that, I think the wave must have carried me inland then sucked me back out again before dumping me there.'

'Oh my God.' She placed her hand on his.

'When I regained consciousness, I just remembered the last thing you said before I left England – *I can't do without you now* – and it gave me extra strength to get up and push on.' He shook his head. 'It's kind of surreal to say it now. But it helped me then.'

He opened his door and stepped out, Hatty quickly coming around to his side, as they walked through the lobby of the Jai Dee resort.

It resembled a derelict building site. and he touched the twisted handrail to the staircase.

'I stumbled down those stairs in bare feet, if you can believe that?' He turned to look at her, red eyed, shaking her head in seeming disbelief. 'Sharp metal and concrete everywhere. The poor receptionist lay dead just here on the floor.'

At the touch of Hatty's arm slipping around his waist, he turned to the love of his life, the sadness hitting him harder than the tsunami. Their life today was irrevocably different. Yet her smile contained only compassion. He sighed.

'I think you're incredibly brave,' she said, squeezing him closer.

'I wish I was. Come on, there's one more thing I want to see.'

The tear-shaped swimming pool was empty, the whale mosaic at the bottom half covered in sand. He admired the verdant trees at the edge of the beach which had weathered the wave far better than the structures of steel and concrete built by humans.

Following a path lined with unkempt bushes and carpeted in vibrant flowers, they passed identical shells of bungalows in various states of collapse.

'This was ours,' Monty sniffed, stepping over loose debris to enter through the hole where the door used to be.

Inside, the wide lounge area was mostly bare but for a thick layer of sand. He turned and walked into the unadorned square of concrete in which he'd slept. The floor-to-ceiling window was now an empty gap. He stared out towards the jutting limestone islands of Phang Nga bay in the distance, the warm sea breeze against his face.

'This was my room. I remember thinking how I'd love to bring you here.' He wiped the corner of his eye, but had no tears left.

Hatty nestled against him. 'It feels like another lifetime.'

He lent his head down gently against hers and sniffed her hair. 'Yes. Time to live again probably. Oi will be wondering where we are.'

'She'll be excited to see you again.' Hatty wiped her face with a hanky.

He smiled, stroking away an errant tear from her cheek with his thumb. 'And you.'

Turning, an object caught his eye and something tagged in the back of his mind that he couldn't shake free. He knelt and brushed the sand away with his fingers.

'Well, I never.' He whistled, pulling the hard rectangular shape free of its anchor, and blowing residual sand off of it.

'Your camera.'

Hatty's voice came to him like a faint echo.

CHAPTER 44

Hatty
26 December 2005

Young children played and the elderly watched from the verandas of their stilted wooden houses as Hatty walked side by side with Monty down the hill towards the beach.

Oi was keeping watch, waiting for them on the top step of the pink house. As soon as she had spotted them, she sprung up and sprinted towards them, arms outstretched, squealing. 'Montyyy.'

In one movement, he lifted her high in the air, joy abundant on her face, cheeks pink with excitement. 'Oh, I really missed you, *Nong* Oi.'

'I missed you too,' she replied in English, before turning her eyes towards Hatty and reaching out.

Hatty ruffled Oi's back with her fingertips. 'Your hair has grown longer. You look so pretty.'

The little girl's face broke into a toothy grin. 'Thank you wery much.'

Pe Tik called down from the veranda. 'Lady, hello, welcome,' she said, waving her hand at Hatty to usher her and the others up the wooden steps to where she had laid out bowls of food for lunch.

That afternoon, while Monty went into town to buy supplies for the school building, Hatty washed Oi's hair and tied it in a traditional bun. Unable to resist, she'd bought a few dresses in London, and Oi chose a yellow one for the evening.

'Yellow is good colour for Monday,' Oi explained in her lilting English with a serious expression.

That night, they all walked hand in hand onto the beach, with Oi in the middle. Monty carried a large wire hoop at his side, wrapped in gossamer thin paper.

A dais had been set up where earlier in the day Buddhist monks had offered a blessing to the deceased. Now, loud karaoke music blared out and the villagers congregated, to drink and eat together noisily.

Monty held the paper canopy aloft, the wire circle making a large opening at the bottom with a hexamine block suspended within it.

Hatty knelt by the little girl. 'Shall we send a fire lantern into the sky to respect the spirits of your *Por* and *Mae*?'

Oi nodded solemnly.

She knelt and struck a match, holding its flame against the white block until it burst into flame, filling the canopy with light and hot air. 'Look at the fire, it's so beautiful.' She stood and held the top of the canopy as Monty lifted Oi into his arms to hold the other side.

After a minute the lantern began to float and support its own weight.

'Ready?' Monty smiled at Oi.

'Let go!' She clapped her hands.

'Three, two, one,' Hatty counted down.

As one, they let go and watched it slowly drift up into the clear night sky.

Hatty looked up as the illumination grew smaller and joined the stars, pressing her hands together in a *wai*. She thought about Oi's parents, giving thanks to them for bringing such a beautiful little girl into the world. As she looked down, Oi stood at her side, hands together and staring into the sky, with her own prayers for the *por* and *mae* she must so dearly miss.

'Come on, shall we go back to *Pe* Tik and eat sweets?' Monty said.

'Yes, yes!'

They walked back off the beach, Oi insisting that they lift her by the arms and swing her every few steps.

28 December 2005

Oi's birthday had been magical. Monty drove them to Phuket where they visited a fairground before a colourful and vibrant Thai culture show. Dinner was taken at a small, local restaurant by one of the non-tourist beaches, where the seafood was fresh, simply spiced and delicious. Monty had snapped loads of photos with the camera Hatty had bought him the previous Christmas.

She marveled at the love and care he took with the little girl and what a wonderful dad he was shaping up to be. And yet, they were now one thousand kilometres away from Krabi, to the west of Bangkok. And tomorrow night, after a brief stay with Aek and Mai, she would fly back to London.

'Look, it's just here on the left,' Monty said, slowing the pickup to a stop by the kerbside of a busy through road. He stepped out of the driver's seat and came around to get her door.

'It looks so beautifully maintained,' Hatty said, pulling on her wide-brimmed hat.

'Here, take this. It's really hot.' He passed her a bottle of water.

They walked along the sidewalk for twenty yards to a set of white stone arches. *Kanchanaburi War Cemetery* the sign read in brass letters.

Inside, low angled stones were laid out in rows on perfectly mown grass and in the centre, a memorial cross.

'I think he's in this first bank on the right,' Hatty said.

Monty walked with her along the row, as she considered the names, regiments – mostly British, Australian, and Dutch – and the inscriptions on the brass plaques. There were heart-rending personal tributes from families. Some stones bore what appeared to be standard pieces of memorial text from a War Office recommended list, while others were empty. To her, they were equally sad. How hard it must have been to grapple with the enormity of commemorating a loved one killed thousands of miles away in a war few people understood? What tragedy if living relatives couldn't be found?

'This is him,' she said quietly, looking at a bronze plaque with pretty flowers sprouting around it. She knelt to read the inscription.

Darlingest Victor,
What grave sadness your sacrifice. Our broken hearts are held together by pride. Our love will comfort us until we meet in heaven. We miss you every moment. All our love, always. Your wife Marion and your baby boy, Malcolm.

She remembered the photo at her grandparents' house of Grandad with his brother Victor, dressed in the uniform of the Royal Northumberland Fusiliers. Marion had died before she was born, but she had met her cousin Malcom a couple of times. He was a quiet, gentle man who had trained as a nurse and worked at a hospital in Birmingham that specialised in tending to military personnel injured in the line of duty. Placing a small bunch of flowers by the stone, she brushed the corner of the plaque with her fingers then stood.

'I hope wherever he is, he knows we never forgot about him,' she said, wiping a tear from her eye.

Later, Monty zipped along at a good speed on the uncrowded road.

Hatty stared out at the rolling, gentle landscape stretching away for two hundred kilometres to Three Pagodas Pass and the border with Myanmar. 'Hard to think that there was so much suffering here to build a stupid bridge and railway during the war.'

'Common sense and human kindness go out the window in times of war. That's it up ahead.' He turned off the road and down a track to a low white building among the trees.

After a brief tour of the museum dedicated to the allied Prisoners of War, they descended the steps, into the shade of the valley below.

'Can you believe they did all this by hand?' She stared at the narrow passageway, cut through the sheer rockface, for Japanese military trains to pass through.

They followed a section of disused track and then into the cool, eery heart of Hellfire Pass.

'Excuse me, would you mind taking our photograph, please?' an elderly lady asked in a soft Australian accent.

'Yes, of course,' Hatty smiled. 'You sound like you've come a long way to get here.'

'We came from Queensland, Australia. My husband Joe wanted to visit before we get too old to travel.'

Joe wore a narrow strip of trimmed white hair around his bald pate, the wisps around his temples damp from the effort. Dressed smartly in a short-sleeve button-down shirt and cotton trousers, he seemed sprite-ly despite his advancing years. He towered over his wife and protectively put an arm around her shoulder, as Monty took several snaps.

'You look so wonderful together if you don't mind me saying so,' Hatty said.

'Gee, thank you, love. We've just celebrated our sixtieth wedding anniversary.'

'How lovely. You must have been married just after the war ended.' It was beautiful to see that their true love hadn't been diminished by his terrible war experience.

'That's right, just after Joe here got back. All scars, skin and bones he was. Hardly got a word out of him for the first little while. But look at him now. Eighty-six and still fit as a flea, hey Joe?'

'I'm slowing down a bit now though, love,' he said quietly.

'And where did you serve, sir?' Monty asked.

The old soldier stood upright, his voice strong. 'I was here, mate. In Hellfire Pass.'

He reached forwards and shook the man's hand. 'It's an honour to meet you. You're a hero.'

'Nah, mate. The heroes are the poor buggers we left behind.'

'Do you want me to take your photo, love?' the lady asked. 'You're such a handsome couple. Where are you from?'

'We're from England. My great-uncle Victor was here too.' She didn't have the heart to counter the lady's assumption about their relationship as she posed next to Monty.

'Did he make it through, miss?' Joe asked softly.

Hatty blinked slowly. She offered a quiet prayer of thanks for bringing William and his troops home safe, and of remembrance to those who had made the ultimate sacrifice. 'No, sadly he didn't. He lays at rest in the cemetery in Kanchanaburi.'

'Jeez, I'm sorry about that. I'm sure the lads in his company took good care of him; the best they could have, anyway.'

'There you are,' the lady said, passing Monty the camera.

'Oh thank you so much,' he replied, with a big smile. 'Would you mind if I took a photograph of you with my camera?'

'You certainly can, love,' Jean replied, her soft, wrinkled face breaking into a smile.

Joe, her husband of sixty years sidled to her again, a youthful sparkle to his mien.

Hatty looked at Monty and her heart melted. Focused on the lifelong loving couple, camera fixed to his eye, he memorialised their unbreakable union with one click.

'Do you want us to help you back up those steps?' he asked after.

The man chuckled. 'You're alright, mate. I'm stronger now than I was back then.'

They bid farewell and Hatty watched the couple wander off, hand-in-hand, her heart aglow. 'After everything he went through, to still be with his sweetheart and in love sixty years later is just fabulous.'

Monty put a hand on her shoulder. 'I'd like to hope you and I will still be as fit and active in sixty years.'

She imagined Monty aged eighty-seven and smiled at the hope he should be so spritely as Joe, the prisoner of war who survived a death railway and found perfect love in Jean.

'Love this place,' Monty enthused, as they walked down the hill towards the river.

On the fast-flowing waters of the Kwai, low wooden structures with pitched rooves sat on pontoons, moored to the shore.

'It's so dark now. The raft looks like a painting, the boardwalks lit up in fairy lights and the rest cast in darkness and shadow. Barely a sound but the water and the cicadas.'

'The rooms are basic,' Monty explained. 'But I've always found it calming to sleep on the river in the middle of the jungle.'

The gangway bounced gently as they stepped onto the pontoon. They sat on a bamboo sofa in an open lounge, and she sat beside him, content with the sound of rushing water. The floor rocked as two other guests crossed the gangway.

Hatty was uplifted after their day, yet their time together was racing to a close. Taking a deep breath, she sat upright. 'I might shower and change before dinner. I reckon there's a beer in the mini-bar with my name on it. Can I bring you a cold drink, like a lime soda, or something?

He squeezed her hand. 'Think I'll do the same. And I will join you for a beer. Haven't had one for months.'

Refreshed, she pulled the cool fabric of a clean dress over her head, tying it at the waist. She admired herself in the mirror, and relaxed. She'd spent too much time reliving what had happened, blaming him, blaming herself, for how things turned out in their relationship.

She clicked her door shut and followed the twinkling lights to the lounge area. 'I've got your beer.'

Shaved and hair combed back, Monty rose from the wicker chair, anxiety riven in his face.

'Everything okay?'

He flicked a thin folder between his fingers. 'I got the pictures from my old camera developed in Krabi. I just . . . haven't been able to look at them since Boxing Day.' He hesitated. 'I dunno, I thought maybe you could help me?'

Hatty put the beers down and joined him on the sofa. She could almost hear each heavy thud of his heart as he stared at the glossy envelope in his lap. Placing her hand on his she asked, 'Would it help if I took them out?'

He nodded and she gingerly removed the photographs, careful not to smudge them.

The first image was of Alan, bathed in sunshine and smiling before a vibrant display of tropical flowers.

'The last photo of Dad,' he whispered.

'It's lovely and something to really cherish and remember him by.'

'I took that just before we had breakfast on the day it happened. Seems incredible now.' He rubbed his eye, but there were no tears.

There were ten pictures of Monty's final family holiday with Alan, including a beautiful shot of father and son with Mai and Aek at a riverside restaurant in Bangkok.

When Hatty flipped to the final photograph, she gasped. Through bleary eyes, she considered the image of an almost forgotten self, cuddling Monty and illuminated by Tower Bridge, huge smiles on their faces and true love in their hearts. The night before he flew to Thailand. The night before everything changed.

'That was the happiest day of my life. The most beautiful, talented, amazing woman in the world had chosen me,' he whispered, almost inaudible.

She gritted her teeth against the anger that bubbled up inside. 'Monty, what did you remember me saying when you woke up after the tsunami?'

Tears now flowed down his face. 'I can't do without you now.'

'And I couldn't. I thought we had our life planned out. Then I spent two whole days thinking you'd died, crying myself to sleep, only to see you die in front of my eyes as you pushed me away then left.' Bashing her leg with her fist, she burst into tears.

'Loving you is what kept me alive.'

'But it didn't make you stay,' she climbed onto his lap, gripped his shirt and shook him.

'I'll never forgive myself.'

'I forgave you ages ago, Monty, but I just want so desperately to see you embrace life again and enjoy every precious moment.'

'I've been trying my best, Hats, but I'll never be quite the same as before.'

'I know, and it's okay.' She sighed and wiped her eyes, before pressing her forehead to his, reflecting on the unimaginable horrors he'd faced. Yet, here he was now, just as kind as ever before, if not more so. He hadn't meant to hurt her, even if that didn't make it okay. She stroked his face, breathing the comforting scent of the cologne he always used to wear, a smile playing across her lips. 'I didn't especially like you when we first met anyway.'

'What?' He laughed, snapping the stubborn, unforgiving tension between them in an instant. 'I flipping voted for you!'

'Then you made an incredibly wise choice, Montgomery Wiles.' She brushed the tip of her nose against his, a shudder spiralling through every dormant part of her.

Consuming her with his eyes, running his fingertips down her cheek, he said, 'No one's ever moved me, just the way you move me inside.'

Lowering her face, she brushed her lips against his, the tips of their tongues dancing unhurriedly, making her want everything she'd denied herself for too long. 'Are you wheeling out Belinda Carlisle songs in a bid to win me over?'

Drawing her into a deeper kiss, he stroked a lock of hair behind her ear. 'Just don't pass out on me, okay? Not sure where the nearest hospital is.'

Fireworks went off in her heart to see the Monty she had fallen in love with, his eyes more brilliant than the stars, as they were in their beautiful photo, before everything changed. She unfastened a button on his shirt, and traced kisses up the side of his neck. 'It was so lovely how you took care of me when I was sick.'

He touched the jewel encrusted amulet at her throat. 'I was petrified of losing my penguin.'

She pursed her lips, unfastening another button on his shirt. 'I was miffed that we couldn't spend longer half naked, flapping around in the sea.'

He chuckled deeply, running his hands over her hips, tracing the lace pattern of her knickers through the delicate fabric of her dress. 'You looked incredible in that bikini, although it did make me think . . .'

Giggling, she lay a finger on his lips. 'Ssshh, Montgomery Wiles, we'll get arrested if we carry on in public like this. We should go somewhere private.'

He kissed her throat, nibbling her collar. 'How about the tiny bed in your tiny room?'

The full moon casting a romantic glow across the deck, his arousal reignited flames in her that the vile tsunami had drenched. 'It's actually a huge bed and incredibly soft.'

Now, he tipped his head back and laughed. Gripping her bottom he sat up then stood in one flowing movement, her legs and arms wrapped around him, their lips melded by fire.

At her doorway his hard body as one with hers, she lost herself in his kisses, moaning as he loosened the bow at the side of her dress.

'Didn't you leave a light on for me?'

'Stop it,' she laughed, fiddling awkwardly with the lock to her room.

The pontoon rocked suddenly to announce the approach of others.

'Oh, gosh, quick . . .' Finally turning the key, she grabbed Monty by the shirt and pulled him obediently into her room.

Hatty gazed sleepily at Monty, dawn light slanting through the window. He lay on his side, his powerful chest rising and falling with every breath, long eyelashes brushing his cheeks, his hand against the bare skin of her tummy. His bed hair was messy and particles of sleep dust caked the corners of his eyes. She smiled, imagining them showering together, then getting distracted as they had several times in the night.

Monty opened his eyes and gazed at her, a tired smile brightening his face. 'You're here.'

'Where'd you think I'd be?' She snuggled up close, her body fitting perfectly against his like a two piece puzzle.

He stroked his fingertips through her hair which was intensely soothing.

'I love you, Hatty. Everything about you.'

She snuffed contentedly. 'And I love you, Monty.'

Hugging her closer, he kissed her forehead. 'I wish we could turn back time. Like today we were waking up in your apartment one year ago, me bringing you coffee and croissants in bed.'

'All we have is now.'

He let out a heavy sigh. 'I'm sorry I didn't talk to you more, you know . . .'

'Ssh.' She rolled on top of him and playfully placed a finger on his mouth. 'You did an awful lot of catching up last night.'

He ran his fingertips along the valley of her back. 'I've found an American counsellor in Bangkok that I can meet sometimes to talk stuff through.'

The next kiss was slow and lingering before they came up for air and she stroked her fingers now through his hair. 'That sounds like a good idea. Just know that I'm always here for you. Even if you don't want to talk, you can just be silent sometimes and that's okay too.'

'But you have to go back to London.' His jaw trembled.

'Don't be sad.' She gazed at the fine hairs of his chest, struggling to keep her breath steady and her heartrate calm. This time tomorrow she'd be high above the clouds, somewhere over the Persian Gulf. William would be waiting for her at Heathrow. Yet she felt he'd understand her decision, as they'd settled into friendship since Alan's funeral.

Composing herself, she said, 'I'm not ready to give up my career, and you have responsibilities in Thailand, with Oi.'

'I've started a distance learning post-grad in teaching, so I'd be able to get a job in England, or teach anywhere you were. The adoption should hopefully be finalised in the next twelve months.'

'You're not worried about taking Oi away from Thailand?'

He shook his head emphatically. 'No. We'll visit every year. I'd never let her forget her culture. Anyway, we talk about it a lot and what she wants most is to be with me. Her daddy,' a fat tear rolled down his cheek, 'one day.'

Hatty brushed away the tear with her thumb, her heart fit to burst. 'You know how difficult it would be to keep this alive from five thousand miles away, don't you?'

His eyes blazed, focused and determined as they had been before the tsunami. 'I really believe in us. All this time we spent apart. How much time have we spent together over the past three years? Our love can hold out a while longer, can't it?'

Nodding, she rolled off Monty to grab her handbag from the bedside. How blessed she was with this beautiful man who would love her unconditionally through the huge obstacles and setbacks they had faced. She opened the flap and withdrew a slender wooden box with silver gilt lettering on the lid. 'If you're going to be a teacher, you'll need to be really good with time keeping.'

He sat up, gingerly opened the lid and smiled at the shining gold case and polished leather strap of his dad's watch. 'Thanks for picking it up from the jeweller's.'

'Try it on,' she said evenly.

He fiddled with the clasp at his wrist as she sat up facing him.

'I've been offered a new job, running a department at the office in Singapore,' she continued. 'I was wondering if you thought I should accept?'

As he looked up, she blinked rapidly, her voice shaking. 'It's not Thailand, but if I came up at weekends we could make it work for a year or so until things are settled with Oi.'

'Would you really do that for me?'

'I'd do it for the three of us. We're a team, after all.' She wiped her eyes and held up another, smaller, square box, gently flipping its lid with her thumb. 'I thought about buying you a ring, but I feel your dad would want you to have his.'

He stared transfixed at the warm golden glow. 'I've dreamed for so long of becoming your husband.'

'Then when we are married, I want you to wear it every day for at least sixty years, so we can revisit this wonderful place when we are old and in love, just like Jean and Joe.'

EPILOGUE

27 May 2006

Stone walls soaked with centuries of Anglican prayer reverberated to the soft, lilting music of Thailand. The congregation stood with a collective rustle of fabric and the scrape of leather.

Bert clapped Monty on the shoulder and the friends turned. Monty was conscious of the guests filling the pews but stared straight ahead. Sunrays streamed through the stained glass windows as the ancient oak doors opened.

Oi stepped into the aisle dressed in ankle-length gold sarong and tunic, her hair in a traditional high bun adorned with purple flowers. She sprinkled orchid petals before her from a golden basket.

Hatty followed arm in arm with her father, face veiled, bathed in light like an angel, followed by her bridesmaids, Connie and Serwah. She held a bouquet of lilies and orchids.

He clenched his jaw, forcing back the tears, and looked at her face.

Her eyes met his. *I'm here for you. You'll never be scared again for I'll protect you as long as I live.*

His hot heart was calmed, hope replaced despair, and joy cast sadness aside.

Oi turned away to sit with Aek and Mai and after what felt an eternity, Hatty was beside him. Her strapless dress fitted in the bodice of pure white silk embroidered with Thai temples and flowers. From her slender waist, the dress billowed in gossamer waves. She let her dad lift the veil to kiss her cheek, then turned to Monty.

'Hello,' she mouthed, revealing her perfect smile, eyes sparkling.

He took her soft hands and smiled with happiness he never knew possible. ‘Hello.’

The vicar intoned. ‘In the name of God, Father, Son, and Holy Spirit, we have come together to witness the marriage of Montgomery Alan Wiles and Harriet Agatha Campbell, to pray for God’s blessing on them, to share their joy, and to celebrate their love.’

The most sacred service of their union – ‘*til death do us part*’ – passed so quickly.

Hatty’s eyes were rimmed with tears as she looked up at Monty and rubbed the warm ring on his finger that once more glistened gold.

The vicar said, ‘In the presence of God, and before this congregation, Montgomery and Harriet have given their consent and made their marriage vows to each other. They have declared their marriage by the joining of hands, and by the giving and receiving of rings. I, therefore, proclaim that they are husband and wife.’

Monty bent and kissed Hatty Wiles, as the congregation stood to applaud the newly married couple.

The church choir burst into a heavenly song as *Pe* Aek and John Campbell walked to the front of the church for the signing of the register.

‘*Ubi caritas et amor, deus ibi est.*’ *Where charity and love are, God is there.*

'Ladies and gentlemen, put your hands together for Mr and Mrs Montgomery and Harriet Wiles who will take the floor for their first dance as a married couple.’

To the sound of cheers and whistles, Monty placed his right hand in the centre of Hatty’s back and held her right hand aloft. ‘I’m sorry, my love, we’re dancing to up tempo rock and not ballet.’

‘And our wedding dance is the lesser for you not wearing tights,’ she replied, arching an eyebrow.

He laughed hard and kissed her cheek. ‘God, I love you so much.’

Belinda Carlisle opened up with 'World Without You' as they held each other close, Hatty's head against his chest, and moved easily around in circles, as if on sand.

Oi ran across the floor and, barely missing a beat, Monty scooped her in his right arm, and the three swayed through to the end of the song.

Towards the end of the evening, Hatty slipped her arm around Monty's waist and kissed him on the cheek. 'Come on, the crowds have gathered in the foyer and I have to throw a bouquet of flowers at them.'

'Try not to hit any of your friends, won't you,' he chuckled.

'I'm more worried about the girls from the bank hitting each other.'

He hitched the fabric of her dress up a fraction to help her walk up the grand staircase of the hotel.

'Okay, here goes then,' she announced. Turning her back to the assembled crowd, she tossed the bouquet in a high arc.

'I got it,' Connie leapt with Olympian prowess, catching the flowers yet stumbling, brown eyed and beautiful into the arms of a handsome Englishman.

Monty caught William's eye, and the men nodded without rancour.

A warm hand slipped into his and he turned into the glow of Hatty's effervescent smile, blessed, uplifted and hopeful of a long life with his one true love.

'Come on, darling, time to change into our honeymoon outfits.'

5 December 2006

The bronze statue of Queen Victoria was visible through the iron gates, glimmering under the tropical sun.

A thirty-something man in shirtsleeves and green tie, emerged from the pedestrian gate and nodded. 'Monty, Hatty, nice to see you both again.'

Hatty reached out and shook his hand. 'It's so nice to see you again, Nick. And thank you for everything you did to help Monty in his time of need.'

'You are very welcome.' He dropped onto his haunches and looked at Oi, who hugged Hatty the bear close. 'Hello, what is your name then?'

'My name is Oi,' she replied.

'And how old are you, Oi?'

'I'm seven, soon be eight.'

'And who are these people?' He pointed to Hatty and Monty.

She beamed. 'They my pair-wents.'

He ruffled her hair and stood and handed a brown envelope to Monty. 'There you go, your daughter's new British passport. Congratulations. Will we be seeing you in Thailand on holiday next year?'

'Monty and *Nong* Oi will undoubtedly visit next year,' Hatty replied with a smile, stroking the bump on her tummy. 'I'll be on maternity leave for much of the year in Singapore. Though I'll be back as soon as our baby is big enough to travel.'

'That really is terrific news. Very best of luck.' The diplomat bowed his head briefly and ruffled Oi's hair again, before walking back along the tree-lined drive of the British Embassy in Bangkok.

The Wiles family walked down the bustling Ploen Chit Road, hand in hand. Hatty said, 'There's a nice department store here, *Nong* Oi. Did you say you wanted a hockey stick?'

'Yes please, Mummy!' she clapped.

A song from Hatty and Monty:

(We Want) the Same Thing (Summer Remix)
Belinda Carlisle, 1989

About the Author

Across a twenty four year career in His Majesty's Diplomatic Service, Ian Proud became one of the most experienced crisis managers at the Foreign Office. He worked on the UK response to the 2001 Gujurat earthquake, the 9-11 terrorist attacks, the first Bali Bombing in 2002, and the Indian Ocean Tsunami on Boxing Day 2004, which struck while he was serving at the British Embassy in Bangkok. He led teams through the Egypt and Libya crises, the New Zealand earthquake and the Fukushima disaster in 2011. In 2018, he was in charge of the crisis response at the British Embassy in Moscow at the time of the Salisbury nerve agent attack. He organised the repatriation of British citizens stranded on cruise ships and in India, at the start of the Covid pandemic of 2020.

Ian took early retirement in 2023 and now spends much of his time writing, baking and gardening, a stone's throw from where Jane Austen was born, in the Hampshire countryside. He is married to Katharine, and they have two teenage children and a needy labrador.Having spent much of his life living overseas, he speaks several languages, including Thai fluently, and has a black belt in karate.

Ian's experience of working on the tsunami in Thailand left him with Post Traumatic Stress Disorder, a subject explored in his debut novel, Searching. If you feel that you have been affected by this debilitating illness, or would like to find out more information, please visit www.ptsduk.org

A song from the author:

Real to Me
Brian McFadden, 2004

www.ingramcontent.com/pod-product-compliance
Ingram Content Group UK Ltd.
Pitfield, Milton Keynes, MK11 3LW, UK
UKHW041820080226
467811UK00001B/2

9 781739 543136